GW00372919

THE DEAN IT WAS THAT DIED

Barbara Whitehead

Constable · London

First published in Great Britain 1991
by Constable & Company Ltd
3 The Lanchesters, 162 Fulham Palace Road
London W6 9ER
Copyright © 1991 by Barbara Whitehead
The right of Barbara Whitehead to be
identified as the author of this Work
has been asserted by her in accordance
with the Copyright, Designs and Patents Act 1988
ISBN 0 09 470440 6
Set in Linotron 10pt Palatino by
CentraCet, Cambridge
Printed in Great Britain by
Redwood Press Limited
Melksham, Wiltshire

A CIP catalogue record for this book
is available from the British Library

To my friend Carol Woollcombe, who inspired this book, and who throughout the writing of it gave me advice, encouragement, joy and laughter

AUTHOR'S NOTE

The cathedral in this book is based, in its
architectural aspect only, on our much-loved
York Minster. I have, in tribute and affection,
peopled it with imaginary characters acting out
a fantasy of imaginary events. Both as individ-
uals and as members of institutions, the characters in this book are invented and are not
based on real persons, whether living or dead.

B.W.

Dean (Nigel) Parsifal — Henry
          Nephew
Canon George Grindal — now Acting Dean
              Lucy   "   daughter

Chapter Clerk Herbert Barkston

  Canon Sam Oglethorpe

Organist Edmund Jason   Terry

Verger   Soames with step son Michael
                                      Killarney

Surveyor of The Fabric

  Assistant Holdernesse
                                    Julia Brass
Tom Churchyard Telephone engineer   Textile exp

DCI { Bob Southwell — detective
    { wife Linda

1

Leave off from wrath, and let go displeasure,
fret not thyself, else shalt thou be moved to do
evil.

—*Psalms, 37, v. 8*

On the day he was to die the Dean of the cathedral woke well
before eight o'clock. He lay quietly for a few minutes, looking
towards the bedroom window. He always opened his curtains
before getting into bed, and now the gradually lightening
darkness of an early November morning showed him that the
still, golden days which had been such a pleasure in late
October were indeed past. He could just discern the simple,
massive grandeur of the central lantern tower of his cathedral,
a darker space on the greyness of the sky.

His hip had been hurting him for some time. He threw back
the bedcovers, wincing as he eased himself to a sitting position,
then stood up slowly and limped over to the window.

He had thought so – the first of the autumn mists hung in the
air and the cathedral towers seemed as if in soft focus. The great
central tower was reasonably clear but the elaboration and
pinnacles of the twin western towers further away were so
vague and woolly in outline that he could hardly make them
out at all. Between the Deanery and the cathedral lay Dean's
Park, where among the dark trees the air was loaded with
moisture, but the Dean could see plainly a large woman and
two small dogs on the shorn grass.

Letting out a yell of anger, he pushed his legs into trousers as
quickly as he could and grabbed a dressing-gown, slipping his
arms into it, and tying the belt as he rushed from the house.

Had Dean Parsifal known what the day held he would have
realized that a little loving-kindness towards humanity might
have been in order. This knowledge was not given to him so he

acted and went on acting as was natural to an irascible man with much to try him, including an arthritic hip.

'Lucy Grindal! Lucy Grindal! What on earth do you think you and your dogs are doing?'

The large woman jumped and turned around. She looked unbelievingly at the slippered and half-dressed figure of the Dean looming nearer in the misty dimness.

'You can see what we're doing,' she said with bravado.

'Not here you don't,' shouted the Dean, bending down to grab hold of the two long-haired dachshunds, who were stationary, fixed at right angles to one other. Lucy was too quick and too strong for him. Holding his wrists firmly she hissed, 'You mustn't touch them while they're in the tie. To interfere in any way would cause great damage.'

'That's just what I want to cause,' hissed back the Dean, but he was helpless, locked where he stood by Lucy's grip.

'I'm awfully sorry, Dean, but I just can't let you try to separate them.'

The Dean, who could cheerfully at that moment have separated both Lucy and the dogs from the world of the living, spat through his teeth, 'This is the last time, Lucy Grindal, do you hear me? This is the very last time.'

Lucy was a pleasant-faced, untidy, middle-aged woman. She looked as though she had picked up various leftovers from a jumble sale for charity and put them on and round her body with not much regard for comfort and without any regard for appearance. It was doubtful if she had combed her mop of wiry hair since getting out of bed. At that moment the two dogs parted company. Lucy let go of the Dean's wrists.

'It's all right now.'

'Haven't I told you, Lucy?'

'But there's no one about at this time in the morning.'

'If you must breed dogs – though I don't see the necessity – can't you mate them in the house?'

'This is a visiting bitch – she came by train and only arrived last night – she was a bit stand-offish – and it's much better for them running around and doing a bit of courting first. Otherwise it's like rape.' Looking down at the bottoms of his trousers she said, 'Do you know that your pyjama legs are showing, Dean?'

'Get those animals out of the park,' he shouted.

'Of course, Mr Dean.'

Lucy bent and clipped leads on to the collars of the two dogs. She was beginning to regret grabbing hold of the Dean like that – she'd had to, of course – but it might rebound on her father, who was a Canon Residentiary and so under the authority of the Dean of the cathedral. Her hands still retained the sense of her adversary's wrist bones, tightly gripped. He was too thin, she reflected. On this cold morning his skin had been warm to touch; of course, he was straight out of bed. He might catch cold, rushing out like this.

The Dean was limping away. She hurried, caught up, and whilst walking beside him said in a conciliatory tone, 'Isn't it the Chapter meeting today?'

'Certainly it is.'

'I thought father said so. How is your arthritis, Dean? Only four weeks to your hip op, isn't it?'

'That is correct.'

They left the park, walking away from the mist-laden trees, the moisture-spangled grass, the towering cathedral. They crossed the gravel, and the Dean turned from Lucy into the garden of the Deanery.

'Good morning, Dean.'

He swung round to face her again, his voice harsh.

'Never again, Lucy. I mean it. That is the last time one of your dogs sets foot in Dean's Park.'

The two dachshunds trotted obediently along by Lucy, now and then looking at one another as if exchanging doggy observations on the morning and the various scents they encountered. She ignored them, not noticing what would normally have given her pleasure. She passed the pleasant white-walled houses without a glance and did not pause as she usually did to look in at the wrought-iron gateway of the National Trust's Treasurer's House, to see its garden which was beautiful even in winter with its well-proportioned layout and a little statue.

Close to the east end of the cathedral she opened the gate of a house tucked away in a corner. Lucy always thought it looked a dear little house, with its steep gables and complex of roofs, though inside it was surprisingly large, rambling up and down; but it had no garden – only the two narrow flower-beds at the front – and a small paved yard at the back. Opening the door she smelt bacon frying.

'Is that you, my dear?'

It was a deep, masculine voice – a voice which seemed to sound in chords, and not in single notes.

'Yes, father.' Lucy took off a mauve knitted hat and unwound a long dangling grey scarf from her neck and hung them up beside the nail for the dogs' leads. She pushed her own dog into the dining-room and shut the door. 'You shouldn't have started cooking breakfast, I would have done it.'

'But I enjoy frying bacon, my dear. Was all well?'

By now Lucy and the guest dog had passed through the spacious square hall with the Elizabethan stair of dark wood rising round it and were in the tiny breakfast room. It was the shape of a shoe box and much the same size. Facing east, it was filled now with the first beams of weak hazy sunlight.

'Far from well. I wasn't early enough. The Dean caught me.'

George Grindal was serving the bacon. He looked sympathetic, even though his ugly, squashed-looking face was bent towards what he was doing. At their first sight of him people often wondered whether he had gone in for boxing in his youth.

'It was awful, father. He grabbed at them while they were in the tie. I had to stop him. I held him off.'

'There are times when our dear Henry shows a certain lack of knowledge of natural history.' George passed his daughter her breakfast.

'It may all rebound on you, father.'

George Grindal glanced at his daughter and nodded, his mouth being full of the large piece of bacon he had just placed in it. He knew her expressions well; she had the pleasantest of faces, but it was like a landscape which is often shadowed by clouds, clouds of anxieties which troubled the surface of her life. He wished that he could teach her not to be so affected by these little troubles. The clouds were thick this morning. 'Read Luke,' he murmured to himself. He was convinced that everyone could be helped in life by reading Luke and often recommended it, although sometimes Job might seem more appropriate.

'He says my dogs are never to set paw in the park again.'

'Don't worry, Lucy.'

'I really hate him, father. How could he try to hurt the animals? And he looked so ridiculous with his trousers on over his striped pyjamas and no socks.'

'I don't believe you could "really hate" anybody.'

'I could cheerfully murder the Dean,' replied Lucy with venom.

Canon Grindal, as was his habit, switched on the radio for the eight o'clock news and for a while there was silence between himself and his daughter as the two ate their breakfast. The headlines over, the newsreader began to go more fully into the various news items. *'In Amsterdam today a young British serviceman was shot dead when his car was waiting at traffic lights by two men dressed in black with balaclava helmets. It is believed to be an IRA attack. The serviceman, twenty-one and engaged to be married, was driving a car with British number-plates.'*

'Please turn it off, father,' said Lucy. 'I can't bear all this IRA business.'

'I want to hear the item about the homeless in London,' he answered. 'Anyway, my dear, it's no use shutting our eyes to evil. It's here in the world with us. Because you don't want to listen that can't wipe out the fact that in this crazy series of IRA attacks another has happened. You can't live in a never-never world filled only with good people and nice things.'

'I wish I could,' returned Lucy.

'Following the armed robbery in central London last week in which a man was killed, the police have issued the following description of a man whom they wish to interview in connection with their enquiries. Anyone seeing this man is asked to inform the police but not to approach him because he may be armed and is dangerous . . .'

Lucy listened to the description . . . *'six foot tall . . . heavy build . . .'* 'That could fit hundreds of people,' she commented. 'Perhaps they'll put a photofit on the news tonight, that would be better.'

'Shhh!' Canon Grindal listened for a few minutes intently while Lucy poured the coffee.

11

The spokesman who had come on to talk about the homeless in London was difficult to hear because his speech was so full of 'ers' and 'ums' that the effect was like the buzzing of a bluebottle and the words were almost lost in the hum. At last he finished and Canon Grindal turned off the radio.

'Evil is here, we have to fight it.' He picked up his discussion with Lucy.

'The only person I want to fight is the Dean. Why can't the Irish live in peace? Why do they have to be so vicious? What had that young boy done to them? He wasn't even in Northern Ireland.'

'That isn't how their minds work.'

It was not until they were settling back with their second cup of coffee that Lucy said, 'Isn't it your special day today?'

'Our new festival. Yes. The service is this afternoon and the whole Chapter should be staying on for it, as they will be here anyway for the Chapter meeting.'

'We hear far too much of All-Hallows E'en.'

'And All Saints' Day – All-Hallows, what a pleasant sound that has! – following on, is not forgotten. But All Souls' – which after all concerns each one of us, we can't all be saints but we will all be souls – was definitely due for rehabilitation. I backed the Dean on that. It is a good idea and I'm looking forward to the service.'

'What will there be?'

The Canon reached for his prayer book.

'The Epistles are from Revelations 20, eleven to fifteen, and the Gospel according to St John 11, twenty-one to twenty-seven.'

Lucy nodded. The Bible was woven into the fabric of her life, its lovely cadences familiar as old friends. Into her head came the verse, 'Then said Martha unto Jesus, "Lord, if thou hadst been here, my brother had not died," and she thought of the young soldier who had died so suddenly: she gathered up into her thoughts also other people whose deaths she remembered, and wondered about death.

'The music will be good too,' went on Canon Grindal. 'I heard Edmund Jason practising yesterday.'

'He's first class, isn't he?'

12

'He was a real find. As he develops I'm sure he'll get better and better. He lives for his music. You can see he puts his whole being into it, his whole soul.'

'Well, on All Souls' Day that's appropriate.'

Her father went on, 'We'll be singing the Russian Contakion for the departed, and the Miserere.'

'Oh, with those lovely alleluias?' cried Lucy. 'With that marvellous minor chant which keeps recurring?'

'That's the one.'

'Do you know, it makes my hair stand on end?'

The Canon could not resist singing very softly under his breath. 'Give rest O Christ to thy servants with thy saints, where sorrow and sighing are no more, but only light everlasting. Thou O Lord art the Resurrection and the light, and we who go down into the dust make our song unto thee.'

Lucy joined in, humming quietly. 'Alleluia . . . Alleluia . . . Alleluia. Lord God Almighty. I like that, father. Thy servants with thy saints. It gives one a wonderful family feeling, of being protected.'

'If the service goes off well the Dean's hoping to make it an annual event. He was talking to me about it yesterday. This afternoon we're using some of the music from Fauré's *Requiem* and he thinks next year we might have a said evensong and then the whole *Requiem* in the evening.'

'That's a super idea,' said Lucy enthusiastically.

The Canon was pleased at the way he had managed to lead his daughter's thoughts away from the radio news and the quarrel over her dogs.

The community which served the cathedral in many different capacities was like a village or an extended family. Everyone knew one another's faults, failings and virtues and somehow managed to live together. Because they knew their importance in the spiritual life of their county their lives had an extra dimension. They were proud of their service to something higher than themselves, but that did not prevent the rubs and quarrels of any community.

'It's a little brighter,' said Lucy as she got up and went to the window. 'Are you going out?'

'I'm going out with Sister Agape.'

13

'Give her my love,' said Lucy, and began to clear the table.

'And what are you doing today?'

'This morning I have an appointment with Julia Bransby.'

'Do I know her?'

'She was costume designer for the Mystery Plays in the summer.'

'I remember. Isn't she a textile specialist? I think we've asked her advice from time to time.'

'That's right. She asked if she could look at the vestments so I'm meeting her at half-past nine to show her what there is. She's going to write an article.'

'There's that very good book, *Thread of Gold* – doesn't that cover it all? Why does she want to write an article?'

'Some magazine has asked her. People always find something else to say, don't they? Books and articles go on for ever.'

There's no escape for a wife, thought Mrs Guest, the Dean's housekeeper, as she left the Deanery dining-room after having served his highness with his breakfast. She had carried out the task without a word, of course. The Dean didn't like talking in the morning. He'd be busy with his own affairs soon enough; then she could settle down to the newspaper for half an hour before tackling the bedrooms. She had no great respect for her employer. She was not surprised that the Dean was not married. How would anyone have put up with his pernickety ways if they weren't paid for it? And all his fault-finding? Being his housekeeper was all right – you could forget him in off-duty hours, sit in front of the telly in the housekeeper's room with your shoes off, and eat Rowntree's chocolates washed down by the odd glass of sherry. But being married to someone like the Dean! Strange things he did sometimes. This morning she was sure she'd heard the front door close while she was starting breakfast, and when she went in to turn back his bedclothes to air she'd moved his pyjamas and the bottoms of the legs were all wet. She'd put them on the radiator to dry.

It would have been a surprise to Mrs Guest to know that the Dean had indeed once been married. It had all happened so quickly, so long ago, and been over so soon, that even people who had known at the time rarely remembered. Still less was it surprising that recent acquaintances thought him a bachelor. They might have known him for years and still thought so. A crusty, confirmed bachelor, they would have thought. Even the Dean hardly remembered. He had smothered the memory, drowned it out of sight, for good enough reasons.

With a relish of his own abstemiousness the Dean ate sparingly of toast, thinly scraped over with margarine, and drank two cups of milkless tea. He considered that the flesh should be subdued as often as possible. He could hardly wait to finish his second cup before hurrying out to the cathedral workshops, where the foreman joiner arrived by eight o'clock.

He should of course have waited and put the matter through the proper channels – through a committee, and the Superintendent of Works, and gone into no end of explanations and justifications. At the very least he should have gone to the Treasurer or the Chapter Clerk. But he was not inclined to go through any channels at all.

'Three notices, Mr Thomas, straight away, please,' he said. "NO DOGS." Can you make them at once? I want to put them up.'

'You, sir? We can put them up for you.'

'No; no. I want to put them up. Make them straight away, please.'

'With painting and lettering – even quick-drying paint, nothing will dry fast this weather – it'd be several hours, anyway, Dean.'

'Borrow your wife's hairdrier, Mr Thomas. I'll call for them after Matins. They'd better be ready.'

'Better be ready!' echoed Mr Thomas when the Dean's back was turned. 'Better, had they, Mr High-falutin! What's wrong with dogs anyway?'

He cut into the wood he had found for the notices with such viciousness that he caught his thumb on the saw edge and hopped about the workshop, sucking it and swearing, and wishing that the Dean were in a warm and painful place. Then a bright idea struck him. He could not refuse to make the notices, but he could notify the Superintendent of Works on the internal phone. A few minutes later he carried on with the job with a much better grace.

15

After giving his orders to the foreman joiner the Dean found that he had nearly two hours with nothing much to do, and this irked him. He was an active man, irritated by the disability of his hip and by his loss of speed. It had been his delight to walk faster and more nimbly than younger men. All his paper work was in order. His notes for the remarks he intended to make at the Chapter meeting that afternoon were ready and lying beside his copy of the agenda. His hands itched to fasten up the notices on the gates of Dean's Park.

Dean Henry Parsifal had few close relatives. He had had no sisters and his only brother was dead, leaving a son; in addition the Dean had a bevy of distant cousins to whom he was the rather awe-inspiring head of the family.

His nephew, Nigel Parsifal, had lived in York for longer than the Dean, and was married with four daughters. Nigel had had a career in the army for twenty-one years and when he left went into the antique business with great relief. At last he was able to follow his true instincts. He enjoyed seeking out beautiful things and trading in them. He enjoyed living in the heart of an ancient city.

He found though that no pleasures are unalloyed and when his uncle came to the city as Dean the difficulties of their relationship gave him much to agonize over, because when the Dean appeared it meant trouble. The Dean went to see Nigel when he felt frustrated and there was no one else on whom to relieve his feelings.

Nigel could not hit back. Apart from his natural good manners, there were other considerations. The Dean had a large amount of money but only one close relative and was growing old. Nigel had his army pension, a small amount from his father's investments, his antique shop and his expectations from his uncle. He had an expensive wife, expensive daughters still at school and an expensive mistress. He would have hated to see the Dean's money go to that bevy of distant cousins.

Today after a brief walk through the cathedral the Dean left through a small door on the south side and crossed the busy road by the zebra crossing, starting straight out on to it autocratically without waiting to see whether the cars were inclined to stop or not.

Then he limped in the wakening morning down the narrow ancient road of High Petergate, a canyon between medieval and Georgian shops. Sometimes the old street still echoed with the clatter of hoofs as tourists were taken on horse-drawn trips round the city, but this morning there was no such reminder of bygone sounds because the trips had stopped for the winter. All was quiet and calm.

'There you are, Nigel,' pounced the Dean.

Nigel was of medium height, dark-haired, with stiff straight eyelashes an inch long round his large grey eyes. 'An inhabitant of Sodom if ever I saw one,' thought the Dean, but could not get over the evidence of the wife, the daughters and the mistress.

'Come and buy a book, uncle,' said Nigel. 'Or have you got one?'

The Dean looked hard back at him. Nigel bit his lip, remembering that he had promised himself to be nice to his uncle.

'Has my binding come back?'

One of the things Nigel carried in his shop was the work of his friend Lacy, who was a craftsman bookbinder. He also kept a few of the books which came his way in sales as parts of lots. Books in themselves did not interest him but he loved a fine binding, and the look of well-bound books filling a bookcase.

Murmuring something he led the way into the shop. On a shelf at the back was a bundle which he lifted down and laid on the counter in front of the Dean.

Ignoring the young woman who sat at the desk Dean Parsifal unwrapped the newly-bound book. Nigel and Jill exchanged a look past his bent head. Jill had not expected the Dean to appear to notice her. She stretched out her slim legs provocatively so that her black spiky heels dug into the carpet a good six inches on the Dean's side of the sales desk. She got out her bag and checked her appearance, adding a dash of colour to the rainbow over her eyes. Then, determined not to be ignored, she rose from her seat, posing prettily in her high-necked, mini-skirted knitted dress.

'Can I make you and the Dean a coffee, Nigel?' she asked.

'Coffee, uncle?'

Two things stopped the Dean refusing. He suddenly felt like

17

a drink of coffee – but he could have overcome that. He wanted Jill out of the way. So at last he grunted and agreed.

'Do you have to flaunt that girl in here?' he asked.

'She's my assistant, uncle, very efficient and popular.'

'Assistant my clerical foot.'

'Definitely my assistant. I don't know what I'd do without her.'

'Your wife or one of your daughters could be your assistant perfectly well instead of that – floozie.'

'The floozie will hear you – it's only a cubby hole at the back.'

'Let her, her and her legs.'

'Anyway Maureen has plenty of work with the house and the girls to look after. She does help sometimes on Saturdays and other times if I need her, and the girls help in their holidays. They *are* still at school, you know.' Nigel sounded very mild.

'Milk and water, you are, my boy,' announced the Dean. 'Don't know how Maureen puts up with you. Nice woman, that.'

'With difficulty, I suppose. Are you pleased with the binding?'

All this time the Dean had been turning the heavy calf-bound volume over in his hands. There was no doubt it was beautifully done. The tiny gold-leaf stars here and there at the junction of the lines of blind-tooling gave just the right effect – a hardly noticeable twinkle which relieved the gravity of the plain leather. They formed the shape of the constellation Andromeda. The whole thing was dignified and elegant.

'How much?' he asked.

Nigel named cost price.

'You know how to profiteer out of me, think I'm made of money,' remarked the Dean as he wrote out the cheque.

Nigel bit his lip and counted to ten, thinking of the future welfare of wife, daughters, and the delectable Jill.

Jill came back with the coffee.

'Dean,' she said softly, placing a china cup near his hand. She passed Nigel a mug and took her own to the desk. A regular customer came up to pay for a Chelsea cup and saucer.

'Damp and miserable this morning.'

Jill agreed, deftly wrapping the china in tissue paper, then

18

putting it into one of the shop's own elegantly designed paper bags and giving him his change.

'Yes, it might rain. The weather man forecasts rain.' She fluttered her eyelids and smiled.

'I'll have a look round while I'm here,' said the Dean, who had glanced at his watch and discovered there was more time to fill before Eucharist at ten thirty. He browsed along the shelves, snorting and exclaiming now and then at the high prices and the vast profits his nephew must be making.

'I'll just go off for half an hour if that's all right,' Jill said quietly to Nigel.

When a few minutes had gone by and the Dean decided to leave the shop he looked round but there was no sign of the outrageous girl. His thoughts were so filled with wondering where she had gone that he forgot to pick up his newly bound book.

It was when the Dean turned out of the short pedestrian street of Minster Gate, where once the barrier into the cathedral precincts had been locked every night, that he saw Jill again. Arrested by a twang of pain he had involuntarily paused, then excused the pause to himself by twisting his head to watch for the traffic, instead of limping straight out on to the zebra crossing in his usual impetuous way. It was then that he caught a flash of her short scarlet skirt. She was with someone. They were standing close together, near the round pillar which had once loomed over frightened native miscreants brought into the main building of the Roman fort. She was holding hands with a man, he was certain. And she'd seen that she was observed, too. The Dean smiled grimly. Serve her right, the painted Jezebel. Let her have a bit of worrying about whether he was going to tell Nigel or not. Pay her back for some of the worrying Nigel's wife must be doing.

Back in Petergate Nigel was standing outside his antique shop and looking in the direction in which the Dean had vanished.

'I could kill him,' he thought viciously, repressing a longing to jump up and down and scream. 'I could kill him, kill him, kill him.'

Where had Jill gone to? He was sure that it was the Dean's presence which had made her leave the shop. Where was she,

that was what he wanted to know, and who was she with?
There had been times in the last few days when he had felt
unsure of her and wondered if there was someone else, but
there was nothing he could do. He could not close the shop and
follow her. There was something in the way she had walked
out – something provocative . . .

2

I am clean forgotten, as a dead man out of
mind; I am become like a broken vessel.
— *Psalms*, 31, v. 4

The gleam of hazy sunlight which had irradiated the breakfast-
room for Canon Grindal and his daughter was soon lost in the
rising mist. After the Canon left the house he paused to put on
his gloves and look around him. He liked the frequent winter
mists, and now he was enjoying the softening of all hard
outlines, the mysteriousness lent to all distances.

It was only a step to the house where the three Anglican
Sisters lived and Sister Agape was ready to accompany him.
She was a tiny woman but vibrated with energy. Her face was
unlined and serene; in earlier life she had been a games mistress
at a girls' grammar school. They were planning to visit the
centre recently established by St Lawrence's Church.

'Why are we going this way?' she asked.

They had plunged down a narrow pedestrian inlet to the little
street called Bedern and were passing the pillaged remains of
the medieval chapel of the Vicars Choral.

'I thought we'd just visit the Brunswick Street Shelter *en route*.
There's someone there who may have a claim on our help.'

'They all have, of course.' Sister Agape was well acquainted
with the shelter for the homeless, which catered for tramps and
other vagrants.

'They all have, true. But this man it seems was once a verger
of the cathedral and so we have a special concern.'

'But how sad! What has happened to him?'

With Agape skimming at his side Canon Grindal had
stumped past the new buildings which were filling the gaps in
the peaceful old streets and reached the road called Aldwark.
They had passed the medieval Hall of the Merchant Taylors and

21

the eighteenth-century Oliver Sheldon House and they were now passing the ancient Guildhall of St Anthony. York whatever its changes was still a city of enchantment where a little narrow inlet took you into times past, where the shape of its streets and the outlines of the surviving old buildings in the quietness and mist had magic more powerful than words.

George Grindal and Sister Agape knew the place so well that at the moment it was making no conscious impression; the present was all they were caring about. The close air held them in their own small world.

They reached the bottom of Aldwark and stood waiting to cross over the busy road where twentieth-century cars, buses and lorries were belting along regardless of the poor visibility.

'I don't know what his story is.' The Canon sounded abstracted. 'Now,' he said, suddenly plucking hold of Sister Agape's sleeve and pulling her across the road through a gap in the traffic. 'We're going to get a new shelter, did you know?' he asked. 'The city council are planning a purpose-built building on the Haymarket car-park facing on to Peaseholme Green. It's going to be very posh.'

'I don't like the idea,' said Agape. 'What's wrong with the shelter as it is? Start going upmarket and you will get bureaucracy and all that nonsense.'

'I'm sure we won't. It will be much better.'

They turned into the car-park of the ancient timbered Black Swan Inn and came to a gate in a wire fence, then passed through to a big old hut. Inside, in the cubby hole of an office, two shabby men were sitting chatting to some of the voluntary staff. The warden got up and came with Grindal and Agape past a tiny kitchen where a comfortable smell was coming from the enormous pan of stew gently simmering on the stove, then into the big dormitory which was scattered with people sitting around, reading, talking, and playing dominoes.

'Your man is in the little screened off bit at the back,' the warden said.

'Ought you to get him to hospital?' asked George Grindal as they stood by the bed where an old man was lying with his eyes shut.

'He'll be perfectly all right. He's only tired and confused,' replied the warden. 'He carried on walking all night, not realizing it was time to rest.'

'So sad, when our last days are clouded like this,' whispered George.

'Pitiful,' whispered back Sister Agape.

'You needn't whisper, you know, I'm not asleep,' said the man on the bed without opening his eyes or moving.

'We didn't want to disturb you.' George spoke extra clearly.

'You won't, and I'm not deaf. Neither deaf nor daft,' added the man on the bed.

'I'll fetch you all a coffee,' said the warden and tactfully vanished.

George Grindal sat down on a scarlet plastic chair and crossed his legs. 'We hear you used to be one of our vergers at the cathedral,' he said conversationally.

At that the man's eyes opened as though the lids were on wires. He took in George's cassock and Sister Agape's coif and veil, then sat up. 'Do I know you?' he said aggressively.

'Canon George Grindal, Sister Agape.'

'They didn't used to allow women in the clergy when I was there,' said the man, who looked extremely old. His face was weatherbeaten and wrinkled, as might be expected in a tramp. His hair streamed down his back in white rat-tails and his bushy tangled beard streamed down his chest. George was reminded of the Old Man in Edward Lear's comic verse, who had so many things living in his beard. 'Four larks and a wren, two cocks and a hen' was it? The old man's jacket was tied round at waist level with the coarse string used as bailer twine.

'You must remember lots of things which were before my time at the cathedral,' George said to him, at the same time accepting a cup of coffee from the warden.

The old man sat up and also took a coffee. He looked at it suspiciously before drinking, like a dog who is sure you intend to poison it.

'Oh yes! I could tell you some tales!'

'How long ago were you one of our little community?' asked Sister Agape.

'I was never one of *your* community,' said the old man, and cackled with laughter, much amused at his own drollery.

23

'I think you'd do better without me.' Sister Agape rose to go, looking rather offended, but George put out his hand to detain her and the old man looked ashamed of himself.

'You lose your manners on the road,' he said. 'Sit down, lady.'

'Well . . .' Agape still stood.

'Please,' said Canon Grindal gently. She sat.

'Oh, I remember everyone! Archbishops and everybody!' The old man began to talk rapidly. 'I remember Cosmo Lang. He'll be before your time. And now there's Temple. What a fine man he is!'

'Yes, indeed. Was,' nodded George.

'And there's that Mrs Hassock, I could tell you a few tales about her. And that young stonemason, he's a fly one. Clever, but there's something wrong about him. Untrustworthy, that's what he is. What's his name?'

'I'm not sure which one you mean.'

'The lady who used to do the flowers – Hassock, was it?'

'Mrs Hassock, yes?'

'Aha! And there's Verger Soames – I bet he's popped off!'

'No, luckily he's still with us.'

'And there's that Dean – oh, he's a caution, he is! Milner-White, his name is!'

'Unfortunately we lost Dean Milner-White some years ago.'

'Oh. Sorry to hear that – he was all right . . . He put the cathedral first, there's no doubt about that. You'll miss him . . . stained glass was his speciality! I haven't forgotten that! But I thought he was best making his sermons. A wizard with words, that's what I heard a bishop call him.'

'We missed him a great deal, he was much loved.'

After a pause, the old man started again.

'There'll be some changes since my time, oh my word! I started as a stonemason you know, apprenticed before the war. It was no good, I'd got no talent for it, so I did odd jobs around the place instead, couldn't leave the cathedral, it gets you like that, and then the war came . . .' His mind jumped rapidly. 'There is the choir master who brings a hip-flask under his cassock, thinks nobody knows about it, what's his name?'

'I'm afraid I don't know.'

24

The old man laughed in a tittering he-he-he. 'Been given the push, has he?' His mind jumped again. 'Times change. I remember when we were lads we used to go for a swim in the Foss where the warm water from the power station comes out. Stark naked we used to be. We used to swim as far as Leedham's mill.'

'Boys don't seem to do that any more.'

'Swimming-baths!' The old man sounded strongly disapproving. 'The Foss was good enough for us. And you could get caught by the bobbies if you didn't look out. Swimming-baths, they'll be the ruination of this country.'

'You're probably right,' said Sister Agape, feeling that she ought to show that she had forgiven him and share the burden of conversation.

'Women!' The old man bent his wild stare on her. 'Women will be the ruination of this country. Smarming round you, getting your money off you, and then making out you're potty. My Ellen would have turned in her grave. My own daughter and that fellow she married – all my savings she got, and then had me put in a mental home. Rotten daughter.'

'When was this?'

'What's that to you? I've finished with her, do you hear me?' His anger flared.

'How can we help you?'

But the old man only looked at her with deep suspicion and began his rapid talk again.

'That Mrs Hassock. Things I could tell you about her. And those guides. Those cathedral guides. Get it all wrong, you know. Not that it matters. The tourists don't know no different. Some foreigners asked me once "Who's that statue of?" they said. "Saint Swithin," I told them. Some old gentleman in a bath towel, lying on his elbow, all written underneath in Latin. "Just fancy," they said, "our only day in York and it's St Swithin's Day and here's his statue!" That made them ever so happy. Are you in the cathedral cricket team?' he asked George abruptly.

Sister Agape was pleased that her sex protected her from that sharp-shot question and the accompanying stare.

'I'm afraid it's not my game.'

'Canon Marten, he was the one who started the cricket team.

25

We played the Yorkshire gents at Escrick and beat them. All out for 85,' he chuckled. 'Do you know what happened to that young chap?'

'I'm afraid I don't know who you're talking about.'

'Apprentice stonemason and the best bowler we had – knew it, too.'

That must be the young man he was on about before, thought George, and replied, 'If you can remember his name I'll try and find out for you.'

'We used to play cricket in St George's Fields when I was a lad. Killarney, that was his name. I knew his father. Now, there was that time Mrs Hassock got stuck up the tower – the central tower, you know – with the curate . . . I'll never forgive him, you know,' remarked the old man.

'Who?'

'That other verger. Ben Deep. He told the Dean I'd been accepting tips from the tourists. It's no use him coming smarming round. I'm not having anything more to do with him.'

'We really want to know how we can help you,' said George Grindal firmly, remembering that he hadn't got all day to listen to this kind of thing. 'We're very sorry that you are in this state.'

They found that if they made any attempt to bring him to the present, he refused to talk. In the end – because they had an appointment at St Lawrence's – George Grindal and Sister Agape had to leave, promising to look in again next day.

They found the warden and stood talking for a minute.

'I suppose we could get him to Casualty,' said the warden, 'but our district nurse can clean him up and check his health.'

'I think his experiences have made him afraid of hospitals,' said Sister Agape. 'His daughter seems to have put him in a mental home. I'm not sure I blame her if he always sounds as batty as he does now. He probably got released because they're closing so much residential mental care.'

'He's a bit feverish. Only the result of a chill.' The warden turned to George. 'If he was really a cathedral employee for all that time, shouldn't he have a pension?'

'He probably has. I expect his daughter and her husband are

receiving it at this moment. He should have a state pension too.'

'He will have sold the book to buy food,' said the warden. 'He may have been afraid the daughter could trace him by it.'

'We'll be in touch and get him taken off your hands,' promised George.

As they walked down the street George said, 'He's so muddled, he talks about things which happened years ago and then more recent events as if they all happened together. Swimming in the Foss, and cricket in St George's Fields! But Marten *was* an Honorary Canon, Vicar of Pocklington; he died in harness about sixteen years ago. He was a keen cricketer, too.'

'He is like Shakespeare's King Lear. I'll see the Social Security people about him,' volunteered Agape, who felt she had been uncharitable.

'Well, Goneril is not going to get him back, if she wants him.'

'Let's see if we can disentangle his continuous present. Archbishops Cosmo Lang and Temple and Dean Milner-White are dead,' Agape counted them on her fingers, 'so is Verger Ben Deep and Canon Marten, you say, Canon. I don't remember him myself. Verger Soames and Mrs Hassock are very much still part of our community. Does it ever occur to you, Canon, that round the cathedral we are like a village – a society of our own within the larger one of the city?'

'We are. And in the old days we could have found some nice widow to look after this poor old chap, in a little house, but the little houses are all upwardly mobile and the widows are busy fulfilling themselves.'

Sister Agape stopped abruptly and George nearly ran into her. 'Mrs Hassock,' she said. 'She's in a cathedral house, widow of a policeman, with one lodger already, and if she won't take him in I don't know who will. She's got a heart of gold, you know, even if she does drive you mad at times.'

George smiled. 'She does have a talent that way.'

He remembered Mrs Hassock's whispers after morning service. 'What rite are we having, Canon?' and the way she officiously took the service books from the verger on duty and distributed them herself, making irritating remarks to people

27

like, 'Rite A of the ASB, no, I know *you* don't like it, Mrs Coneyton, but the Dean does.'

Aloud, George said, 'This old man seems to know a bit about her from the past, do you think she'll mind?'

'Not her, she'll be delighted,' said Sister Agape firmly. 'You know how she giggles and has coy little jokes with everyone. She'll love having a reputation as a *femme fatale*. I've even heard her being arch with the Dean and Mr Barkston.'

'That must have gone down like a lead balloon, as Lucy says . . . We must get him cleaned up before Mrs Hassock sees him.'

'Sister Lauren will cope with him. He's been through a bad time and lost his self-respect.'

George grinned. He remembered the large and formidable figure of Sister Lauren swooping down on noisy tourists just before service time. He felt some sympathy for the old man, who was liable to have self-respect dinned back into him forcibly.

'I'll look up the records,' he said aloud. 'If he started as a stonemason and then became a verger I should be able to trace him. He was very keen on talking about that other person – Killarney, didn't he say? An apprentice stonemason who was good at cricket?'

'He'll probably tell us his own name when he learns to trust us. If you do find one of them in the records you might well find the other.'

They sped on to St Lawrence's, where a social centre was being established which was going to be a boon to the retired people of the parish.

Later, they got back to the cathedral just in time for Eucharist.

Lucy Grindal had met Julia Bransby at half-past nine and shown her where the vestments were kept. They looked at them briefly.

'This is the one,' said Julia, indicating the green set embroidered with gold thread and known as the Benedicite.

'It's modern,' said Lucy doubtfully. 'Of course we haven't got anything really old – none of the Opus Anglicanum, which filled the cathedral before the Reformation, survived. Dean

28

Milner-White bought a lot of early work in, but it had to be mainly Continental, that was all that was available. There's that lovely Portuguese chasuble of about eighteen hundred, don't you like that? I love the little figures rising from the centres of the flowers, all among the birds and butterflies and bees.'

'I think they are souls,' said Julia. 'They remind me of the design on the pall of St Gregory's Church in Norwich where angels hold human souls in their hands. You should be using that piece today, as it's All Souls.'

'It's rather precious to actually wear.' Lucy was cautious.

'No, this is the one. The magazine is interested in modern work and this is the nineteen twenties, isn't it? That's modern by church standards, and it's English, and I love it.'

'Well, I love it too,' said Lucy. 'I must admit it's my favourite, though they're all so lovely and interesting.'

'I wish they were worn more often. Look at the simplicity of the embroidery of these words, BENEDICITE OMNIA OPERA, just two parallel threads of gold, simple shapes, yet how right they are, here on the shoulders.'

'I like the bee.' Lucy pointed to it.

'Worked direct on to the green damask,' Julia muttered to herself. 'Outlined in two threads of gold, black velvet head and three stripes on body.' She wrote busily in her notebook.

'And the snail and deer.'

'Padded, worked separately, and applied,' wrote Julia about the snail and deer. 'Couched gold thread. Outline covered in a couched green silk thread. Whoever designed that deer was a genius.'

'I'll leave you to it.' Lucy had been thinking for some time of all the jobs she had to do. Julia had got out her sketchbook and was selecting pencils. 'Will you be all right?'

'Thank you. You've been very kind. Will I be in anybody's way?'

'They know you're going to be here. They'll come in before Eucharist.'

'I haven't such a lot of time myself this morning. I'll stay until ten fifteen.' Julia looked at her watch. 'And then come back tomorrow at the same time if I may.'

29

'See you then,' Lucy said. 'Don't forget that in the Benedicite set there's a maniple and burse as well as the chasuble.'

Returning from Nigel's antique shop the Dean stood for a moment by the steps and looked up at the cathedral and the welcoming, though awe-inspiring, six-inch-thick richly moulded door in the Early English south transept. 'NO ENTRY' said the sign, because the south transept had been badly damaged by fire. The tourists were told to go in at the west. The Dean went whichever way he liked going into his own cathedral, but even he thought twice before going in among the builders and the rubble, and he turned left to the door from which he had come out earlier, the simple unassuming door near the notice about Miles Coverdale, who had been associated with the cathedral centuries before and had translated the Bible into the mother tongue. Unlocking the door and then locking it after him, the Dean arrived in the narrow corridor space among scaffolding and huge pieces of plywood which had been constructed to allow access to the cathedral shop and the Undercroft and the stair up to the central tower. It was crowded but the Dean expected the mums and dads to move themselves and their children out of his way.

Entering the nave of the vast building filled with the soft murmuring of the crowds of tourists, he took no notice of them. As far as he was concerned they did not register on any of his senses. To him the place was empty. He reached a point where he could look over to the Five Sisters window shimmering very dimly at the end of the north transept in this day of mist. From where he was standing the five lancet windows which made up the whole appeared to consist of silver-grey, but he knew that as he drew nearer he would perceive glowing spots of ruby red and that close up many other colours would become perceptible among the ancient grisaille glass. He had plenty of time in hand before the service. It was lucky that he had; two people were waiting to accost him.

As he crossed the floor of the great soaring nave the Dean met a tallish, bulky man dressed in rough-surfaced grey tweed;

30

the sort of man with a natural presence which makes him notable even if you know nothing about him.

'Mr Dean . . .'

The Dean remembered that Tom Churchyard had played God to great acclaim in the York Mystery Plays in the summer and that they had come across one another recently on the committee of the Friends of the Cathedral – such a useful institution – so he smiled graciously, and said, 'Hello, Tom.'

There was no answering smile from the big, serious-looking man, only a troubled and hesitant look. 'Good morning, Mr Dean. I'm so pleased I caught you. The Friends don't want to appear ungrateful . . .'

The Dean's smile slipped just a little.

'And we do like the piece of sculpture . . .'

'Eighteenth-century.'

'It does appear a very suitable item on which to spend Mrs Wilmott's bequest . . .'

'Excellent.'

Then, prayerfully, Tom got to the crux: "If only you could see your way to asking the Friends *before* you buy something instead of *after* . . .'

The Dean frowned.

'We do prefer to sanction a purchase with our money before it is made . . .'

'You've made your point, Mr Churchyard. Thank you. Tell the Friends the Dean will of course come grovelling to them before he purchases something suitable for the enrichment of our heritage which comes up unexpectedly at a sale, a unique opportunity. Oh yes.'

'You do usually arrange it with us first.'

'Of course! Of course! And you normally have a say in what is purchased. But you must remember that a bequest is different. It is not money gained in the usual way by the efforts of the Friends. The cheque came made out to me, as head of the Friends. The piece was put into the sale at the last moment – it did not even get into the catalogue. There was no time for consultation.'

The Dean's whole attitude put over the idea of the man of action, prompt, bold, purposeful. His angry and disdainful tone carried no promise of improvement. As he went off, sweeping tourists wholesale from his path by an imperious wave of his arm, Tom Churchyard looked after him and sighed.

A meek little elderly woman popped out of the choir stalls where she had been hiding and appeared through the middle of the famous screen of medieval kings.

'Have you done it?' she asked.

'I tried, Mrs Hassock, but I don't think I got very far.'

'He should listen to *you*, Mr Churchyard.'

'The Dean doesn't listen to anyone. I don't think he'll change his ways one iota.'

'But we don't want to keep on fund-raising and getting no say in how it's spent – all the bits of old stone and wood he keeps wishing on us are so *expensive*! The rest of us don't see that they're anything so wonderful.'

'He said a bequest was different, and that the cheque came made out to him.'

'The bequest was made to the Friends.'

'My dear Mrs Hassock, I agree with you. The whole committee agrees with you. Perhaps we'll tame him in time. At present he's a new broom still, although he's been with us about a year.'

'Dear Mr Churchyard, I know you did your best.'

'I'll tell you something, Mrs Hassock. I could strangle him sometimes.'

'Oh, you shouldn't talk like that. Not even in joke, you know,' and Mrs Hassock peered up at him looking quite shocked.

'I could, honestly, I could strangle him.'

With a farewell smile to the horrified Mrs Hassock Tom walked away down the length of the superb north nave aisle. Above his right shoulder was some of the finest medieval stained glass in the world, glowing and telling its myriad stories, but it could have been modern float glass at that moment to him. Tom felt ill. The Dean always produced this feeling in his inside. Frustration, he supposed. Well, he'd done what he could – what he'd promised to do at the last committee meeting. He didn't feel he could keep up a conversation about it.

He passed near the statue of St Peter without a glance. This particular St Peter held but one key instead of the customary two, one for heaven and one for hell. Tom Churchyard usually looked up with a glance of amusement and wondered, is it the key to heaven or hell he has with him? The two keys should be different patterns and when Tom saw St Peter with two exactly alike that amused him too. How was the saint to know which was which when he had to admit a sinner? There was no need to wonder anything today and Tom did not feel like searching out his usual sources of mild private joy. The pain in his inside could only come from hell.

His bicycle was chained to the railings near the west door. He left the scene with a feeling of defeat.

The Dean's second encounter was with the Chapter Clerk, Herbert Barkston. Herbert approached carrying a file of papers in his hand. Forty years before, Barkston had discovered that if you carry a file of papers in your hand you can walk about an office how you please and no one asks you what you are doing, and the habit remained even after retirement. The file now with him might have been the file he always carried, although acute observers had noticed that the colour of the cover varied from time to time and assumed that the contents also varied. Others were convinced that the file was a carry-over from his civil service days, and that in it was material relevant to income tax or unemployment.

'These notices, Mr Dean,' he said. The Superintendent of Works had been in touch with him.

The Dean looked enquiring.

'NO DOGS. I do so agree with you over the matter.' Barkston found it best always to begin by agreeing with everyone. 'But there are rules laid down for the conduct of cathedral affairs. You shouldn't have approached the foreman joiner yourself like that, most irregular. The matter should have been dealt with through the proper channels.'

'Have I or have I not got the ultimate authority over cathedral affairs?'

'Of course you have, Mr Dean. But the rules say – '

'The notices are for the Dean's Park. Not, mark you, the Chapter Clerk's Park. Not even the Cathedral Park. Dean's Park, Mr Chapter Clerk.'

'Yes, sir, but the procedure is – '

'Mr Barkston, the church of Our Lord does not run on your rules and procedures.'

The Dean's hip was behaving itself well enough for him to sweep off, rather magnificently.

It had reached ten thirty. The Dean, still very much alive, was enjoying the Eucharist. He was pleased that he had remembered to put his antacid tablets in his pocket. His digestion had been playing him up a little and now with the second tablet in his mouth he was beginning to feel much better altogether. A virtuous glow enveloped him, as one who has a little righted an unstable world. Many would agree with his intentions – suppressing dogs in his park, upholding morality in his family, collecting beautiful rare things for his cathedral. And after the service the notices should be ready.

In spite of quick-drying paint and no undercoat they were still a bit tacky, but the Dean was too pleased to see them to mind the smears of black paint on his fingers. He took up one of the notices, a backing block of wood for the other side of the wrought iron, some screws and a screwdriver and went off happily to the back gate into Dean's Park – the gate Lucy Grindal usually used. In spite of not often doing this kind of job the Dean was deft with his hands. With a sense of achievement and delight he fastened up the notice:

NO DOGS

then went back for the second and third notices.

It was lunch-time and he felt that he well deserved his meal. The hour of death, unheralded approaching him, had not yet come. The bell called Great Peter had been swung in its tall tower, following the chime for twelve, and the sonorous mist-muffled notes had boomed out over the shrouded city as the tons of bell-metal clashed to and fro for some ten minutes before coming to rest. The mist had thickened steadily, to a peaceful milkiness. All was well with the world.

34

3

There be many that say, who will show us any
good? Lord, lift thou up the light of thy coun-
tenance upon us.
—*Psalms*, 4, v. 6, 7.

'And now,' said the Dean after his lunch, 'for the Chapter
meeting.' Metaphorically he rubbed his hands in anticipation
and physically he sucked another antacid tablet. It would not
do to be distracted by indigestion when he wanted to be at his
most alert.

The mist made the day dark. When the Dean re-entered the
cathedral, this time through the west door after a short stroll
through the park checking on the absence of dogs, the indirect
lighting had been switched on above the nave.

The whole stately series of huge arches and groined vaulting
was warmed to the shade of pale honey in the soft glow, which
made the gilt carved bosses of the vaulted roof shine gently and
lit up the dragon-headed gilded wooden shape which the Dean
believed to be the prow of a Viking ship. Perhaps as old as the
cathedral itself, it projected into the vast, airy, vaulted space.
Dean Parsifal thought little of the theory that the prow-like
carving was an old roof beam, and that the pulley in its head
was a cantilever which pivoted up into the triforium to lift the
lid of a medieval font which used to stand below. It was
perfectly obvious to him what it was. A prow or a tiller. He
remembered seeing a tiller in the museum at Hull ending in a
similar beast-like head.

Greeting one of the cathedral policemen as he passed, the
Dean made his way along the north nave aisle.

As usual the building was full, not only with tourists, but
with workmen and cathedral staff – the Anglican Sisters, the
joiners, glaziers and stonemasons, and the vergers.

Looking towards the east end, the Dean could hardly see his

favourite window; it was obscured by the wonderful carved screen of medieval kings and the mass of organ pipes rising above.

He passed the stacks of folding chairs in the north nave aisle, regretting for a moment the old fashion of a vast open rush-strewn floor and picturing the building as it must have looked then.

As the Dean was walking as briskly and straight as he could up the aisle – his arthritis was granting him a temporary remission – he came face to face with Verger Soames, Mrs Soames and a young man whom the Dean did not recognize.

They stopped and Dean Parsifal could not avoid speaking. The thought that nevermore should dog set paw inside Dean's Park was giving him a feeling of content. He smiled.

Verger Soames was a good sort of man – by which the Dean meant that he was unobtrusive, quiet, did as he was told, looked forward to his roast dinner on a Sunday and took a good tenor part in the choir if so requested. Mrs Soames he had hardly noticed previously, she being one of the less significant half of mankind. Pleasant, he was sure, indeed she looked pleasant. Useful, he understood, for washing surplices. But the young man with them – their son, he supposed, remembering that they had one – was not the kind of young man he approved of. He had heard that the son was away travelling the world and now assumed that this strongly-built young man was he.

'Mr Dean,' said Verger Soames, 'may I have the pleasure of introducing . . .'

'My son Michael, just got back from Australia,' Mrs Soames broke in, and she made a curious open-palmed gesture with her hands as if she were offering this grown-up youngster to the Dean.

'Nice for your parents to have you home,' said the Dean, who could not avoid responding. 'Now you must excuse me.'

The smile had frozen on his face. He did not like the look of Michael and found himself prejudiced against him simply by his appearance. Track suit trousers and a parti-coloured anorak too big even for that hulking frame. The Dean ought to have approved the short cropped hair, cut to give the head a box-like squareness on top, but as it was the latest thing he did not. No wonder the West Riding woollen industry was down the drain, he thought. Men should be clad in dark decent woollen suits, not this bright cotton rubbish which you saw everywhere nowadays. He didn't like Michael's expression either. Truculent was the word that came to mind. He looked just the restless kind who would set off to roam the world, not heard of for years at a time and causing his parents no end of anxiety.

As the Dean turned and walked on, Verger Soames almost ran after him. 'Mr Dean . . .'

'Yes?'

'Mr Holdernesse was asking me if I knew anything. He is very concerned. There's a rumour that the de Vere tomb might be moved.'

What business is that of Soames, thought the Dean.

'I just hope it isn't true, sir. I told him I didn't know anything about it.'

'I decide these things, Soames.' The Dean went on his way.

What were vergers coming to, these days?

The reunited Soames family continued walking towards the west doors and the thick outside air of the November afternoon.

'What did you want to introduce me to him for?' grated Michael.

'He is the Dean. It's an honour to be introduced. You should have looked cheerful, Michael, and tried to please him. There might have been a job in it for you.'

'He's just another of these old farts. They get up my nose. I can find my own jobs, thank you.'

'Michael! Don't speak about the Dean like that!'

'Michael! Speak more politely to your mother!'

'Well.' He shrugged his shoulders. 'They're all alike. Should be bumped off before they get to that age.'

Verger Soames saw two of the cathedral Canons approaching, Grindal and Oglethorpe. He smiled and nodded but this time did not venture to introduce Michael. Canon Grindal knew him, anyway.

*

37

The Dean was caught by Colin Holdernesse, the young architectural assistant, near the Astronomical Clock in the north transept which commemorated the air-force dead of the 1939–45 war.

'As Dying and Behold We Live,' proclaimed the clock. The gentle blue of the clock's heaven with its rising constellations gave the Dean, as always, pause. Once, long ago it seemed, the Dean had flown an aircraft in defence of his country; he had been one of the lucky survivors from those gallant air-crews. They had known that their chances were slim, known the number of missions the average airman survived. They had been young and innocent and brave, and counted their lives well lost in the saving of their homeland. He could not pass this clock without a momentary vision of a group of faces, young faces, his comrades when the world was young with them and England was a patchwork of tiny fields under their feet; faces he would never see again on this earth. 'Do Not Go Away Without Saying a Prayer,' advised the Astronomical Clock, and as always when he passed this way the Dean's lips moved in a swift prayer. It was to be the last prayer to spring directly from his heart in his lifetime. He saw so clearly before him the face of his friend, the navigator, sighting Betelgeuse.

His privacy and peace were then immediately broken into by Colin Holdernesse, but his prayer had finished and had taken its place in the scheme of things. Perhaps it was enough.

'Mr Dean!' said Holdernesse.

'Yes?' The Dean looked far from pleased. He was beginning to consider the appointment of Holdernesse a mistake. The fellow was decidedly above himself. How could he be got rid of? The last time they had met there had been an altercation.

It had been on a sunny day a month before, outside the Deanery. Greenness and creamy stone made a setting which was a poem. It was one of the perquisites of being Dean that one lived in a delightful house in superb surroundings. All around the house lay its garden, backed by the time-worn limestone wall which was the historic defence of the city it girdled, and fronted by the equally old palimpsest of a building which had gradually through the centuries been built up into a great monument of visible praise to the Creator.

38

It was thus the Dean thought of it. Holdernesse had argued with him on that day. 'There is very little re-worked stone,' he had explained pedantically. 'The present cathedal was built outside the previous building, with newly quarried stone.' 'A palimpsest is written over anew,' the Dean had replied, 'after erasing the earlier writing. I think my simile was apt, Mr Holdernesse. We can no longer read the prayers of our ancestors expressed in their many previous buildings, but imprint over them our own souls' traces. Yet together, the generations have created praise in stone.'

The thought of that argument came back to him now.

'What do you want?' His voice was distinctly ungracious. 'Not the de Vere tomb again?'

'No, Dean. Though I must say that your decision does seem to me rather – '

'Is it your place to tell me what to do with the monuments in the cathedral?'

'No, sir – that wasn't what I wanted to mention to you – '

'De Vere was a strong contender for canonization in the medieval period. Had it not been for the greater political pull of St William he might well have been the York saint of the time. Having rediscovered his tomb – believed by those who had seen it previously to be merely a chance collection of carved stone – I wish it to be enjoyed by everyone. Is that clear?'

'It was something else, Mr Dean.'

'I haven't got all day, Mr Holdernesse. There is a Chapter meeting in five minutes. You do realize that this is a busy time for me.'

'This will only take a moment, sir. It's about the tell-tales I've been putting on the stonework of the north-west tower.'

'Tell-tales?'

'You remember, sir. They show if there has been any movement in the stone.'

'Had you any authority to put these things on the tower?'

'They do show slight movement, sir. The position is extremely serious. I would not trouble you like this if I did not feel immediate action should be taken.'

'Are you trying to say that there is danger?'

'There certainly is, sir. All our towers weigh thousands of

tons. This is one of the lesser ones, I grant, but all the same, if it starts to shift . . .'

'Mr Holdernesse. You are merely the assistant to our Surveyor of the Fabric – colloquially known as the architectural assistant, I believe. As I understand it, you have only been qualified for three years. Yet you take it on yourself – do you have the authority of your superior?'

'I'm going to inform him today, sir . . .'

'Without, I say, the authority of your superior – to stick these "tell-tales" on the tower?'

'It is recognized practice, sir. It is as well to keep an eye on things.'

'Then, on your rapidly assumed conclusions – to which you have, no doubt, jumped without justification – '

'Similar tell-tales did warn us of the danger in the case of the central tower, sir. That's safe, now, thank God.'

'I am aware of that fact, Mr Holdernesse. That was a great danger averted but, no doubt, proper procedures were followed – we are not anarchists, Mr Holdernesse, there are channels – you must take them; there are rules – you must keep them. You come and speak to me – without an appointment – when I am extremely busy – with this scaremongering of yours: Mr Holdernesse, I am really very annoyed. Very annoyed indeed.'

The Dean turned on his heel, his cassock swinging round him. The faces of his long-dead comrades were still in his mind's eye. What right had this young upstart to be alive, when better men than he were dead?

Holdernesse stood still, completely nonplussed. What could he do now? He could feel his blood seething.

'Damn you,' he muttered. 'Damn you for an uncaring, blind, self-important bigot. But I'm not going to be beaten by you – this matters too much. The welfare of the cathedral concerns not only me but all Yorkshire, England, no, the world! I'm going to fight, Mr Dean. The matter is not going to rest here.'

A few minutes earlier just inside the more northerly of the west doors, two of the Canons, Grindal and Oglethorpe, had met on their way to the Chapter meeting.

'Sam!' George Grindal had stretched out his hand.

'George! Nice to see you. How's your daughter – er – er, Lucy?'

'Very well, I thank you. She would be pleased if you could eat with us tonight.'

'Well, I don't know . . .'

'We're never late with our meal. Six o'clock? Would that suit you?'

'Oh, well, then. Yes. Please thank her for me. I would enjoy that.'

They walked on together. Ahead of them were the black skirts of the Dean, vanishing down the vestibule to the Chapter House.

Passing them and heading out of the building was the family group of Verger Soames, Mrs Soames, and Michael. Canon Grindal smiled and nodded at them.

'Isn't that . . .' Sam Oglethorpe laid a hand on Grindal's arm. 'No, he's gone now. I thought I saw someone I knew . . .'

A moment later a woman came up to Oglethorpe with a smile, obviously delighted to see him. She plunged at once into talk. George Grindal, watching the look on his friend's face and knowing how much difficulty he had in remembering names, guessed that he could not for the life of him think where he had seen this voluble lady before or who she was, although judging by her accent it must have been while he was in his Leeds parish.

Sam Oglethorpe said at last, very carefully, 'Do tell me, how is the family?'

'Oh, Ada died, you know, and Jim went to New Zealand, and . . .'

Oglethorpe's face lit up. This had reminded him. 'And how,' he asked, 'is dear little Connie?'

'All was well!' joked Grindal as they walked on. Oglethorpe sighed ruefully.

'I always remember faces, George, but as for where I saw them, or the names attached to them – well – let's say I need reminding by something. Like that face that went by as we were walking up the nave just now. I've seen him somewhere, in fact I know him well, but where? And who?'

41

'You had just about forgotten your god-daughter's name!'

Canon Grindal's interjection stopped Canon Oglethorpe's train of thought. Otherwise much which was to happen might have been totally different.

'I must confess I had. Poor dear Lucy!'

Herbert Barkston the Chapter Clerk, a man with a round head, thinning hair and an earnest look through his spectacles, who was always super-efficient, had laid out spare copies of the agenda on a small table near the entrance to the Chapter House in case anyone had forgotten their own. They should already have received these through the post. He was pleased to see as they filed in that most of the Chapter were indeed carrying their own agendas. He liked it when the Dean decided to have a full meeting of the Chapter in the Chapter House; he loved the extra ceremonial and the feeling that the beautiful building was fulfilling the purpose for which it had been created. For was not this the building of which it was said, 'As the rose is the Flower of Flowers, so is this the House of Houses'?

The Chapter meeting began with a short prayer, then the Dean said, 'Gentlemen, we are met here on the occasion of All Souls' Day to consider a number of things; but this day has been chosen, and this time has been chosen (as you know we commonly meet in the mornings) in order that you may attend the special service this afternoon with the least possible inconvenience to yourselves.'

'Get on with it,' muttered the Chapter Clerk under his breath. He was anxious for the Dean to pass on to the next item.

'We begin as usual with the minutes of the last meeting.'

Dean Parsifal gestured to the Chapter Clerk, who rose as impressively as he could to read the minutes. He liked this bit of the proceedings particularly and looked round at the men assembled. Above them soared the amazing roof which needed no central pillar to sustain it, but by a miracle of engineering skill was completely supported on its many-angled outer walls and buttresses.

'Are these agreed as a true record – may I have a motion that they be accepted, please – a seconder – thank you, gentlemen – I will now sign the minutes.'

'If the Dean brings up the matter of my statue, I am going to make a fuss,' Canon Oglethorpe whispered to Canon Grindal.

'Matters arising – perhaps the principal matter arising is the special service this afternoon for All Souls' Day. The subcommittee you chose at the last Chapter has organized the service, and music. We will have the opportunity of enjoying the fruits of their labours later this afternoon. Are there any other matters arising?'

There weren't.

'We pass then to the other items on the agenda.'

There was a slight rustling of papers as the members of the Chapter found their places. Canon Oglethorpe, who had his finger on the correct line, let his gaze wander round the building for a moment. I expect the public appreciate the carved as much as I do, he thought; the carved capitals, pendants, and bosses. One day I really will spare the time to study them all: I'll look for the various devices through my binoculars – the ivy, the maple, the buttercup, the hawthorn with its flowers, the speedwell and the strawberry, the vine leaves with their grapes, the stone cat forever chasing the stone mouse through the stone leaves. I'll find the knight, and the smiling lady. He recalled his thoughts swiftly to the meeting. The Dean was speaking again.

'There are several matters before us,' declaimed the Dean. 'First of all, I would like to tell you that the Friends of the Cathedral have presented us with a magnificent piece of eighteenth-century carving with which to beautify the house of God. It is a very rare and lovely piece and will, I am sure, help to give that richness and sense of continuity which only these surviving masterpieces can provide. We have it here, in fact, for you to examine after the meeting.' He waved at it and enlarged briefly on the provenance and aesthetic qualities of the carving.

'We have some small points before us: the removal of a medieval statue from St Helen's to the cathedral, the re-siting of the de Vere tomb – we should be able to deal with those quickly – and a slight alteration in cathedral procedure, on which I'm sure we will agree. None of that should take much discussion. Then I would like to invite you all to a cup of tea at the Deanery before our special evensong, to which we are all looking forward.'

George Grindal, sitting with the other Canons Residentiary, found himself thinking of his daughter and the new notices on the gates of Dean's Park. All lunch-time he had had to bear Lucy's silence and tragic eyes.

'The Dean has the authority,' he had told her, but it had not made any difference. Her cooking had not been up to the usual standard. George could feel the rather hard plain boiled potatoes and underdone mutton bumping about disagreeably in his stomach. It was lucky Lucy was not providing the afternoon cup of tea or it was likely to contain hemlock. He hoped she would recover a little before cooking the evening meal to which he had invited Oglethorpe.

When the chance arose, Oglethorpe spoke out vehemently against the moving of his church's statue.

'I object to the whole scheme of moving our beloved saint into the cathedral,' he said, anger giving an edge to his voice. He was the Rector of the small city church of St Helen's on the Walls, an honourable harbour after a hardworking life in a large inner-city Leeds parish and more recently a good spell as a prison chaplain.

'I have explained to you, Canon Oglethorpe,' – and the Dean sounded all sweet reasonableness – 'that your statue is believed to have come from the cathedral originally. There can be little doubt that it represents not a saint but John de Vere, who was indeed put up for canonization, although never canonized, and who was widely believed to have worked miracles. You can have no objections to your parish returning what is not yours to keep.'

'The statue is believed to have been in St Helen's on the Walls since at least the year 1500,' protested Oglethorpe.

'And it is of thirteenth-century date, designed originally for here, until the devotees of St William managed to have it ousted. You must agree, Canon Oglethorpe, that last winter one of your gargoyles was damaged by boys playing football, and that a small fire was started in the nave. We can provide much better security here at the cathedral.'

The matter had, in the end, to be left for future discussion.

'They get that statue over my dead body,' muttered Ogle-thorpe. For so long he had had to stifle his longings for beauty in his place of work; he was not now going to hand over his delightful statue, with its serene but harrowed face, without a fight.

'The matter of the de Vere tomb need not delay us long. As you know, this tomb was recorded by early historians but appeared lost, until recent maintenance work in the crypt brought it unexpectedly to light. It is very beautifully carved and of historic importance and I suggest that we move it to a site in the north choir aisle. The statue from St Helen's will make a splendid companion; no doubt they were always meant to be seen together.'

The Dean unrolled a large diagram and pointed out the suggested site, which was outlined in red. 'Have I the agree-ment of the chapter?'

No. He did not have the agreement of the Chapter.

'It's that confounded fellow Holdernesse,' thought the Dean as one by one the canons made their objections. 'He's been priming them with what to say. Dratted antiquarians, don't they know these things belong to the church and not to them?'

The de Vere tomb was another matter on which decision had to be deferred.

The Dean wished to stop decorating the altar with mistletoe at Christmas time. Surely, he thought, no problem would arise here. But today the Chapter seemed determined to thwart him. Were they going to prove die-hard traditionalists? They were.

'It is our most ancient custom!'

'This is our cathedral's alone – a special thing to us!'

'Completely pointless innovation!'

'Sacred tradition!'

The Dean had been doing his best to do away with the mistletoe surreptitiously, by allowing the bunches to be much smaller the previous Christmas, and by banishing them from the altar itself to the tall candlesticks which stood on either side. A thousand years of tradition – perhaps fifteen hundred – meant little to him, unless he could use it as an argument on his own side. The uniqueness of the custom also meant nothing to him. He was the new broom, was he not, and he had to sweep clean, and what he had decided to sweep was the mistletoe, because he thought he would have no opposition.

Now, a furore began which after half an hour the Dean was forced to quell.

Fortunately there were other matters on the agenda. No one cared passionately about these, so with a high hand the Dean pressed these further proposals through. Exhausted, the Chapter let him. If he did not have at least some triumphs they knew he would be unbearable.

The Dean closed the meeting with only just enough time for the Chapter to go to the Deanery for tea before the All Souls' Day service.

Chapter Clerk Herbert Barkston found that he was shaking from head to foot. Why had he thought he would enjoy being part of the cathedral community? It was worse than working, much worse. He had never before had to deal with anyone the least like Dean Henry Parsifal.

'You did extremely well,' said George Grindal, pausing beside him. 'Beautifully organized. Your first Full Chapter, wasn't it?'

'The second, actually.'

'Oh yes. You really are most efficient, and to be congratulated.'

The Chapter Clerk stopped trembling and smiled weakly. He began to feel distinctly better.

'Splendidly arranged.' Oglethorpe supported his friend although he had no thoughts one way or the other on the organization of the meeting.

'Do come and have a cup of the Dean's tea,' went on Grindal. 'Mrs Guest's scones are always very good. Canon Oglethorpe and I are walking over together, if you would care to join us.'

The Chapter Clerk postponed his mental decision to resign. It was very pleasant to be appreciated. Perhaps he was going to enjoy working for the cathedral after all. He walked out between the two canons into the misty afternoon.

4

For mine enemies speak against me, and they
that lay wait for my soul take their counsel
together, saying; God hath forsaken him; per-
secute him and take him, for there is none to
deliver him.

—*Psalms*, 71, v. 9

Luckily for the peace of mind of Holdernesse, the Surveyor of
the Fabric had phoned him at lunch-time and arranged to come
to look at the tell-tales that very afternoon, while all the clergy
were in the Chapter meeting. The two architects went up
together to the tower, Holdernesse explaining as they went the
unforgivable attitude of the Dean.

'Not to worry,' said the Surveyor of the Fabric, giving his
young assistant a smile and making a gesture that said, even
more clearly than his words, 'the Dean knows nothing at all
about structure.'

'I don't see how I can help worrying,' Holdernesse replied,
not at all ready to be mollified.

They reached the tell-tales and spent half an hour examining
the tower and discussing the minute fractures which had
appeared in two of the small pieces of glass attached to the
stone.

'In my opinion,' the surveyor said at last, 'the trouble is due
to this north pinnacle. It has been on my mind for some time.
No, I don't think the whole structure is affected at all. Quite
safe. But we must take the pinnacle down and rebuild it. Now
let's go to the office and have a look at the financial forecasts for
this year, and see if we can fit it in.'

When at last the Chapter meeting was over and the clergymen
were filtering in ones and twos to the Deanery for their tea, the

Dean did not immediately go with his guests. He went back into the body of the cathedral, drawn by the sound of tentative chords. He remembered that he had a bone to pick with Edmund Jason, who was due to play later at the special evensong for All Souls' Day. Edmund Jason was a very different kettle of fish from that uppish architect, Holdernesse. It would be rather satisfying to put him down.

Once again the Dean was interfering with things which were considered outside his province. It was the job of the Chapter Clerk, Barkston, to investigate the matter of Jason's morals, not the job of the Dean at all. He ought to have maintained a magisterial impartiality and stood ready if necessary to give Christian guidance to the young organist.

The Dean stood for a moment reviewing his opinion of the Chapter Clerk. He discovered that it had not altered.

Delegation, he decided, was wrong, however according to precedent it might be. A particularly vicious and prolonged increase of pain in his joints made him immobile for a while longer, enduring. He gasped and glanced upward towards heaven, then he grabbed for a handhold on the nearest monument. As the pain ebbed slightly the Dean found that his resolve had strengthened.

Climbing the stairs to the loft, the Dean found that it was indeed Edmund Jason who was there with his hands picking out chords as he studied a piece of music propped before him. 'A word with you, Jason,' said Dean Parsifal.

The young man turned, a pleased smile on his rather earnest face, his eyes swimming up behind the thick lenses of his glasses.

'It has come to my notice that you were dismissed from your last post – at that direct grant school,' said the Dean sternly.

The young organist began to speak and was halted by the impossibility of utterance. The words refused to come out. At last he managed to say yes.

'So you were appointed under false pretences.'

'Well, no, Mr Dean. I just applied for the post here and won it. It is true that I was under notice at the time. There seemed no reason to mention that.'

'It has also come to my notice why you were given your

48

dismissal. Do you not think that fact should have been mentioned?'

The young man blushed deeply.

'I can see nothing that is wrong, sir.'

'Do you think we would have appointed an assistant organist – to be closely in touch with our choirboys – who we knew to have been suspected of homosexual practices?'

'It wasn't anything like that, Mr Dean . . . I wasn't . . . it was only . . .'

'We should have been told that you were a man with a past, Jason. You should have made a clean breast of it.'

'But I wouldn't have been given the job, sir.'

'That is possible.'

The Dean felt he had said enough to strike fear into the young man and that to say any more would be superfluous. He drew himself up and looked very forbidding. He turned and, taking care how he placed his feet, lowered himself slowly down the steps.

Behind him Jason shivered. He had thought misunderstanding and reproaches were behind him; now the knowledge of things which had been said before and might be said again threatened to spoil the ideal way of life he had been lucky enough to win for himself. He wouldn't have minded if the accusations had been true. But because a friendship with a young man of nearly his own age had come about, a young man in the sixth form at the time, the whole thing was twisted into the suggestion that he was capable of approaching small boys! The bare idea revolted him. His relationship even with Simon was chaste. How much more so his dealings with innocent children!

If he left Edmund Jason shattered by the encounter, the Dean was, to his surprise, amazingly disturbed himself. Putting down the humble, unsure young man should have been a pleasure after the encounter with that self-confident Holdernesse, but instead of a glow of satisfaction he was as uneasy as if he had been in the wrong, which was of course impossible. Certainly the young man did not seem repentant. Everyone who has responsibility for children must be aware of the risks and dangers they run from those who are supposed to have their

49

best interests at heart, thought the Dean. He concluded that the worry over the choirboys was a real one, even though he had only invented it as a stick with which to beat Edmund Jason. Suppose Jason were to lay an unholy hand on the little one with the thick fair hair, for instance . . . patting his shoulder in a brotherly way . . . If the bare thought of casual friendly caresses made the Dean shudder, how much more horror – and also prurient fascination – lay in wilder speculation!

The Dean, carried out of himself by these ideas, was able to summon the resources to conquer his enemy arthritis. He walked along firmly, which took a lot of determination. Deep in furious thought he soon found himself stalking into the door of his own home.

A mirror showed his face, rigidly set, the brows drawn together. It took a further great effort of will to drag his thoughts back and speak politely to his guests, who were being served by the housekeeper with their cups of tea and scones.

Mr Barkston the Chapter Clerk, who had been enjoying himself, now hurriedly drank up his tea. He spoke to those canons who were near him and then hurried off on the plea that he had a lot of work in the office. He did not say goodbye to the Dean.

The Dean's visit to the organ loft had not gone unnoticed by Mr Barkston, who had seen him heading that way and who had also heard the chords of music. He felt uncomfortable and even ridiculously guilty. He had known all about Jason's dismissal, even before he was appointed assistant organist, but, liking the young man, having a very real respect for his musical ability, and unable to believe that there was anything basically corrupt about him, he had not shared his knowledge with the Dean. He had felt fully justified in this, but now that the matter had come out and everybody knew, it looked as if his silence might mean more trouble for Jason. He told himself that the Dean had probably wanted to have a word about the music but he did not really convince himself. He hurried over to his office in part of St William's College to forget his worries in work.

'Are you going to evensong?' asked his secretary as she laid the letters before him for signing.

Mr Barkston said sharply, 'No. Far too much time is wasted

50

in going to the cathedral services by non-clerical staff, in my opinion.' True to his local government training he had long ago lost sight of the real purpose of the institution he was supporting.

His secretary sighed. If only dear old Mr Long was back, they would have gone together, and had a good critique of the music and singing afterwards and told each other who was in the congregation. Mr Barkston just did not fit in. Why, oh why, had the Dean appointed him?

Towards the time of evensong Sister Agape was walking over to the cathedral from the Sisters' house when Lucy Grindal emerged from her own front door, unaccompanied for once by the dachshunds, and saw her. With the quarrel with the Dean on her mind and those horrid tacky-paint notices trumpeting her shame to the world, Lucy felt she could not face Agape. She dodged round the end of her house towards St William's College and pressed herself against the wall until she was sure Agape was out of sight.

Verger Soames came quickly past her in his cassock and said, unnecessarily loudly, 'Good afternoon, Miss Grindal.'

Lucy thought she must have looked an idiot and with her colour rising (how she wished she did not go pink on the slightest provocation) walked on. As she passed the College, Holdernesse rushed out of the time-blackened carved oak doorway with the heraldic arms on either side of it – the seven red mascles on a golden shield of Archbishop Fitzherbert on one side and the two crossed silver keys of the see of York on their red field on the other – and nearly collided with her.

'So sorry, can't stop,' he said.

Lucy gazed after him and then, because he had behaved so unlike himself, retraced her steps so that she could see where he went. Whatever was he doing? She watched him make for the north door, the 'back door' closed to the public, open for cathedral employees and clergy. 'It's not like him to go to evensong,' she reflected. 'His interest in the cathedral is purely professional. He always says he's an agnostic, and he doesn't really enjoy church music.'

51

She went on her way towards Goodramgate, thinking, 'I'm not going either, and I am not an agnostic, and I do like church music, especially the music they are having today, but I just can't feel in the right mood. I am sure it's wrong of me. Hullo, there's Mrs Hassock, well, she is certainly off to the service. I hope she doesn't stop.' She didn't. Lucy walked on, wishing to carry out her shopping in peace without encountering anyone else.

The east end of the cathedral lay wrapped peacefully in the milky dim afternoon light. Suddenly the door of the Old Residence – now a school – opened and a crowd of green-clad children came out on the steps with a harassed-looking girl in charge of them. At the same time a fleet of cars, which had until then been held in check by the police, swept in front of St William's and mothers and children were noisily united.

Nigel Parsifal, walking negligently past the College in the opposite direction to Lucy, was swept up in this hubbub and spent some minutes extricating himself and the parcel he was carrying. Lucy saw him from across the road but hoped he had not seen her. She was far too upset to want to see anyone at all.

As he went on towards the Deanery Nigel saw the Chapter clergy walking across, in full cry, as he described it to himself. He slackened his pace to avoid them.

The Chapter were straggling back to the cathedral immediately after their refreshment for it was now nearing four o'clock. They were looking forward to donning the vestments of purple embroidered with silver, to processing to the music of the special introit into the beauty of the choir with its carved seats of oak, to helping in the weaving of a stately celebration and remembrance on earth of all those departed. As in the vestry they put on their robes they put on with them timelessness, stateliness. They collected everything they needed to carry.

The vergers were placing a rope across the aisle so that the casual tourists were kept back in the nave and did not disturb the service. The builders' shuttering, closing off the south transept which was under repair, hindered the tourists' view. For this reason, so that the visitors could enjoy seeing some of the pageantry, the procession was planned to pass round the whole of the east end, coming finally down the north choir aisle

52

into the nave and into the choir through the central door in the medieval screen of kings.

The bell immediately over the vestry door rang out, signifying that the service was due to begin.

George Grindal was one of the last to leave the vestry, passing his friend Sam Oglethorpe busily re-tying a shoe-lace.

Above them, the cathedral clock prepared to strike four.

The procession assembled in the south choir aisle with the Dean at the back of the line. After a few seconds of impatient delay, waiting for the organ to sound out the introit, the Dean decided not to wait.

'Set off without the music,' he commanded.

They moved forward very slowly, forming as they went a single spaced out line.

Their heads were slightly bent, their thoughts concentrating themselves towards the coming act of worship.

As the Dean passed up the south choir aisle, alone, at the end of the procession, a knob of carved stone fell and with a dull faint thud knocked him to the stone-flagged floor.

He gave a short cry which was swallowed up by the distant sound of the first of the four o'clock chimes which went before the striking of the hour. The cry was only heard by George Grindal, walking ahead of him, who swung round.

Sister Agape, who had been respectfully standing at the side with the verger, rushed forward and dropped on to her knees by the Dean's head. He was gasping, but lying very still. His cheek seemed to press into the paving stones gratefully, as if they were downy pillows where he could seek rest. She looked down wordless, her eyes wide with shock, her hand reaching out to touch him.

'A heart attack?' whispered Grindal. The rest of the procession were slowly pacing further away, not aware that anything had happened.

Sister Agape pointed to the stone lying by the Dean and then reached out to his head where between the temple and the crown the skin was broken and a trace of blood was showing.

The Dean was still gasping.

'He must be going to be all right,' said Grindal quietly. 'It doesn't look much of a bump, and he's breathing. It's knocked him out, that's all.'

Sister Agape put her hand flat on the Dean's head and moved her fingers very slightly. Under the Dean's skin she could feel the now overlapping fragmented free bones, as if she were touching a bag of marbles.

There was an almost imperceptible movement of the head as if to nestle closer into the stone and the hands palm down on the paving seemed to caress the comfortable bed they found there.

The troubled gasps for breath went on.

'Is he still breathing all right?' asked George Grindal doubtfully a few seconds later. The gasps seemed to have stopped.

'The Dean is dead,' said Sister Agape.

The last stroke of four had just faded away.

5

Who will rise up with me against the wicked, or
who will take my part against the evil doers?
—*Psalms*, 94, v. 16

'Conmen, defaulters, fraudsters, they wouldn't have minded,'
Detective Chief Inspector Bob Southwell remarked to Detective
Inspector Dave Smart. 'We could have housed hundreds of
those without a protest. But give a prison a maximum security
wing – and they're worried to death.'

'It's what they read in the papers that does it,' DI Smart said
reassuringly.

Bob Southwell had enough to preoccupy him.

A new prison opening at Full Sutton, near his area, had
meant a lot of thought. It was not the prison itself or its staff,
for that was part of the national prison service and not his
responsibility – thank goodness. But the movement of prisoners
into and out of the area, the interest created in the criminal
world by a new centre of detention – these needed
consideration.

It meant visitors to the prison arriving and departing, usually
via York. The local population had been disturbed because
house prices had jumped upward in response to the sudden
demand from prison staff. People were not keen on the presence of criminals in their peaceful rural community – particularly of violent and dangerous men.

'We've had several letters asking if famous criminals are
coming, like the Black Panther, or Ian Brady, or the Great Train
Robbers,' Bob Southwell went on. He was glad that DI Smart
had come in. He could speak what was in his mind in Dave's
presence.

'They've been reading the tabloids, thinking of rapists and
murderers. They'll settle down,' replied Dave. 'Anyway, the

Great Train Robbers aren't in prison any more, are they? One of them's in South America and I heard one's selling flowers on Waterloo station. Probably the others are out by now.'

DI Smart was one of the large, stolid type of police officers. When he still wore uniform he was the sort of policeman that people felt they could approach to ask the time. In his early days on the beat he had rapidly become a kind of agony uncle to his community. Those days had long gone, but even out of uniform he still bore the aura of serenity and safe harbour about with him.

Bob Southwell, his boss, was totally different. Keen and blade sharp, he was physically and mentally restless. Now he went on, 'They think in picturesque terms. Real danger is prosaic in comparison. It's the unusual crime, the sensational trial, that makes the difference to the public. But once a man is condemned, danger is something as simple as power, and money is power. Clout. It's the prisoner with influence and cash who is likely to get sprung, not one who is likely to endanger the community.'

'Train robbers or IRA,' summed up DI Smart.

'You've said it.'

'That isn't what I came to speak to you about, Bob,' diffidently remarked Smart.

'What? Oh. No. What is it, then?'

'CPS have got a date for the Crown Court on that hijack job on the A1. They want to know if Jim Wilson and Bob Morrison can be available on the 4th. It'll probably be a three-day stint.'

'Of course they can't have Jim, he's on the theft from the exhibition at Beningbrough – silver on loan from somewhere. And Morrison is on that escort job for Full Sutton prison, that's top priority, and the Home Office'll go spare if it's changed again, they've altered it a few times already, you know how jumpy they are about anything with an IRA connection. Can't they get the defence to agree to a statement about the hijack?'

'They might for Morrison. But they'll definitely need Wilson. Can't you take him off that silver for a day or two, put someone else on?'

'No, I can't. He's the only one of you who knows an heirloom from a Habitat offering, ring CPS – '

'You can't ring CPS.'

'Oh, sorry, I forgot they don't know about telephones. Ring Processing then, and tell them no dice. Try for a three-week adjournment.'

'They won't like it.'

'They can damn well lump it.'

The phone rang. Bob Southwell snatched it up.

'It's for you, Dave.'

As Smart took the phone Bob Southwell rose from his desk and walked over to the window.

'You'll want to know about this, sir.'

'What is it?'

'Accident in the cathedral. The Dean killed by a falling stone.'

Bob turned to face him, with a crease between close-drawn eyebrows.

'Accident, you said?'

'Certainly looks that way.'

'Been passed to you for investigation.'

'Right.'

'I seem to remember a flake of stone narrowly missing a choirboy last year.'

'Yes.'

'Sounds like a nasty tragedy. No need for me to be involved, I take it.'

'No.'

'I'll just walk along with you, anyway. It pleases the authorities if they think something like this has had a bit of high-level attention. It'll give me a break. That makes it three unusual things today. First, the theft of that silver. Second, the names of the first high-security prisoners for Full Sutton. Third, the death of the Dean.'

'They say things come in threes, sir.'

'When I get back I'm going to do nothing but ordinary things. I'm going to OK that leave list and deal with those inter-office memos, and keep office hours and leave at five o'clock.'

'You do that, Bob,' said DI Smart.

*

The two big men entered by the main south door, ignoring the notice which told them to use the one at the west.

Detective Inspector Smart walked up the steps to the door heavily, ponderously; but, exuding more presence, Bob Southwell was as light as a panther, with a dancer's grace which reminded a passer-by of Fred Astaire. The broad forehead, the narrow jaw, carried forward the likeness. Bob was wearing police regulation spectacles that day and so had not quite his usual characteristic look.

When they passed through the door it was to find themselves among a mess of rubble and scaffolding and in an air thick with dust.

'Hey!' A man in overalls and a hard hat was sitting drinking a mug of coffee. 'You can't come in here! Who's left that bloody door open?'

'My fault,' said Bob meekly. 'I'd forgotten you're working here. Police.' He got out his identification. 'Can we come through? There's been an accident.'

'We need to be in the south choir aisle,' put in Dave Smart. 'This is the quickest way, isn't it?'

'Forgotten?' said the man incredulously. 'The whole world knows the south transept was burnt out and you've got your eyes in your head. You can see the scaffolding and the temporary roof well enough I should hope. I haven't heard about an accident.'

'It's only just happened. To one of the clergy.'

'You'd better come through then,' said the man. 'But for heaven's sake go the other way next time. No one's been allowed in here since the fire, you ought to know that. You haven't got hard hats on. But we've knocked off for tea-break while the service is on and most of them have gone to have a ciggy, so come on quick.'

He opened part of the shuttering and they went through. As soon as it closed behind them it looked as if it had never been opened, no latch or handle showed. They were in the claustrophobic corridor of shuttering leading from the nave to the area near the gift shop and the entrance of the Undercroft.

'Come on,' said Bob. 'It would have been quicker to go round to the west.'

58

They jostled through the sightseers, who were chatting and strolling as usual, not knowing anything tragic had happened; and came out into the open nave.

As always Bob caught his breath on realizing the vastness, the spaciousness, of the great cathedral church, even when one of its arms was burnt out, boarded off and useless. It seemed a desecration that violent death had entered this place; yet here death was only a continuation and fulfilment of life and the contribution of dead hands lived on. Death was accepted, not fought; so, after all, there could be few better places from which to pass on to another world. As he gazed up into the heights above he noticed a faint thickening of the air as if some of the mist had seeped inside.

They turned right towards the south choir aisle and were greeted by a verger putting up solid barriers to keep the public out of the area. The rope which had protected the service from intrusion was no longer enough.

Only a quarter of an hour had elapsed since the Dean had died.

It had taken that time for the shocked Canon Grindal to fetch Tockwith, the cathedral policeman; for Canon Oglethorpe, who came limping up as all was over, to go back to the vestry to fetch a surplice and cover him; for Tockwith to ring the police station in Clifford Street, for Smart to tell Southwell, and for the two of them to arrive.

Had they used a police car, it would have taken them longer, for this was the autumn term. Parents had brought their children to York in desperation for there was something to do there even if the weather was wet or wringing with mist as it was at present. The consequence was that even in late afternoon there was not a single parking space in the city. All the roads were as cram-full of cars looking for somewhere to stop as the pavements were full of tourists.

Southwell and Smart approached the group round the Dean as the last of the congregation who had gathered in the choir for the service were leaving through the screen of kings, well away from the south choir aisle. They had been told that an accident had taken place and that the service was being postponed for at least an hour. Some of them had been reluctant to go, particularly when the organ was still playing.

Now the choir and the south choir aisle were empty except for the Chapter clergy and the cathedral policeman.

Sister Agape had gone back to her post in the nave, selling certificates to tourists to prove that their financial contribution had kept the ancient building going for one minute of terrestrial time. Whatever she was feeling of shock and horror she had the self-discipline to hide. The public must not know that anything out of the ordinary had happened – not yet. The crowds would thin out soon, it was November after all; they would not want to be late home. If she could keep up a normal front a little longer it would be to the good.

Canon Grindal was standing with his head bent and his back to the approaching detectives. He was reciting in a quiet melodious voice the first Collect for the service: 'Oh Lord, the Maker and Redeemer of all believers, grant to the faithful departed all the unsearchable benefits to thy son's passion, that in the day of his appearing they may be manifested as thy true children through the same thy son Jesus Christ Our Lord. Amen.'

It was the first thing by way of prayer which had come into his head, partly because the All Souls' Day service had been running through it since early morning. The others had fallen in with his lead and were either listening or in even quieter tones speaking the words along with him.

As George Grindal ended he looked up and saw the two policemen standing beside him.

'Mr Southwell!' he exclaimed. 'This is kind, to respond yourself.'

'The least we could do.'

'A dreadful accident, we fear.'

'May we see? Would you stand back, gentlemen?'

'I don't think we're all needed,' put in Canon Oglethorpe.

'Could most of us go and wait in the Helpers' Rest Room?' asked Grindal.

'Certainly. I would like you to stay. You, perhaps, Canon, if you would be so good.'

With backward glances the rest of the Chapter filed silently away.

'I have taken it on myself to send the choirboys across to their

60

school again,' Grindal confessed. 'They're waiting there if you need them but none of them saw anything, they were at the front of the procession.'

Bob Southwell lifted the covering over the Dean.

'No doubt about cause of death,' he said, looking at the stone which lay beside its victim.

'No.'

'Fairly quick, I should think.'

'That is at least a blessing.'

After finding out from Canon Grindal just what had been happening that day, and what was planned to happen next, DCI Southwell turned to the cathedral security man, Tockwith.

'Where did the stone fall from?' asked Southwell. 'The builders in the south transept are a long way off, it can't have had anything to do with them. Were there any of the cathedral's own masons working in the vaulting?'

'No. And they always take the strictest safety precautions. Look, sir; they're working on the north side of the nave at present. There's a platform built out, and it's all netted in, so that no stone can possibly fall.'

Tockwith was a member of the private force, the cathedral police, which had existed before Robert Peel invented the modern bobby. Relations with the younger force were always exceptionally good. Tockwith looked upset, but not worried.

'But this stone did fall.'

'In humid weather like we're having at present the limestone is affected and it can happen that a piece drops off.'

'Yes. Didn't some nearly hit a choirboy?'

'Last year. But that's very unusual. The masons keep a strict eye on the condition of the stone.'

'This piece seems to have escaped their notice.'

'I'm afraid so. It isn't very big, of course.'

'He was doing what?'

'They were walking in procession.'

'And he fell where he is lying now?'

'Yes. Dropped in his tracks.'

'Is there some kind of walkway up there?'

'Yes. You can see. He's just about under it.'

'Did the stone fall from there?'

61

'We haven't had the masons up yet, sir, but it does look as if it must have done.'

'There wasn't an odd bit lying about from work?'

'They're so careful you'd hardly believe it. No chance.'

Southwell and Smart together stepped back and looked up to where, they could see, it was possible to walk at an upper level.

'If a piece of stone was left on that walkway and accidentally kicked over . . .'

'You can question the masons. But I'll stake my life they wouldn't leave anything about, and there was nobody up there.'

'How can you be so positive, Tockwith?'

'Two things, sir. One, we carried out a search of the roof area at two thirty this afternoon. Regular practice. Parties go up the tower, and although they can't get into those walkways, we check thoroughly to make sure that all is well. Two, to get to that part you have to go up the narrow stone stairs set in the piers, and the entrance doors to those stairs are kept locked. The keys are in our custody.'

'Let's see them.'

Inside the Cathedral Police's little cubby-hole of an office in the thickness between the panelling of the choir and the south choir aisle was a key board with labelled keys, and Tockwith produced the Key Book, where any key issued was signed for.

'None of the relevant keys signed out today, sir, and the whole set present and correct.' He waved his hand to indicate them.

'No one could borrow one without your knowing?'

'This place is kept manned. If it should be empty even for seconds it is locked.'

Bob Southwell had indeed just witnessed Tockwith unlocking the door. 'What's your interpretation, then, Tockwith?'

'Can't be anything other than a freak accident, sir. The care the masons take is phenomenal. But the air is very damp indeed today.'

'You're positive that no one could have been up there and accidentally dislodged it or kicked it off?'

'No way. As I've explained, no one had been up at all today

apart from us doing our routine search. The masons have been working in the stoneyard.'

'I'd like to have a look, all the same,' insisted Bob Southwell. Tockwith took down the relevant key. As he left the office he locked it behind him, with a pointed look at Bob.

Bob felt like twitting him because he hadn't signed the stairs key out, but because of the proximity of sudden death decided that to do so would be unfeeling and flippant. He could see that Tockwith was in shock, as was everyone else who knew of the tragedy. He hadn't known the Dean himself and was used to sudden death and corpses, so he reminded himself not to forget that to other people the event was both personal, unfamiliar and shocking.

A narrow door in what looked like a solid pillar opened to show a cramped circular stair. The three climbed it. Then they had to follow a complicated route before reaching the walkway over the south choir aisle.

'I'm glad we're no fatter,' Bob commented.

Then they moved slowly along a stone walkway with pierced stone parapets on one side and a solid wall on the other, which stretched across the south choir aisle. They looked down at the floor far below, and the surplice-shrouded figure there. They spent a few minutes looking around, in what Tockwith realized was a very experienced way. He felt that their eyes missed nothing. At last after what seemed a long time to Tockwith, Southwell declared himself satisfied. The place immediately over the body, where the piece of stone must have fallen from the moulded arcading above the walkway, had been examined intently, and the floor of the walkway scrutinized.

'There doesn't seem to be anything else to do up here,' said Dave Smart after a while. With shared relief they edged their way back and then at last down the circular stair.

Once returned to the patterned paving of the floor of the great building Southwell stretched out his arms and filled his lungs with a great inrush of breath. The contrast between the restricted stair and the spaciousness around the pillar concealing it was striking. Tockwith left them to go to speak to Canon Grindal.

'What do you reckon, sir?' asked Smart.

'Accident. Tockwith is a good reliable security man. So is his shift mate, Cullis. The cathedral is well cared for by its security staff. Act of God.'

'Like the lightning strike after the consecration of the Bishop of Durham?'

'Just like that. Though why the Good Lord didn't strike Durham itself beats me, instead of causing us all this trouble. They are going to be years repairing that transept. I didn't realize what a big job it is until we stood there among it all. They have to work to such a high standard, too.'

'Right, sir. So, inquest, but we presume accident. Act of God, if you want to put it like that.'

'We do.'

And then Detective Chief Inspector Southwell went back to his office and his desk, to whip through the rest of his routine paperwork before going home to his wife Linda, children Susan and Paul, and the evening meal. Paperwork was always with him; it was one of the constant features of his life.

Left in charge in the cathedral, Detective Inspector Dave Smart remembered that the Chapter had been waiting for him in the Helpers' Rest Room for what must have seemed to them a considerable time. He had radioed earlier to the station, in fact almost immediately after arrival, to ask for an assistant, a doctor, and an ambulance. Detective Constable James Jester had arrived and was standing about unobtrusively, while the police doctor bent over the body and the ambulance men stood ready. Canon Grindal was waiting. Dave passed over temporary authority for the body to the doctor, spoke to the verger about keeping the barriers up, and turned to Jester.

'Will you lead the way, Canon?' asked Dave. 'Come on, James. Let's have a word with the clergy,' and, as they followed Canon Grindal, 'You got a notebook?'

When Canon Grindal opened the rest-room door the buzz of conversation abruptly ceased. All heads turned towards Dave Smart. He found the sight of the Chapter daunting; all the members were still wearing their processional clothing; they were sitting rather stiffly and with alert expressions.

'I am very sorry to have kept you waiting, gentlemen,' he said. 'I am Detective Inspector Smart. The Detective Chief Inspector, Mr Southwell, and I have been carrying out an examination of the scene. This event has of course been a great shock to you all. I'm happy to be able to tell you that the DCI and myself feel, on the evidence of what we have seen and learned so far, that the death of the Dean was purely accidental, and not due to negligence on anyone's part. So, distressing as it is, at present there seems to be no cause for blame. However, in all cases of accidental death, an inquest must be held, and I would like to take the opportunity of making a few notes of anything you can tell me, as guidance in preparation of that inquest.'

'Is the Dean still lying there?' asked one of the canons indignantly.

'The ambulance has arrived and the Dean is being taken to the mortuary until arrangements are made. The area is remaining sealed off from the public at the moment.'

This answer seemed to calm the assembly. They were impressed by solid Dave Smart with his air of authority, and the considerate tones in which he had spoken.

'Was there any need to keep us shut up here?' one of them asked, but in a fairly placid voice.

'It is always important to have as few people as possible trampling around' – Dave caught himself up – 'standing round a body, in the case of a sudden death. We always have to consider the possibility of carelessness or malice having been contributory factors, and . . .'

'You don't want the clues destroyed by being trodden on,' put in an elderly clergyman whose main reading was detective stories.

'Exactly.'

'Can we go now?'

'If you don't mind, gentlemen, first giving me a picture of what happened this afternoon.'

The Chapter was remarkably clear on the whole. The members of it shrank away from saying anything critical of Dean Parsifal, and Dave Smart gained the impression that the Chapter meeting had been all harmony and brotherly love. The tea

65

provided for them by the Dean came in for a great deal of praise. They all said how much they had been looking forward to the All Souls' Day service. As they had all been together since two o'clock, it was not difficult to put down a coherent account of the chain of events, but so many voices were busy in telling the story that it was well after five o'clock and tipping towards six when Dave Smart finally left them.

Once the Chapter clergy were alone the Precentor turned to George Grindal. 'While we were waiting we elected an Acting Dean, Canon Grindal,' he said in a formal manner. 'The Chapter unanimously voted for yourself.'

For a few seconds George said nothing, then he thanked the assembly for their confidence in his powers to tide things over. 'But in my absence and without my prior agreement I don't think it was correct procedure,' he could not help adding. 'Mr Barkston, the Chapter Clerk, should have been present and organized it.'

The Precentor, who was on the verge of retirement and in poor health, could still be firm and overrule mere striplings like Grindal. 'We felt in the circumstances that action ought to be taken. We telephoned the Chapter Clerk and he came and conducted proceedings. He wanted to remain but his mother is ill and he felt he had to return home.'

'We don't want to have to formally assemble again tomorrow,' put in an elderly canon who had had a long journey.

'I can see it was very sensible,' said Grindal. 'And I'm glad that I won't have to mollify Mr Chapter Clerk.'

'And now, Mr Acting Dean, I suggest that we return to the choir and conduct evensong,' said the Precentor. 'In your absence it was decided that I should take the service. Jason!' The young organist rose up nervously from the unobtrusive seat he had found. 'Come along now. We thought the plainest and simplest service,' he went on, 'none of the extras which had been planned. But evensong itself must be carried out – statutory, I don't need to remind you, George, and it has been advertised as sung, not said. Can someone slip across for the choirboys, if they are still at the school? It will help us all, I feel, to carry God's service out as normally as we can.'

Evensong took place. None of the congregation who had

gathered earlier had returned for it. Although conducted with reverence and not rushed, it was still completed very quickly.

They walked to the vestry to disrobe, and finally dispersed quietly. What there was to say had been said, many times.

'They were all in front of him in the procession,' Dave said thoughtfully to DC James Jester. 'So no one really saw the accident happen except Sister Agape. We'd better talk to her if she's closing her little stall. Canon Grindal turned at hearing the Dean's cry and saw him just as he flattened on to the ground. The verger was keeping his eye on the public. Canon Oglethorpe was late and came out of the vestry door more or less at that moment.'

'You would have thought some of the tourists would have seen it happen,' said Jester.

'The verger had moved them well back, and the builders' boards and screens round the burnt-out south transept reduce visibility to almost nothing from where they were standing.'

Sister Agape had been watching the procession and she had seen the stone fall and strike the Dean on the side of his head. No, she hadn't been looking upward, she saw the stone first when it came into view on its downward path, a fraction of time before it hit the Dean.

'Straightforward, then,' said James Jester.

'Nothing to it,' replied Dave Smart.

6

They gaped upon me with their mouths and
said Fie on thee, we saw it with our eyes.
—*Psalms*, 35, v. 21

'We have to carry on,' George Grindal had said, and it had been
what all the Chapter felt. Life and its processes, the life around
the great cathedral, must flow on.

George had said the same words again after he had spoken
of the news to Lucy. He and Oglethorpe had arrived just as she
was beginning to fear that dinner would be forgotten. She
already knew what had happened, for Mr Barkston had come
over before going home, to break the news to the Dean's
housekeeper and to other cathedral people concerned.

By mutual consent George Grindal, Lucy and Oglethorpe
avoided the subject of Dean Parsifal over their meal. Canon
Oglethorpe enjoyed his dinner. The atmosphere in the dining-
room was pleasantly civilized; there was a fire in the Elizabethan
fireplace with its elaborately carved dark oak overmantel; the
chairs and refectory table were reassuringly solid; there was a
thick Turkey carpet underfoot. The wine had been good and
the meal excellent.

Lucy had been in as great a turmoil while cooking it as she
had been while cooking lunch, though for very different reasons. Turmoil goes well with the preparation of cheese omelette
followed by tossed salad, rice, and lightly grilled fillet steaks.
The pudding had fortunately been prepared the day before and
was a kind of mousse, rich and chocolate-flavoured with a hint
of Cointreau, set in boudoir fingers and accompanied by cream
in a silver sauce boat. This was just the kind of meal Oglethorpe
enjoyed, and his friends enjoyed pleasing him.

'But I won't be late home,' he said.

'You've time for coffee by the fire upstairs?'

'You've not lit two fires?' To the frugal Oglethorpe this seemed the limit of extravagance.

'It does the house good.'

They settled round the sitting-room fire. It could not be denied that there was a lightness of atmosphere seemingly incompatible with sudden death.

'The police seem convinced that it was an accident,' said Oglethorpe comfortably.

'A dreadful thing! An extraordinary thing!' exclaimed George.

'It makes me feel awful for being so angry with him,' said Lucy.

George Grindal, after his exclamation, was quiet for a long time – all the time Lucy was pouring and serving the coffee. Oglethorpe's words kept recurring to him.

'The police are convinced it was an accident, you said?' Lucy questioned at last, and Oglethorpe answered her. 'When Detective Inspector Smart came and spoke to us, he said as much.'

'What else could it have been?' said George.

No one spoke – they did not even sip their coffee. At last, Oglethorpe said, 'There is no alternative.'

'No thinkable alternative. There is an alternative.'

Lucy jumped up with a cry, her coffee jerking from the cup to the saucer. She set it down shakily.

'You mean me, father – you're remembering what I said at lunch-time. I keep remembering it too. I said I would like to murder him.'

George Grindal's beautiful voice was sharp.

'Never be so absorbed in yourself, Lucy, that you take things personally which are not meant to be so. If our Dean's sudden death was not accidental, it must have been purposeful. Someone must have intended it. He was a man who irritated many people, including you.'

'Count me in,' said Canon Oglethorpe. 'God rest his soul.'

'It is not really our business to enquire into the matter of his death, and the police have apparently decided, very reasonably, that it was an accident. What troubles me is that should they be wrong – should this have been murder – then the cathedral would need to be reconsecrated, would it not?'

'I'd forgotten that aspect,' said Oglethorpe.

'For that reason we must be sure.'

'But the police are experts, father,' put in Lucy. 'I can't imagine why you should think it was not an accident. They think it was. You can't enquire better than they can. Why say that awful word? Why even think that it might be . . . murder?'

'I can't explain it,' said George Grindal a little helplessly. 'I just have a great feeling of unease about the whole matter. A strong, underlying disquiet. All right, it isn't logical. I know that, Lucy. But I have had this feeling ever since it happened and it is growing stronger all the time. I have to satisfy myself that this unease is justified – or that it is not justified, and I'm only a silly old man with fancies in his head.'

Both his daughter and his friend objected to this description of himself.

'And you said that I could not enquire as well as the police can, Lucy. There is a difference, my dear. They are from outside, and, however concerned they feel, they cannot see cathedral matters in the same light that we do.'

'Tockwith and Cullis are of us, father.'

'And, bless them, they can conceive of nothing breaching their security arrangements.'

'But who would feel so strongly against the Dean?'

'Present company, for a beginning. You yourself said to me, Lucy, that you could cheerfully murder the Dean. And your face in Chapter, Oglethorpe, indicated that you felt the same over the matter of the statue.'

'So I did. Had the Dean and I been alone at that moment . . .'

'Let's establish where you both were at the time of his death,' said Grindal in a businesslike way, getting out of his pocket a little blue-covered notebook.

'I don't really believe any of this is happening,' said Lucy. 'It must be early afternoon still and in a moment we'll wake up from our after-lunch naps and realize that it is all a dream and that our Henry is still alive and as irritating as ever.'

'Where were you, Lucy?'

'At what time?'

'At about one minute to four.'

'Arguing with the butcher about the steak, I should think.'

'The butcher in Goodramgate?'

'Yes.'

'Then you were very close to the cathedral, could have slipped in and committed murder.'

'Oh, father!'

'Suspects,' he headed a page as he said the word. 'Lucy: whereabouts not proven.'

'You're just doing this to make me feel awful,' said Lucy.

Her father looked at her kindly.

'Not at all, my dear. I'm doing it because I want to find out the truth, and I can't exempt you from any enquiries I might make. You can't have special treatment. I intend to start by finding out where everyone was at the appropriate time, and by everyone I mean those people who had an antipathy to the Dean, or reason to profit by his death. As soon as you tell me where you were I'm sure that will be the end of it as far as you're concerned.'

Lucy hung her head and fondled the ears of the dachshund Clementina, who looked up in sympathy.

In a light tone, George went on, 'Where were you, Samuel Oglethorpe?'

'You know where I was, George. Tying up my shoe-lace in the vestry. I was climbing up the vestry steps when I heard a faint cry, and the sound of him falling.'

George Grindal gazed at his friend severely.

'You are trying to make this difficult, Samuel. Is there no secret door through which you could have gained access to a stair, run up, pushed a stone over, and come back down very quickly?'

'Not with my leg, and with my shoe-lace flapping, I couldn't,' replied Canon Oglethorpe. 'Even if there were such a route.'

'You didn't murder him over the matter of your small Georgian putti carved in limewood and looking up to heaven in an appealing fashion, which he was coveting in the spring, until the Chapter refused to back him?'

'No, nor over my medieval statue of John de Vere, though I felt like it.'

'I'm rather surprised that you heard him. The clock was beginning to strike.'

71

'My hearing is excellent, whatever may be happening to my memory for names.'

'Who else is there?'

Lucy had recovered some of her usual calm cheerfulness. 'His nephew, I should think,' she put in.

'Poor Nigel. Yes, I believe he has suffered.'

'Doesn't the Dean's money go to him?'

'Probably – though didn't we hear a lot of talk about changing wills?'

'That's typical, isn't it,' said Oglethorpe. 'Even though I've only known the Dean for ten months, I can imagine him saying that. Promising someone that they would be remembered, and then threatening to cut them out.'

'And then telling them that he had cut them out,' put in Lucy.

'Could well drive anyone to fury and loss of control.'

'Nigel Parsifal,' entered Canon Grindal in his notebook. 'Who else is there?'

Canon Oglethorpe opened his mouth to speak and then closed it again.

'Yes, Samivel?' George Grindal was fond of his Dickens, and often, thinking of Sam Weller, used this pet name for his friend.

'It's nothing . . .'

'Oh, yes, it is. Come on, let's have it.'

'Oh well, then – I heard a rumour about the organist.'

'Edmund Jason? Gracious, yes, it's been all round. He's supposed to have been kicked out of his previous job for caressing his pupils, or something.'

Lucy turned bright pink.

'Nothing proved, I understand,' said Oglethorpe hastily.

'No. Just asked to resign. For that matter, it may have been very innocent. Arm round the shoulders – a quick hug – '

'More than that, I fancy.'

'Had it been much more, they would have charged him for sure instead of asking for his resignation.'

'You would have thought so.'

'There is an odd thing. As we stood in the choir aisle before moving off, the Dean said, "Where's the introit? Jason's sulking, I fancy." Then he said, "Set off without the music."

72

'So he'd spoken to him about it!'

'It seems like it.'

'It was really the job of the Chapter Clerk. Trust Henry to butt in where angels fear to tread.'

'When do you think he spoke to him?'

'Jason was all right earlier this afternoon,' put in Lucy. 'I saw him as I came in from the market with vegetables. He smiled and passed the time of day and seemed his normal self.'

'What time was that?'

'About two. I had as much as I could carry so I went out again later to buy the meat.'

'He must have spoken to him after Chapter!' exclaimed Oglethorpe.

'Which was less than an hour before the service. Jason would be in an upset condition, of course. He couldn't possibly have got over an interview like that with the Dean in such a short time. So he was delaying beginning to play. Did he start at all? He did, didn't he? Then we had a job stopping him.'

'Yes. I came out of the vestry door – saw you bending over the Dean – there was all the fuss – you, George, ran to fetch Tockwith – I went for a surplice – it was only as you came back with him that the music began.'

'Oh dear. It doesn't look very good.'

'You can't really believe that Edmund Jason could kill anybody?' cried Lucy.

'I don't necessarily believe anybody killed anybody. But I must be sure. And what other way is there, except by putting forward the proposition and trying to prove it? If it is impossible to prove, then the death must be, as the police think, an accident.'

'I had better go,' said Canon Oglethorpe, heaving himself to his feet. 'Your chairs are too comfortable, Lucy. They make my old enemy relax; a hard one is better for him.'

'Next time I will bring a Windsor in for you.' Lucy was repentant. She had forgotten that the old war wound was such a constant trouble to her father's friend.

'There was that book I was going to lend you,' said George Grindal. 'You be going down. I'll just find it.'

Lucy was helping Canon Oglethorpe on with his coat, in the

pleasant hall, when her father leaned over the banisters on the landing above.

'Found it!' he said. It was at that moment, looking down, that a new thought struck him. He decided not to share the thought with his daughter and their guest. It had, however, been grave enough to strike away his air of gaiety. He thought further, as he descended the stairs and joined the others in the hall, that a falling stone was very much a blunt instrument; it might have hit anyone in the procession that day.

'I feel like a breath of air,' he said, and went to find his own overcoat. 'Get a dog lead, Lucy. I'll take Clementina. I'll walk back with Samuel. Nothing nicer than a chat under the stars.'

'No stars tonight,' rejoined Oglethorpe, putting his head out of the door. 'Still foggy. At least it's not raining.'

The cathedral stood eerily in the swirling water vapour, its towers obscured. As the two canons and the small dog rounded the end of the house they came upon a group of shivering people collected beneath Canon Grindal's bedroom window.

'The ghost of a little girl . . .' they heard the leader of the group say, pointing upwards.

'What's all that about?' asked Samuel.

'Don't say you've been in York nearly a year without coming across the Ghost Walks?'

'I haven't.'

'They take parties round the city to show them the places where sightings of ghosts have been reported. One of them's my bedroom. At least they don't ask to come inside. They're a nuisance at times. Even in the sitting-room where we were tonight you can hear the leaders shouting out their commentary, and the constant flashing of camera bulbs is quite irritating. I would have expected them to have finished for the winter, though. Perhaps it's a special party they're taking round.'

'Have you seen your ghost, then?'

'Oh, no. Not that I would mind. She's supposed to be a little girl whose family all died of plague and she was left alone in the boarded up house.'

'Could not get help, and died?'

'Yes, poor thing.'

'Is the story true?'

74

'I don't know. It might be.'

Canon Oglethorpe silently considered the sad story of the little plague girl. 'Probably things like that often happened,' he remarked. 'Child life was cheap, and it must have been rare to find the nobility and self-sacrifice shown at the Derbyshire village of Eyam. To rescue the child would not save her; she must have been already infected, and would only transmit it to one's own family. It might well seem a useless, even an unkind act; to give her hope, when the end was inevitable.'

But Canon Grindal had gone on to think of other things. 'It's still quite early,' he said. 'Barely eight. Things must be done. I wish I'd had the presence of mind to mention a few of them when we were all together earlier.'

'That's why we appointed you Acting Dean, so that there was someone to deal with what must inevitably be a great deal of troublesome business. No need to call another full Chapter meeting, I think. The Residentiary Canons, and such others as are easily available, will serve if you need to discuss or have additional authority.'

'Someone ought to look into the arrangements for poor Dean Parsifal. His nephew should do that in collaboration with us. I wonder if anyone has told that young man?'

'The police, surely.'

'Yes. Tockwith knows that Nigel Parsifal is the Dean's closest relative.'

All this time the two old men and the dog had been treading a network of back lanes and alleys. The mist lay like sweat on the cold stones. All the streets in York centre were unusually quiet. For the people on the Ghost Walk the mist added to the likelihood of eerie sensations which they were hoping to experience, but most of the local residents who could stay at home had decided to do so. Theatres and lectures were having a thin night, and restaurant staff thought they might as well shut and go home themselves. It was only the pubs which were doing a good trade.

At one point the two old men and the dog did meet other pedestrians. Two young men coming towards them appeared like trees walking, like wavering monsters, with surrounding auras caused by the yellow light of a street lamp behind them.

75

They gradually became more distinct but while they were still only vague forms ahead, one of them seemed to almost shriek at the sight of the older men. For the dark shapes of Grindal and Oglethorpe were likewise wrapped in waving trembling auras of mist and gold from the next of the street lamps. Then as the distance shortened between them one of the young men shouted out 'By Christ!' in astonishment. 'He's alive again!'

Grindal and Oglethorpe, busy talking, had only just noticed the two young men when they heard this cry and in a moment the two had gone, stepping sideways down an entry, and the only thing to prove to the astonished canons that they had not been seeing things was the thump of retreating running booted feet. One had loomed much larger in the mist than had the other, but they had both seemed almost ghostly figures, large at one moment magnified by mist, then shrinking, hidden by swirls of moisture.

'What startled them, I wonder?' Oglethorpe said, looking all around, but nothing seemed to be amiss.

'Perhaps they don't like cats,' said the puzzled Grindal, struggling to keep hold of the dog.

A stray tomcat had sprung out, all claws and hisses, at Clementina Crosspatch, who didn't like cats either, and struggled to get at him, then cried a weird wolf-like cry of frustration.

'Their words were odd, though,' said Oglethorpe. '"He's alive again." I thought they were merely shouting blasphemy as the young of that type so often do, but were they really in some form of religious fit or mania?'

The two old clergymen came to the small, square, decent house occupied by all rectors of the tiny ancient church. On its doorstep Grindal bade his friend goodnight.

Oglethorpe turned into his dwelling the picture of serenity. He had lived too long and seen too much to be unduly stirred by the death of a rather unpleasant man who had had his eye on the lovely statue in the tiny church of St Helen. Art is long and life is short, remembered the Canon. What was left to him of life he meant to spend in enjoying art, in revelling in the products of the pious ages. York was the ideal place for that.

76

He was intending to enjoy the end of his life greatly and in peace.

George Grindal, pacing back alone except for the dog, and listening to the echo of his footsteps bouncing from the walls flanking the alley, had no such serenity. A number of things were stirring in his brain; it was buzzing gently like a piece of well oiled machinery. For him that night the joy of active thought and preparation. Back home he went into his study and began the self-imposed task of ringing the Residentiary Canons and arranging a meeting for next morning. He could not take all the responsibilities himself.

'The Archbishop rang while you were out,' said Lucy, popping her head round the door.

'Oh?'

'He's coming into York to commiserate with Nigel Parsifal.'

'What, now? In fog?'

'Yes. He's been away all day and when he got back and read your message decided to come down now instead of waiting till morning. He's almost certainly at Parsifal's now.'

'Oh.'

'And he's coming round to see you on his way back.'

'Oh, drat.'

'Good of him,' said Lucy.

'Oh, very. But I have to arrange this meeting for tomorrow. There's so much to discuss. Only the Residentiaries.'

'You get on with it, I'll prepare for him, and receive him and take him upstairs, then come and fetch you. Do as much as you can,' advised his daughter. And George Grindal had almost finished his task when Lucy reappeared at his door.

'Look, Lucy, there's only two more to do. Could you ring them for me? Here's the list. Is His Grace upstairs? I'll go up.'

The Archbishop expressed his feelings about what an awful thing it was to happen.

'Young Parsifal's quite cut up,' he added.

'I haven't seen him yet.'

'You must, George. He will need our support. We're all going

77

to miss Henry very much, but probably Nigel will miss him more than anyone.'

'We will feel his loss, certainly.'

'Such a fine linguist! I must admit I relied on him a great deal when dealing with the World Council of Churches. You remember he went to the Polynesian and Melanesian islands for a couple of years after the war, and he always retained an interest in their language and culture. He spoke Dutch, too, rather well.'

George Grindal was no mean Latin scholar, but he found modern languages less interesting, and acknowledged the truth of his Archbishop's judgement; Henry Parsifal had been very useful in dealing with foreign visitors and correspondence. Hadn't he been shot down in Holland, during the war? There was certainly something like that, and Henry had taken charge of that Dutch delegation a few months ago, he remembered.

'He was going to help me over the coming International Conference,' said the Archbishop with gloom.

George Grindal realized that here was someone who was genuinely sorry that Henry Parsifal was gone; and the influence began to spread to himself, too. He was ashamed now of the feeling which had been nothing more nor less than relief, which he had detected in himself earlier in the day. It was true; Henry had been a useful modern linguist . . . and an irritating man . . .

'Pity his physical state rather clouded him lately,' added the Archbishop.

'I shall have to go on my knees, when he is gone,' decided George, 'to ask pardon for forgetting these good things and seeing only the bad. That's the beam in my own eye. I must tell Lucy. Not that it will make any difference at the moment; but ultimately, when she has forgotten the irritation of his presence, she too will be sorry.'

Should he mention his suspicions about Parsifal's death to the Archbishop? It seemed a bit premature. He might find them totally unfounded. On the other hand, if the case was murder, then it was not proper for normal services to continue until some kind of spiritual cleansing had taken place.

George cleared his throat. 'I have been rather worried in case the Dean's death was not accidental,' he said. 'I don't know if the possibility of murder had occurred to you, Archbishop?'

'You're not serious?'

'Well – yes. In which case would not the cathedral have to be reconsecrated?'

The Archbishop took some time to reply. 'You amaze me, George,' he said at last. 'No, reconsecration would not be necessary in such an event. Once consecrated a thing is so for ever. You should have remembered that. But a Rite of Reconciliation would be needed.' He paused again. 'Let us not be premature. The police are investigating, I believe. I understand they are quite convinced it is a tragic accident. Suppose we leave it to the professionals, George. You have had an unpleasant shock, perhaps you are not thinking very rationally. It worries me that you should even have thought of such an idea. Until we know otherwise we go on as usual.'

'Very well, Archbishop.'

On Wednesday morning at nine o'clock the Residentiary Canons assembled in a serious mood. They had had time to take in what had happened. They talked in lowered voices. That the most vital, obtrusive presence among them had gone in such a fashion made everything in the world seem different. They knew that Grindal as Acting Dean would see the cathedral through until a new Dean could be appointed. First there were various business matters to arrange. They had a long, sober, serious meeting, without any conflict or confrontation. Mr Chapter Clerk took notes busily and highly approved of the way things were conducted.

Then the Acting Dean was free to think of the subject preoccupying him. He was pleased to have the temporary power of Dean for it meant that no bar existed between him and the investigation which he was determined to make. He had to satisfy himself that the death of the Dean was really accidental, and that no threat – no danger – existed still, to the members of the little community over which he was to preside. The Archbishop's implied command that he leave the matter alone he decided to ignore.

Turning aside from his fellows as they left the Chapter meeting, George Grindal made his way to the Zouche chapel where, cradled in the peace and simplicity of the place, he could sink on to a pew for meditation for a few minutes before the morning service. The Zouche chapel was next to the vestry and both had a short flight of steps downward immediately inside the door. As George took them gently he saw a man kneeling on the floor, fiddling with large lenses and a camera.

The man looked up. 'Gee, I'm sorry,' he said. 'If you're wanting to use the chapel for private prayer I won't be in your way. I'm through.'

'No hurry,' said George. 'I hope you have had a pleasant visit.'

'I'm just intoxicated with your stained glass. For the whole history of window shapes and the glass that went in them you only have to look round this cathedral and it's all here,' replied the man in a gentle, earnest voice. 'These little panes in this chapel are out of this world.'

'The quarries. Yes, they are interesting. They were collected together by Dean Milner-White who assembled them here where they could be appreciated. Have you seen the modern window at the end?'

'That's not for me . . . But these little ones! I wish I knew all they meant. Where's the one with the monkeys . . .'

'There's one with birds,' said George Grindal, pointing.

'And one with fishes, do you think they are whales?'

'Dolphins, do you think?'

'Here's the one with the monkeys. There's the monkey funeral out there in one of the windows of the north nave aisle and this in here. I'm just mad about them.'

'Three monkeys in procession,' said George. 'One carrying a flag, one a sword and one a cross. Civic authority, armed might, and spiritual strength, perhaps. And what monkeys we make of ourselves, into the bargain. What a lesson for a few square inches of glass . . . I always think when I come in here of Queen Philippa and how she set out, in the absence of the King, to lead an army against the invading Scots, and how they held a great service in this cathedral to pray for God's help, and how Archbishop Zouche of York went with her with a band of warlike clerics.'

'Is that right? Did they win? I must be getting out of your way.' The visitor had picked up his camera and equipment.

'Yes, they won, and took the Scots King prisoner. It is always a pleasure to meet our overseas friends. Have you been touring? Where are you from?'

'I've been touring gardens. Edinburgh Botanics and the Chelsea Physic Garden for example. I'm from Idaho.'

'Ah, the Materia Medica,' George said of the Chelsea Physic Garden. He thought of Idaho and had a vision of giant redwoods and wondered if the correct term was sequoia, a word which had come into his head. He thought he'd better not mention it in case it was wrong. 'Do you get a lot of rainfall?' he asked.

'Not much. It's good corn country. Now I really mustn't disturb you any longer.'

George was quite sorry to see the pleasant American go. But time was getting on. He sat down in a pew next to the cupboard doors with their beautiful oak grain and old ironwork. Covering his face with his hands to concentrate better, he remembered a talk he had given years before to the students of a teacher training college. 'Theologians and scientists are like detectives; scientists ask *how*, theologians ask *why*.' I am a theologian, he thought: I will ask *why*, and leave the police to their job which is to ask *how*.

'The point is,' his thought went on, 'if the Dean was murdered, why would anyone do it?' He pushed from his mind Lucy's voice proclaiming, 'I could cheerfully murder him.' He would have gone to the stake for his belief in his daughter's innocence. Still, he had to find out where everyone had been at the time. The stone could hardly have dropped by remote control. But was that venturing into the police province of '*how*'?

At that moment the door of the Zouche chapel opened again and Edmund Jason, the assistant organist, looked round it anxiously. Seeing Grindal's bent head, he hesitated. Then he closed the door behind him and came to sit in the same pew. He said nothing. George dropped his hands from his face, and very quickly realized that the young man was longing to unburden himself. Looking sideways, he said, 'You wanted to speak to me, Edmund?'

For a moment Jason opened his mouth to speak, but then he blushed deeply and got up untidily from the pew.

'I won't bother you now,' he said, and bolted out.

'Oh dear.' George sighed. 'The young. What troubles they make for themselves. I'll give him time to cool down and then I really must make an effort with that young man. Time goes so quickly. It is already twenty past ten and service is at ten thirty and before that there is so much to get through. I promised Sister Agape I'd have a word with her this morning, too, about that old man at the shelter. I'm not going to have time to look in the records for him. I wonder if Lucy would do it?'

He got up slowly, grateful for what little time he had been able to use in meditation. His mind felt clearer. His conviction that the death was no accident was stronger.

Means, motive, opportunity; what he must concentrate on was motive – but he could not exclude from his busy brain the two other considerations. Means – that the cause of death was the stone was obvious, but how someone had gained access to the walkway, and not been seen, was another matter. He felt he must concentrate on two things: who had been in the general area, and, of those people, who had any motive to murder the Dean.

There were people (in addition to his daughter) who thought George Grindal was next door to a saint. There were others who considered him an interfering busybody. Grindal had interests and experiences much wider than the cathedral close. He was involved in crusades from time to time which took him among the hidden strata of society, among the homeless, the down-and-outs, the mental patients thrown out of closing mental hospitals, the drug addicts, the criminals, and the underworld in general.

It had been while he was away from home on one of these missions that he had met the pop star, Poison Peters, in a sleazy all-night café in London at three in the morning. He was used to investigating, to tracing people. Now this trouble had cropped up in his own patch of territory he could not let it rest.

7

They have taken crafty counsel against thy
people, and consulted against thy hidden ones.
—*Psalms*, 83, v. 3

While the Chapter meeting had been in progress earlier that
morning Julia Bransby had quietly worked away in the vestry,
drawing the embroidery of the Benedicite set of vestments. She
had finished and packed her things when Lucy Grindal came in
with a young woman.

'I was just going, Lucy,' said Julia. 'I wasn't going to bother
you today, you must be overwhelmed.'

'Well, yes, we are rather. How has it gone?' asked Lucy.

'Fine, thanks. I've finished.'

'Are you in a rush to go anywhere?'

'Not specially. Can I help?'

'You do know the building well, don't you, Julia – I am right
– I have seen you guiding?'

'Yes, I guide when I can.'

'Can I introduce you to Jill? She's awfully keen to become a
cathedral guide – I was going to take her round, she has a few
days off work and would like to start learning right away – '

'And you're up to your eyes and would I give her an
introduction,' Julia finished for her.

'Well, yes.'

'Of course.'

'Jill, Julia is a textile expert and historian and travels around
the country a good deal, advising on conservation. She's a
voluntary guide as well and she'll start you off. You don't mind,
do you, if I dash?'

Jill and Julia looked at one another.

Julia was in her late thirties, with a good, slim, neat figure, a
clear skin and dark hair which she wore straight and with a

83

fringe in something of a Twenties style. For someone as ancient as that Jill supposed she looked all right.

Jill was all of twenty. She was wearing the same mini-skirted brilliant red dress that she had worn the day before, the same shiny black shoes with high heels, similar black patterned tights and rainbow of colour round her eyes. Negligently draped on her shoulders was a jacket of soft bloused leather. Her whole air was arrogant and blasé. Julia found her startling, but she didn't dislike the girl. She smiled at her, and wondered why Jill appeared to be tingling with suppressed excitement.

Jill had discovered that she liked living on the edge of danger. It had begun when she had worked for Nigel Parsifal for a while and the attraction had been growing between them. She sometimes wondered if she would have fancied Nigel if he had not been married. The affair had supplied her with all the adrenalin she needed until she realized that Nigel's wife Maureen knew and didn't care. Then the element of risk and excitement had gone out of it. Now she had something new and better, much better, much more real and exciting and dangerous. Also, it gave her a kick to trail her coat.

The two women walked round the great building together. Julia conscientiously repeated the usual things which Jill would need to know as a cathedral guide and now and then put in something of her own.

'Don't you think that fabric is lovely, Jill?' she asked when they were in the K.O.Y.L.I. chapel and standing looking at the altar end. 'You'll never guess where it came from. Do you know that it once belonged to Marie Antoinette and hung in her palace of Versailles? The colours are faded now but I think it must have been a smashing colour scheme, the green background and the embroidery of fruit and little scenes in peach and rose and cream. Really pretty.'

'It wouldn't make a bad dress now,' said Jill, looking at the dossal curtain with her eyes half closed. 'But it seems a funny thing to put in a cathedral.'

'An ancient tradition. In the old days queens would bequeath their most beautiful dresses to be made into altar frontals or vestments, and an embroidered and jewelled girdle might be given and made into part of a cope or a burse or a mitre. This was always a hanging so it is actually less of a change of use.'

'What's K.O.Y.L.I?' asked Jill.

'Don't you know, and you a Yorkshire girl?'

'If I knew I wouldn't ask, would I? Sounds like cauliflowers to me.'

'King's Own Yorkshire Light Infantry.'

Jill swung out of the K.O.Y.L.I. chapel in front of Julia as the organ began to play. 'Fergal Mourne's coming to York,' she said, as if the music had made her think of it.

'A pop star?' guessed Julia.

'Yeah,' answered Jill after a fractional pause. 'He's fantastic. Great guy.'

'Will there be a concert?'

'Some concert.' Jill performed a tiny dance step.

'Jill! Show respect. You must love the cathedral or you wouldn't want to be a guide.'

Jill lowered her painted eyelids slowly over her eyes. 'I've always liked it,' she said, and Julia believed her. 'Doesn't mean I can't like other things too, does it? Music and dancing and pop concerts and sheep.'

'Sheep?' Julia didn't think she'd heard aright.

'Living things – you know – lambs and that.' Jill clicked her fingers repeatedly as if to a rhythmic beat. 'Where's the crypt?' she asked.

'I think we've done enough for today. You won't be able to take it all in.'

'I'd like to see the crypt.'

'Well, the entrance is just here, but look, it's locked at present.'

Jill held on to the wrought-iron gate and peered through. Julia saw to her amazement that the girl was trembling, as if she were a dog on the watch for a rabbit.

'When's your pop concert?' Julia asked.

'Friday. I won't be here then. But I'll be here tomorrow. Will you take me round again and see how much I've remembered?' she asked almost pleadingly.

'If you want me to.'

*

Wednesday lunch-time, and the previous day's mist which had lingered over into that morning had at last dispersed. The day it left behind was cold and raw with the peculiar penetrating rawness of early November. Julia Bransby and Tom Churchyard were warm and comfortable in Ye Olde Starre Inne in its yard off Stonegate. From time to time they met and lunched together. The habit had started when they had become better acquainted during the Mystery Plays earlier in the year – the production in which the plays' director had been murdered. The Starre was not their usual place, but that Wednesday it was convenient for both of them.

'I'm struck all of a heap,' Julia had announced when they met. 'What do you think to the Dean dying like that?'

'Vaguely guilty,' replied Tom.

'How do you mean?'

'Only that I found him so infuriating. Earlier yesterday I had felt like bumping him off personally. I spent all afternoon full of animosity towards him – and then he died in that freak accident. I feel like getting on my knees and saying, "I didn't mean it, Lord," only it's all too late.'

Julia looked serious.

'Shepherd's pie, please,' she said to the waitress.

'I'll have the same. And two half pints of lager.'

'You get the drinks at the bar yourself, sir,' explained the girl.

'Wait a minute, Tom, let me pay for mine.' Julia passed him the money. She knew he earned a good salary with British Telecom but paying for herself was her gesture for women's lib. It was not until he returned with the drinks that she said, 'You mustn't let it worry you, you know. He was the most annoying man. Lots of people must have felt as you did.'

'Not everyone says it.'

'Who did you say it to?'

'Mrs Hassock.'

'Ooooh. Might as well tell the wind.'

'Exactly.'

'It was only an accident, Tom. No need at all to worry.'

They had been speaking fairly freely, but with the arrival of three customers at the next table in the tiny section of the inn which had once been a separate room before all the rooms were thrown together, they both instinctively lowered their voices.

The newcomers were two young men and a girl. The girl was Jill. She and Julia acknowledged one another with a wordless smile.

'If you've got it, flaunt it,' thought Julia, when the long shapely high-heeled legs flashed into even more prominence as the girl seated herself eighteen inches away.

Julia could see that Tom's interest had been immediately aroused and found herself resenting it. She could see that Jill was very attractive in a rather blatant way, and there was nothing romantic in the friendship between herself and Tom, she reminded herself sharply. One of the reasons she liked Tom Churchyard was that he had never made any attempt to flirt with her. Yet she found herself not liking the fact that he was obviously having to make quite an effort not to stare at the girl. Julia had the impression that Tom had also recognized the newcomer.

To put some weight on the other side of the scale she decided to run her own eye over the two young men.

They were both in their early twenties; one had a rather heavy muscular build and she did not find him in any way attractive apart from the general animal magnetism of youth and health. The other was a different matter. He had startlingly blue eyes and dark tumbling curls over his forehead; a narrow face; a skinny body. As for a second his eyes rested on Julia and returned her gaze she felt an undeniable charm emanating from him – yet it made her uneasy. She withdrew her glance instantly and contemplated the shepherd's pie which had opportunely arrived at their table.

Both Tom and Julia then took care to appear absorbed in each other and their meal. They spoke of indifferent things; Julia told Tom about her recent work. She had been visiting a country house to identify fabrics and advise on conservation. Tom, who as a British Telecom engineer had a quite different view of society, told her a few bits of office gossip which he thought might interest her.

At the next table voices were also lowered.

'Still got them hidden OK?' asked the slim young man.

'Fine. No one will find them in a month of Sundays.'

'After that bit of bother no one's going to go poking around?'

'Not down there they're not. Anyway, there isn't any bother.'

'Good on yer, Mike. So it's Friday, then.'

Just then the waitress appeared with more shepherd's pies and a ploughman's lunch. The three stopped their conversation – which had been hissed in whispers – and began to eat and talk about the food in normal tones.

It had been impossible for Julia and Tom to quite ignore the three, although they had talked so perseveringly themselves. They were rather glad when they had finished eating.

'Did you know those people at the next table?' asked Julia as they walked along Stonegate.

'The thickset bloke I've seen around, just in the last day or two. I'll tell you who with – Mr and Mrs Soames – you know Soames the verger?'

'No, I don't.'

'And I've seen the girl before. It took me ages to remember where. She's Nigel Parsifal's assistant in that antique shop in Stonegate.'

'She's also going to be one of our cathedral guides.'

'Is she indeed!'

'I was taking her round this morning. She's got a few days off work.'

'What did you think to her?'

Julia had to be honest. 'I like her, though she's strange.'

'You mean that short skirt?'

'No, I don't mean that short skirt. It's a bit hard to define. I felt that she was playing a part, that I was the audience for an act, yet there's something real underneath the acting, if one could only be sure what. She's keen on pop music. Some character called Fergal Mourne is going to visit York for a concert, apparently, on Friday. I must tell Adam.'

'Your son? Is he keen on modern music? I suppose they all are. Another big pop concert, eh! As if Poison Peters wasn't enough pop star for one city this century.'

'Have you heard from him lately?' asked Julia, remembering the strange young man who had played Christ in the Mystery Plays and who had become so unexpectedly friendly with Tom.

'Yes, I have, as a matter of fact.' Tom's face lit up as he felt inside his jacket, then pulled out a picture postcard from an inner pocket. 'Here.'

'A train. How typical of Poison! I've always thought he must have wanted to be an engine driver when he was a little boy.' She turned it over. 'Canada! That's exciting for him.'

'He's enjoyed the railroad, yes. And the new songs seem to be getting him quite a following.'

'That's good. Well, cheers, Tom. I must fly, and your office no doubt awaits.'

'Fall down without me.' Tom put on a mock groan. 'But I'm going first to inspect that excavation we're carrying out in Market Street.'

The two friends parted without touching – neither a handclasp nor a chaste kiss. It was always rather an awkward moment. Tom turned after a few yards and tried to catch sight of Julia again, but the crowds of tourists were too much for him. He couldn't see the neat grey coat or the black hair, or pick out the crisp walk.

Going on his way, Tom allowed his mind to dwell on the girl in the pub. What legs! And that tight dress!

The other three had been able to speak more freely after Tom and Julia had left.

'I'm not sure of my bit,' said Jill. 'I want to help all I can, Terry. You know that. After all, he is your brother. Afterwards – well – maybe he and I are going to be related – '

Terry squeezed her hand under the table.

'You bet you are,' he said fervently. 'Let's go over it again, girl. Time's the thing. It all has to happen together. Mike and me collect the stuff from where he's put it and come to near where you are, we're driving the Ford. You won't see us till after. The back-up group will be in touch with you by radio. They'll tell you when Fergal leaves Wakefield. We've timed the route. They won't be able to let you know exactly what's happening after that but there'll be the code messages you know about.'

'Superstar,' nodded the girl. 'Superstar travelling to York concert.' Her voice was a clear soprano.

'That's when they set off. They're going to try to keep within sight of Fergal. Then when they pass the agricultural college they'll radio to you, "Superstar on course". You've got to be ready for that. Then it's go, girl, go! Don't worry about anything but doing your bit.'

'I shall be worrying about you,' Jill said with a tender look at the thin young man. 'Don't get cold.'

'Cold! I'd go through hell and back for Fergal. You ought to know that. We're providing the sort of reception committee he needs right now.'

'It's so unfair,' went on the girl. 'When he's only trying to save his country.'

'Working for the cause we all believe in,' put in the thickset lad called Mike. 'Don't forget my father.'

'Your father's an inspiration for all of us.' The thin young man's face burned with intensity. 'Michael Killarney. That's a noble name you bear, Mike.'

Canon George Grindal, Acting Dean, after sitting in the Zouche chapel in the middle of the morning, was not free from immediate affairs again until midday lunch.

'Did you see Sister Agape?' he asked his daughter.

'Yes. She quite understood that you weren't free. She organized Sister Lauren to go with her and visit the old man at the shelter and they got his name out of him. He's called Albert Horncastle.'

'Oh! That was good. Do you know, that name is faintly familiar?'

'Then I began looking through the records for him, but I haven't found him yet.'

'You'll carry on, dear?'

'Yes, father. As soon as I've time. There are a few urgent things.'

'Of course.'

'Oh, and Agape said, he's still talking in the same confused way, but she's decided to make notes of what he says. It may be useful to have a record of his progress towards clarity, if he's properly looked after.'

After eating, George took his cup of tea into his study and

resumed his contemplation, thinking back on the happenings before the Dean's death, looking for the little ends of events, threads of gossip, half-noticed looks and gestures which would lead him to the murderer, if murderer there had been.

Then he remembered the assistant organist, young Jason.

'I haven't seen him again,' he thought. The young man had definitely had something he needed to say.

Walking into the breakfast room, he said to Lucy, 'Remind me where Edmund Jason lives. Didn't he move recently?'

'He's lodging with Mrs Hassock.' Lucy seemed absent-minded. She used the room as her office and had gone in there with her own cup of tea. At present she was struggling with the Mothers' Union accounts.

'And Mrs Hassock lives . . .?'

'You know, father. What's wrong with you today? You know where she lives and that Edmund Jason boards with her. They're round the corner.' She named the street.

'There's a lot on my mind,' replied George. 'Sister Agape and I were going to ask Mrs Hassock if she'd take the old man. . .did you say he's called Albert Horncastle? I'll go and see Jason now, and maybe mention it to her. I won't be long,' said the Canon.

He could not remember having gone to Mrs Hassock's home before; she was so omnipresent in the cathedral that one hardly needed to seek her out. But it was not difficult to identify the house. It even said 'Hassock' over the bell push.

Mrs Hassock's door was a gentle green and the brass knocker was immaculate, gleaming trimly. Grindal was glad that it was a simple double-curved Georgian design, and not in the shape of a fox or a Lincoln Imp. Ignoring the bell, he took the well-balanced weight of the knocker in his hand and thumped with it.

'This is an unexpected pleasure,' cooed Mrs Hassock. George recognized the special manner which she kept for men she found attractive. The thin form gave the impression of supple-ness, the head with its sparse, scraped-back grey hair tilted in a coy manner.

'Is your lodger in?' George floated on a wave of charm into the hallway.

'He was playing the piano until a few minutes ago,' Mrs

Hassock said. 'Rather stormily, I thought. But now it sounds like his gramophone going, or the wireless.' She conducted him upstairs to the first floor.

George knocked, using his knuckles against the dark shining wood.

'I'll leave you to it,' said Mrs Hassock girlishly and started off down the stairs.

There was no answer to the knock. George hesitated. Inside the music was still playing. He knocked again, and, turning the handle gently, pushed the door open an inch after calling out, Mr Jason! Mr Jason! Are you at home?'

Still there was no sound but the music. With a sudden resolve George Grindal opened the door wider.

Edmund Jason was swinging gently from a coat hook on his bedroom door, bent at the knees, suspended by a silk tie. His eyes were open and staring at George, but it seemed doubtful if they saw anything; his face was pale and severe; his tongue protruded slightly between his lips.

George rushed to him and lifted him so that the weight was taken from his neck. Beside his feet was a low stool, which had been kicked over. The young organist's toes were actually trailing on the floor. If his knees had not been bent he would have been standing.

'Mrs Hassock!' roared out George.

Silent prayers were rushing through his head. His first action must be to unloose that dreadful knotted necktie; he pulled at it but it was too tight to move while he held the body in his arms. Righting the stool with his foot, he pushed it under Jason's dangling toes to support some of the weight. That seemed to work. Cut it, cut it, his brain told him. Freeing a hand, George felt desperately in his pockets. Yes, he had his trusty old penknife. Opening the blade with his teeth he then hacked at the tie, giving thanks that the good Sheffield steel was razor sharp. It seemed an age, though it must only have been seconds, before he had sawn through enough of the fabric of the tie to make it give, and could take Jason in his arms and lay him down on the floor.

There had been no response from Mrs Hassock.

Frantically, as he worked at the knot round the thin throat,

George found presence of mind enough to bellow in a voice that shook the house, 'Mrs Hassock! Mrs Hassock!'

Mrs Hassock could be heard running up the stairs.

'Ring for the ambulance!' George yelled. 'And the police! Ring 999! Don't stop to look them up!'

He could hear her footsteps pause, come on, faltering, then turn and descend quickly.

'Thank goodness.' George let out his breath. He had got the tie from round the young man's throat. Somehow George did not consider it was all useless. Jason was very warm, and he did not think he was dead. 'What ought I to do now?' he thought desperately.

He settled the young man down more comfortably on the floor, with his head next to a worn patch in the carpet. He heard Mrs Hassock's voice from below – she was obviously responding to the telephone operator. Leaving Jason, George ran to the landing.

'He's hanged himself but I don't think he's quite dead,' he shouted down.

Barely giving himself time to catch Mrs Hassock's gasp of astonishment he dashed back to Jason. Below, he could hear that Mrs Hassock's voice had suddenly gone high and squeaky. At least she had not panicked.

George felt the young man's pulse. He could detect nothing. He felt for his heart. Was there anything? Ought he to thump his chest like they did on TV or give him the kiss of life?

Looking at the protruding rim of tongue George felt disinclined. He took hold of the face and jawbone and tried to restore a more normal appearance. Then he gave the chest a few firm thumping pressures, before pushing aside his reluctance and lowering his mouth to Jason's.

Blow air into the lungs, he thought. Then press them to expel it. Is his throat so compressed that it will not admit any air? We'll have to try. Blow. Press out again. Blow some more. What good can it do blowing my used air into him? Blow. Press out. Blow. Press out. I'm not sure if I'm doing this right.

The ambulance had screamed along Clarence Street, Lord Mayor's Walk, through Monk Bar and along Goodramgate. It came to a sharp stop outside Mrs Hassock's door and the ambulance men came briskly in. They walked rapidly upstairs and pushed George Grindal to one side. He did not mind at all. Then they both bent over the still body of the young man.

Heaving himself up, George left the room, feeling very old. He went downstairs slowly.

In the shadow of the stair Mrs Hassock stood motionless. She too seemed to have aged in the last few minutes. The coyness was gone. Instead, the true goodness and loving-kindness of her nature shone from her attitude and the care on her face.

'Poor young man,' she whispered, as though to speak normally would mar his chances of survival. 'What can have gone wrong?'

'I think I know,' replied George. 'How long is it since he stopped playing the piano?'

Even in the urgency of the moment George had registered a mental image of the old walnut upright piano by the wall, with fretwork front and candlesticks, open, with music on the holder.

'A few minutes. Not more. I was sitting in here with my door open, enjoying the music. Then he stopped and put on the Brandenburgs – it must have been his gramophone, because it was the beginning, and if it had been the wireless it would have been more likely to be the middle of a piece, wouldn't it?'

'I'm sure you're right – if he switched on at random.'

'Then I closed my door, because I'm not very fond of Bach, and I was trying to finish knitting a shawl for my niece for Christmas and wanted to concentrate. I'd only done part of a row before your knock came at the door.'

'How long does it take you to do a row?'

Mrs Hassock hesitated. 'They're rather long at this point and I have to think about the pattern. Perhaps ten minutes. But I hadn't done much more than a quarter of one.'

'A quarter of one – two and a half minutes, then you let me in and we walked upstairs – a very short time really – and after he stopped playing and put the music on he'd have to get over to the door and string himself up.'

There were sounds from above. One of the ambulance men appeared and came downstairs.

'Any news?' cried George.

94

'Not quite hopeless, sir. Fetching a stretcher.'

'Can I help you?'

'No, no. Quicker on my own,' called out the man with a grin as he went past them through the hallway. In seconds he returned with a stretcher. Deftly the men then carried the inert body of Edmund Jason downstairs, put it on the stretcher, and went out.

'Do you want to come? Give details and so on?' one of them asked George and Mrs Hassock, as the two ran out of the house after them.

'I'll follow along,' said George. 'Be with you in two minutes.'

'Right.'

Without further words the ambulance and all in it sped away.

'Now, I don't think you ought to come.' George turned to Mrs Hassock. 'Make yourself a cup of tea. I'm going to get my bicycle, and I'll ask Lucy to come and stay with you for a bit. Will you do that?'

'Yes, Canon,' Mrs Hassock whispered.

'You've been very brave under a nasty shock. We'll talk about it later. Now I must go after them.'

George jogged the short distance to his own house and spoke hastily to Lucy before jumping on to his bicycle and following the ambulance to the emergency entrance of the hospital.

There was very little he could do there. For a while he sat in a corridor outside the room where the medical team was saving Edmund Jason's life, and he did his bit by praying hard but silently for the young man.

'You can come in now, sir,' one of the nurses said at last. It seemed like hours later.

Edmund had been wheeled into a little room. George Grindal stood by the bed and looked down at him. The pale face lay as if carved on the white pillow. It was not a handsome face; it seemed to be composed of knobbles, the long knobble of the chin, the several joined knobbles of the nose, the group of low rounded knobbles making up the forehead. The young man was connected to all manner of wires and tubes, and obviously still deeply unconscious.

'Is he going to be all right?' George whispered to the nurse.

95

'We hope so, sir. He's very fortunate that he was found so quickly, otherwise there would have been no chance.'

The newspapers loved it. Their headlines made the most of their opportunity, shrieking out DEATH OF DEAN; NEAR DEATH OF ORGANIST, over articles which implied a great deal without saying anything. For what was there for them to say? An accident had killed the Dean and no one told them about the shadow over Edmund Jason's life or the scene between the two men. The bare words DEAN and ORGANIST were quite enough. A few paragraphs mentioning 'romantic gothic towers' and 'booming notes of the organ' and 'this ancient city' were enough to titillate.

The more sober local papers were equally delighted by their scoop about the Acting Dean's part in the affair: 'Acting Dean Grindal, who only the previous day had seen his Dean struck down at his feet, today saved the life of the cathedral organist by giving the young man the kiss of life. "I tried to remember what you're supposed to do," the Dean modestly explained to us.'

'I don't even remember talking to a journalist,' said George Grindal in exasperation to Canon Oglethorpe. George was not to know that the sympathetic young woman who had sat beside him for a while in the hospital corridor was a reporter. 'And the Dean was killed behind me, not in front. I didn't see him struck down, nor was he at my feet. I do think these fellows ought to try to get it the way it was.'

'Far more interesting the way they write it,' replied the worldly-wise Oglethorpe.

8

Yea, even mine own familiar friend, whom I
trusted, who did also eat of my bread, hath laid
great wait for me.

—*Psalms*, 41, v. 9

The only other relevant event of the Wednesday afternoon was
the discussion of the Dean's will, which took place in the office
of solicitor Humphrey Hale. Nigel Parsifal had previously been
in touch with him by telephone and had now been sitting for
ten minutes on a rather nice old Victorian parlour chair in the
waiting room, when Humphrey came down the stairs to fetch
him.

'So sorry to keep you,' said Humphrey. 'Do come up. I've got
the will out, as you see. Yes. You know it was made last year, a
few months after the Dean – the late Dean – was appointed.'

Nigel did not know anything of the sort, but he did not say
so. He stood mute and immobile.

'Do sit. You realize that until probate is granted it is not
official, but I see no reason why you should not know what the
will contains. Indeed, as it touches on the disposal of his body,
you need to know, being his executor.'

'Well, that's why I rang,' said Nigel. 'There's going to be an
inquest but I ought to be thinking about the funeral and know
about any wishes he expressed on that. The police tell me the
inquest should be straightforward.'

'I've had a copy of the will made for you,' said Hale. 'You can
take that away. Do you want to read it while you are here in
case there are any points . . .?'

'I would like to, yes.'

'Cup of tea? We usually have one about now.'

'Please.'

Nigel realized when he was seated and unfolding the docu-
ment on his knee that he was very much in need of a cup of

tea. He managed to skim through the will before Hale passed him a brimming china cup. 'These bequests . . .' he said.

'Yes?'

'How long does it take to get probate?'

'The will is very simple and I made it out myself. It shouldn't take long.'

'We will have to clear the Deanery reasonably quickly. Could I go ahead and hand these small bequests out?'

'I don't see why not. Presumably even if there was a problem – which I'm sure there won't be – you would still want to carry out his wishes.'

'I would.'

'It might be advisable to ask for receipts.'

'Yes, all right.'

'Then, I wouldn't have any objection.'

When Canon George Grindal returned to the hospital to see Edmund Jason again it was later, much later, than George had intended it to be. The early autumn night was gathering. Inside the little side ward the light had been switched on and the outside world looked almost black beyond the window. After a word of greeting to the nurse George busied himself unwrapping his scarf and taking off his overcoat. The temperature in hospitals was necessarily high, no doubt, but George was always convinced that it constituted the major part of the cost of the Health Service.

'I'm afraid he hasn't regained consciousness yet,' said the staff nurse.

'How long?'

'Tomorrow, perhaps.'

'I thought he would come round almost at once. He will be all right, won't he?' George felt anxious.

'We can't say yet. There may be residual paralysis, or some other effect. He's very lucky to be alive. We'll know a bit better tomorrow.'

George peeped in at the door at Edmund Jason, who looked exactly the same as he had earlier in the day.

Stepping out once again into the cold air and discovering that it was pouring with rain and that a wind had sprung up, he was glad that he had put on his thermal underwear that morning. Longjohns were such comforting things. When he arrived home Lucy had news for him.

'Sister Agape rang.'

'Yes?'

'She asked Mrs Hassock about your old man with the beard – what was it, four larks and a wren? I'm sure you're right, though I would have thought four fag-ends and the pull top of a can of lager more likely to live in his beard – '

'What a time to ask her, when young Jason . . .'

'Well, what could she do? You can't just put off asking when there's this old man. The shelter isn't designed for long-term residence.'

'No, of course you can't. What happened?'

'She'll take him, bless her. Seemed quite pleased. She remembered him and Agape said quite a gleam came in her eye. She has a little bedroom he can have, sparse, but something simple seems the best.'

'He's more likely to settle in it.'

'Exactly. And while Jason's away she'll have a bit of extra time to devote to him. So they've probably arranged removal this evening.'

'Splendid.'

'Oh, and Agape asked me to tell you that Mr Horncastle has remembered the name of the young cricketer he was on about – Killarney, she said.'

'Not a name I've come across in the cathedral records.'

'No, nor have I. Probably he's made a mistake.'

'I'll go round to Mrs Hassock's now, Lucy. I want to tell her about Edmund Jason anyway, and I'd like to see what's happened about Albert Horncastle and see how he's settling in.'

'Must you go out again, father? It's a really awful night, blowing heavens hard. And what about your dinner?'

'Keep it hot for me, won't you, dear?'

'Tom,' said Bob Southwell's voice on the phone later that evening. 'Beastly night. Have you seen how the rain's being blown sideways? I don't feel like going to the pub but there's some bitter in the fridge. What about you coming round here for an hour?'

The telephone engineer and the detective lived next door to one another in a pair of semi-detached houses on a small private estate built in the sixties. It was their regular drinking night. The local would be warm and welcoming when they got there, but Tom gladly changed plan. He and the Southwells had an unwritten rule not to pop in and out of each other's houses, but to visit by arrangement. Tom was pleased only to have to walk as far as next door in such a storm. The weather had changed fast in the last hour and there were reports on the radio of gales in the south.

It was towards the end of a very pleasant time by the Southwells' fire, well piled with the last of the smoky coal which they were burning up before conforming with the new smokelessness, that Tom remembered his lunch in the Starre.

'You're having another pop star to look after, then,' he said.

'Another? You mean like Poison Peters? I hope not. One was enough.'

'It was only something I heard at lunch-time. Julia Bransby was telling me that some pop star called Fergal Mourne was coming to York on Friday and there was going to be a concert. She thought her son Adam might be interested.'

'No. I've heard nothing of it.'

'The name sounds Irish, I thought.'

Bob shook his head. 'No pop stars that I know of, Irish or otherwise.'

'What a disappointment.'

'You bloodthirsty devil! Wasn't what happened last time we had a visiting pop star enough for you?'

'Oh, well, yes, of course,' said Tom, who in spite of lunching with Julia thought that life was a bit humdrum these days.

'What more do you want? The Dean killed in the cathedral by a falling stone . . .'

'That was yesterday,' objected Tom.

'Nothing's happened today, is that it?'

'I suppose so.'

'Did you know the Dean?'

100

'Very well. If you'd been looking for a murder suspect for him you'd have had me on the list.'

'I've got a little list. Just as well it's not murder then. When did you last see him?'

'Yesterday,' admitted Tom. 'Just before lunch-time. Tackled him about spending the Friends of the Cathedral's money without so much as a by-your-leave and got a flea in my ear for my pains. He always gave me stomach-ache, that man.'

'New cause for murder. Victim gave murderer dyspepsia. Reasonable, I suppose. An appeal to the jury should get you off.'

'I'd better be going. Many thanks for the beer. Early start tomorrow – have to check on some duct-laying before going in to the office.'

As he put on his outdoor waterproof jacket Tom was startled to hear from the lazy reclining figure of his thin friend a question deceptively casual: 'Where were you, then, Tom, when the Dean had his weird accident?'

Tom came back towards the fire, zipping up his jacket. He felt suddenly flustered.

'When was it exactly?'

'Four pip emma.'

'I expect I was in the cathedral library. I finished early on the job, gave myself a bit of time off and went along there. The Dean had rattled me so much in the morning that I decided to look up a few precedents.'

'So you were in the area of the cathedral?'

'Yes. May have been walking past the east end when the accident happened, come to think.'

'Interesting.'

'Can I go?' asked Tom, with a certain irony. 'Or am I under arrest?'

'Take no notice of Bob,' soothed Linda as she came back into the room after calming down the children, who had been kept awake by the storm. 'He can't help it. He's never really off duty. I get the third degree often enough.'

She winked saucily at Tom, who had been feeling rather upset under a carefully maintained bluff exterior. He was cheered. Linda always cheered him. They got on well, some-how, and he was pleased that the family had moved to York on Bob's promotion and come to live next to him. Linda was a modern young woman – all jeans and sneakers – but the way she wore them had gone some distance towards reconciling him to such gear, even though he was very much a legs man and liked to see high heels and preferably stockings, under fluttery skirts.

The children were nice, too. They were open and friendly and Tom was a bit of an honorary uncle to them. In fact, contemplating the Southwells as neighbours, Tom really felt very lucky. Except perhaps when Bob put on his policeman's hat.

'I'm sorry!' Bob leapt to his feet and came forward to show his friend out, his hand on Tom's shoulder. 'Linda's right. The habit – the tone of voice – become engrained. We've already satisfied ourselves that it was an accident. It's just what Hercule Poirot would have called the little grey cells. They never stop working.'

'Cheers, then,' said Tom.

'Mr Southwell,' said the voice on the telephone.

'Canon Grindal,' responded Bob.

'How clever of you to recognize me.'

Bob smiled. No one who had seen Canon Grindal's ugly face and then heard his beautiful chord-like voice could ever forget.

Then, remembering that his smile could not travel over the wire and realizing that there was an expectant silence at the other end, he said, 'That's my job, sir. Trains our memory for voices. Can I help you?'

'Have you heard that our young assistant organist, Edmund Jason, tried to commit suicide today?'

'No! And it was only yesterday that the Dean . . .'

'Not altogether unconnected, I fear. Before his accident the Dean had created a rather nasty scene with Jason. This – and the cause of it, combined with the Dean's death – seems to have preyed on his mind and in my opinion led to his suicide attempt. He's still unconscious.'

102

'What happened exactly?'

'He hanged himself, but by a lucky chance I arrived to see him and he was cut down in time, we hope.'

'A suicide, after an accident . . . makes one think . . . What was the scene about?'

'The Dean had found out that he was under notice at his previous post for suspected homosexual behaviour, when he applied for the post here. Jason was very upset by his accusations. In fact I did wonder whether he might have dropped the stone.'

Bob Southwell's ears almost visibly flapped. 'So you don't think it was an accident, Canon?'

'Oh, yes, of course I do. I only want to be certain.'

'So . . .'

'I went to see Edmund Jason in the hospital earlier this evening. Then I called on Mrs Hassock – I don't suppose you know her – she helps in the cathedral, and Jason lodges with her. I wanted to tell her how Jason was, also she has just got a new lodger I'm much concerned about. So it was quite late before I arrived home again. The cathedral stonemason was waiting for me.'

'Oh?' Bob was even more alert.

'He doesn't think the Dean's death was an accident.'

'Can you tell me why?'

'He thinks the piece of stone was helped to fall – was aided on its way.'

'I examined that stone,' replied Bob, 'and could see no trace of interference – no chisel marks, or anything at all suggestive of anything but natural splitting.'

'But with all due respect, Mr Southwell, you are no more a stonemason than I am.'

'True. And the expert witness thinks it was dislodged deliberately.'

'He does.'

'This could be merely an anxiety to defend his department from blame.'

'So it could. But I think you should take it into account.'

'Do you still think Jason might have been responsible?'

'No, I'm positive that he was not. He is a humble soul and

was, I believe, agonizing over the Dean's harshness, but I am morally certain that he is incapable of deliberately harming anyone.'

'I really don't think you need have any worries at all on this. In my opinion the stonemason was only worried in case any blame was felt to lie at his door – the natural reaction. There seems to be no reason to suppose anything out of the way. If you don't mind me saying so, Canon, you are suffering from shock and allowing things to prey on your mind.'

'Imagining things?'

'Well, yes. But I'll remember what you've told me and I'll watch out for any suspicious circumstances.'

'Thank you,' said George Grindal, and rang off.

'That was Canon Grindal, Linda.' Bob took a mug of tea from her.

'At this time of night?'

'You remember him?'

'Of course I do. We've met several times. And he was the one Poison Peters got so pally with – you know – when he was in York to star in the Mystery Plays.'

'That's the second time today someone's mentioned Poison Peters. Tom Churchyard earlier. He'd heard another pop star was coming to York – someone called Fergal. Heard of any pop singers by that name, Lin?'

'No. It's an unusual name, isn't it? The only time I remember hearing it before was when that big trial was on, of the suspected IRA bomber – the Brigade Commander from the Ardoyne area. Wasn't he called Fergal Mourne?'

'By hell!' shouted Bob, bouncing to his feet, hot tea flying.

'Bob! Do you have to yell like that?'

'Why didn't I think of that? That's it!'

'What's it?'

'That was why it rang a bell! That was the name Tom said – Fergal Mourne. Fergal Mourne is being transferred to the High Security Wing of Full Sutton Prison this Friday from Wakefield.'

'So?'

'A pop star coming to York on Friday called Fergal Mourne . . .'

Already Bob was dialling Tom's number.

104

'Tom! What do you remember of what Julia told you at lunch-time?'

Tom's deep voice sounded sleepy. 'Look, Bob, I've just climbed into bed. Julia Bransby told me all sorts of things at lunch-time. We were together for an hour.'

'Something about a pop star.'

'She said her son might be interested because there was going to be a pop concert. That's all.'

'Tell me again.'

Tom cast his mind back to the crowded pub. He repeated what he had said before. 'Julia might know more than she mentioned,' he finished.

A couple of minutes later the telephone rang by Julia's bed. 'Mrs Bransby, this is Bob Southwell here of CID. We have met.'

'Yes, and I know Linda quite well,' responded Julia. She sounded less sleepy than Tom had done.

'I must apologize for disturbing you like this, but Tom Churchyard happened to mention something you'd told him at lunch-time about a pop concert.'

'Yes?'

'Would you mind telling me, too?'

'Are you interested in that kind of music?' asked Julia. 'I'd have put you down as a Vivaldi man.'

'I'm not interested personally,' replied Bob.

'I was helping to train a cathedral guide this morning, a young girl. It's nice when anyone her age takes an interest. She mentioned it.'

'Can you remember exactly?'

Julia told him. 'Is anything wrong?' she asked.

'Nothing at all. Just a stray coincidence, I'm sure.'

'I'm seeing her again tomorrow, I can ask her how much tickets are and so on if you like. I was going to ask for Adam – my son, you know – he's omnivorous when it comes to music.'

'I would like to know anything else you hear about it.'

'Right then, I'll ring you tomorrow.'

Bob thanked her and rang off.

'What about sleep?' asked Linda fretfully, appearing in the doorway in peach silk pyjamas with lace inserts. She was retying the long supple belt round the eastern-style jacket, which often slid undone. 'All this telephoning.'

'Who cares about sleep?'

Bob followed her upstairs and slid into bed beside her, into the softness and warmth, and took her in his arms. She turned her head towards him and welcomed him with a kiss . . .

That was when Bob forgot all about Canon Grindal and the accident in the cathedral.

9

He sitteth lurking in the thievish corners of the streets; and privily in his lurking dens doth he murder the innocent.

—*Psalms*, 10, v. 8

At about the same time Canon Grindal was sitting up in bed finishing his hot milk and frowning over his notebook. He still had one or two suspects on his list of people who had expressed their intense dislike of the Dean, but gradually they were being whittled down and the remaining names looked unlikely. Holdernesse, the architectural assistant, had been with the Surveyor of the Fabric at the crucial time. Mr Barkston, the Chapter Clerk, had been in the cathedral, but only to have a word with the manageress of the cathedral shop and she could vouch for his having been with her as the clock was striking four.

He was going to check the remaining people, Nigel Parsifal for example, but his thoughts were more and more insistently taking another direction – the direction which had first occurred to him as he stood on his own landing and looked down at his friend Oglethorpe and Lucy standing in the Elizabethan dark-panelled hall beneath him.

From above, Oglethorpe's head had looked remarkably similar to the Dean's when, during the previous week, he too had been standing in that hallway. Had the stone been intended to strike Oglethorpe? Or someone else? On his fingers George Grindal counted how many of the Chapter in that procession had bald heads naked to the same extent. Most of them had more hair. The thin patches were half-crown size, or palm size, or the hair was in retreat from the forehead and still showing fight on the rest of the head.

'There were only the two of them,' he concluded at last. He himself had a thick silvery thatch.

107

Then, was murder really intended? Could it not have been a minor act of spite on someone's part which had had unintended fatal consequences? The part of the head which had been struck was apparently crucial, from what the doctor had said. A blow on any other part might have been far from lethal. Perhaps it was merely meant to disable, even to annoy.

Who would want to have a go at Oglethorpe? That was the question.

The next morning, Thursday, Canon Grindal attended the early service. It was the time he loved the cathedral most. Not many people realized that the doors opened at eight o'clock, and that at that hour the vast building was empty and dim and private, so that one could stand anywhere one liked and appreciate it. Leaving, he went out by the northernmost of the west doors and instead of taking the shorter way through Dean's Park he decided to circumnavigate the building round its south side, taking pleasure in seeing the town's early mood.

He reached the east end; ahead of him in the road workmen were already busy, their bright yellow plastic jackets showing up well in the grey, wettish morning. The wind of the night before had dropped, although there had been reports on the radio that damage in the south had been severe. George swished along in his black cassock, rather enjoying the feel of its skirts round his legs. He imagined himself one of the woollen-robed clergy who for so many centuries had paced past the side of this holy building. Tom Churchyard brought him abruptly back into the present.

'Good morning, Canon,' said Tom gloomily. He was standing at the side of the garish little British Telecom van, wearing a bright yellow rainproof over his customary grey tweeds and watching the men at work.

'You look as though you were suffering from a feeling of grievance,' George remarked.

'So I am. Not only do I have to work early this morning, I had to put up with an interrogation last night from our friend Detective Chief Inspector Southwell – who seemed to hold me personally responsible for the death of the Dean.' It was surprising that Tom had not been able to shake off the effect of Bob's very mild and momentary checking. He had woken up in the night thinking of it and now it had come pouring out when he saw Grindal.

'Were you responsible?' asked George Grindal in an enquiring tone of voice.

'Of course not. But I did tell Mrs Hassock just what I thought about the Dean and felt like doing to him. He always upset me. And I did spend part of the afternoon trying to find ammunition for a show-down with him, and I was nearby when he was killed.'

'It seems to me,' replied George, 'that many people were antagonistic to the Dean and they were all floating round the area at the time.'

'I was. I'd been in the cathedral library. But that's the trouble with policemen. They're never off duty.'

'In fact I rang Mr Southwell last night, to tell him that the foreman stonemason believes that stone to have been deliberately detached.'

'You can't mean someone murdered him?'

The Acting Dean cleared his throat expressively. 'That was what we were just discussing, wasn't it, Tom? You were saying that, had the Dean been murdered, you might have been a suspect?'

'You didn't phone while I was with Bob.'

'It was late. I was lucky to find him up.'

Tom was only in his mid-thirties but he was built on a massive scale which made people assume that he was older. He had large dignified features which would come into their own when he reached his fifties. They did not show emotions as plainly as more mobile faces did. His friends learned to notice the tiny changes which told them how he was feeling. George Grindal looked at him now and read consternation.

'I can hardly believe this. I was suggesting just what you say. But not seriously any more than my threat against the Dean was serious.'

'Just for the moment working on the supposition that the Dean's death was murder – only a supposition, please don't let the idea go any further – there were several people who would have preferred his absence to his presence. That is not quite the same thing as killing him. You are one of the lesser contenders, I feel, about on a par with my daughter Lucy.'

'Lucy? But she wouldn't kill anyone!'

'No, of course she wouldn't. But she voiced that desire.'

'So did I.'

'But in neither of you is a passing exaggerated phrase likely to indicate either the capacity or a sufficiency of will to do murder. Both of your characters are too bounded by the knowledge of what is right, to have broken those bounds on account of the provocation you were given.'

'The very idea that Lucy could kill anyone is ridiculous, if you don't mind my saying so, Canon.'

'Lucy might strike out if she saw someone inflicting pain on a child or an animal – on anything defenceless; she would rush to their aid and her anger would be terrible. But the Dean's actions were not enough. She bitterly regretted having grasped him firmly by the wrists earlier in the day, and her reaction to his forbidding her dogs the park was to weep and spoil our next meal.'

'Of course she would never do such a thing.'

'Nor do I think his provocation enough for you, Tom. The Dean's attitude made you give up some of your free time, planning how to defeat him, when you could have been doing something more fruitful. That's all. I don't know what would rouse you to the point of hitting out murderously, but it was not our irritating Henry Parsifal.'

'You seem convinced it was murder?'

'Yes. Though I can hardly explain that belief.'

'You are suggesting there are other people . . . whose motives would be sufficient?'

'I thought at one time of our young assistant organist. But no. He is absolved. It is too out of character altogether, and I don't think he could have surmounted the practical difficulties in the time available.'

'Then?'

'There are more likely people. Just to state a hypothetical case – the nephew: the Dean inflicted countless small harassments and constantly threatened to cut him out of his will, yet his

110

inheritance from the Dean is his only real hope of affluence. The antique shop seems to be doing quite nicely, but that is a living only.'

'And he has Jill to keep happy.'

'Who?'

'That girl with the startling legs. Jill, the assistant in Nigel Parsifal's shop. She is supposed to mean more to him than she should.'

'The painted Jezebel, as Dean Parsifal referred to her.'

'Painted, yes. I wouldn't know about the rest. She was in Ye Olde Starre Inne at lunch-time yesterday.'

'With Nigel?'

'No. They stagger their lunch-times, I imagine. She was with two young men. One of them I knew, I've been introduced to him – by Mr Soames the verger. He's his son, Michael.'

'Step,' said George Grindal.

'I beg your pardon?'

'Step. I think you'll find Michael is Mr Soames's stepson.'

'"My son Michael," he said, when he introduced him to me. I can't say I took to him much. A bit of a bruiser. Tough type. Been travelling about abroad, I gather.'

'Yes. He would say "my son Michael." He formally adopted the boy when he married the widowed mother. Don't you think when you see people in a different place, not where you expect them to be, one tends not to recognize them?'

'I did recognize him. He was one of the young men Jill was with.'

'Odd,' commented Grindal. 'Strange mixture of tastes some people have. Lucy told me that only yesterday Jill was here in the cathedral offering to be a cathedral guide. Very urgent about it – she wanted to be taken on and trained at once.'

'She looks more likely to be interested in discos than in ecclesiastical architecture. I wonder what the attraction is? Although – ' Tom was following his own train of thought, 'she does work in Nigel's shop and so can't be altogether stupid. He specializes in some quite obscure things, and she'd have to know about old china, glazes, the different factories.'

'Why, Tom, because she's young and pretty with sex appeal

111

and likes to show off those facts, did you assume that she is stupid?'

Tom looked embarrassed.

'Did I? Yes. I did. Male chauvinism, I suppose.'

'Definitely. Now that would make Lucy cross. I don't think she's much time for girls like Jill, but she would not equate good looks with lack of brains.'

'Right. Point taken,' said Tom. 'Odd though, that Jill should suddenly want to be a cathedral guide.'

'Perhaps it's something she's long wanted to do. We may be misjudging her. She went to Queen Berengaria's.'

'Really? Isn't that rather county?'

'Very expensive.'

'And now she suddenly wants to be a guide, coinciding with Michael Soames's arrival back in his parents' home after several years doing goodness knows what? Will it be a coincidence?'

'And she has been lunching with him?'

'If you're implying that she's fallen for Michael Soames, Canon, she seemed more interested in the other one.'

'Really?'

'I'm pretty sure they were holding hands under the table. She seemed quite sweet on him.'

'The Dean credited her with being Nigel Parsifal's mistress.'

'I should have thought that likely,' said Tom uncomfortably. He had never before discussed such matters with his friend in holy orders.

George Grindal had been so worried by his theory that Canon Oglethorpe had been the real target of the attack – if it had been an attack – that he had sent Lucy over with a trumped-up message to Canon Oglethorpe's house first thing that morning, before either service or breakfast.

'He was all right, was he?' George asked when he reached home. Today it was Lucy who had been cooking the home-cured bacon which she took great trouble to obtain.

'Right as ninepence. Why, father?'

'Nothing. I expect I'm a silly old man. It's just a thought that crossed my mind.'

George ate rapidly and drank his coffee as if there was a prize for being first to finish.

'Before I do anything else, Lucy, I'm going along to the hospital. If Jason has regained consciousness I want to see him. I'll take the bike and won't be long.' George dashed off into the dark morning, leaving Lucy sitting there shaking her head and wondering when he would realize that he was growing old.

'You can come in,' said the nurse.

As George Grindal went over to the bed he could see that there were fewer tubes and wires attached to his young organist than there had been the previous day.

The protuberant eyes fluttered open.

George looked down kindly, pressing the young man's long hand as he tried to convey moral support.

'It's all right, Jason,' he said. 'Everything's going to be all right. I shall see that it is. You are not to worry about anything. You remember the words of Our Lord, "I shall not leave thee nor forsake thee." He has not left thee nor forsaken thee, and neither shall I.'

Although Edmund Jason did not speak, George felt sure that his words had been heard and understood. He pressed the bony hand again.

'Rest now,' he said. 'I must go because I have things to do. But I will be back later.'

Outside the door he told the nurse how pleased he was that the young man was awake and could understand him.

'He has a lot to thank you for,' she told him. 'Do you know, the doctor was saying that in all his twenty years' experience it's the first time he's known a hanging case recover consciousness? Usually they linger for a few days in intensive care and then we lose them. You must have rescued him very quickly.'

'Yes.' George was going to say more, but found that he could not.

'Now we must see if there are going to be any lasting effects,' said the nurse cheerfully. 'Partial paralysis or any damage to the brain.'

It was impossible to take in this further horror.

'He looked *compos mentis*,' said George.

'We will hope for the best.'

113

With that bright tone ringing in his ears George pedalled back home as fast as he could go, arriving there in under five minutes. Lucy was still in the kitchen, washing up after breakfast.

'You look terribly serious,' she said. 'He's not worse, is he?'

'No, he was conscious, though he didn't speak.'

'The muscles of the throat must be awfully sore.'

'I'm sure they are.'

It was at eight-thirty on that same Thursday morning that the officer from Full Sutton Prison was sitting in Bob Southwell's office in Clifford Street. In front of the two men was an open book of mug shots.

'That's Fergal Mourne.' The prison officer turned a page. 'He's the one you're escorting through, Friday afternoon – tomorrow, isn't it. That's Bill Banklin, who is coming next week. That's Tommy Harcher, who's coming the week after. Once they're in our high security wing that'll be the last anyone sees of them for a good few years.'

'It's very impressive. I've been over it, you know. Best security I've seen. Turn back a minute. Let's have another look at this week's gentleman, Mourne.'

The two men looked at the thin face, lit by great fanatical eyes, shaded by a lock of hair falling in a curve on to the forehead.

'Funny thing,' said the prison officer. 'We had his brother Terry in Parkhurst when I was there. Petty criminal. Mind you, that's what the IRA recruits from more and more these days. The youngsters get into petty crime – out of work, most of them – and because the IRA has taken over the crime network in Ireland, they're in it before they know where they are.'

'You mean the IRA have got like the Mafia?'

'Pretty much. Protection money, the lot. Most building sites pay ghost gangs, to get protection. That's why they've not had a strike in years on construction – because the IRA control the labour force. Little shopkeepers shell out. Belfast businesses pay extortion money.'

'I didn't realize it was as bad as that,' said Bob. It took a lot to

114

astound him, but he'd been too busy with his own patch to keep up to date with events overseas.

'The IRA controls illegal shibeens, prostitution and drugs, gambling machines – you name it. Not much idealism around these days. Fergal Mourne's one of the few idealists left at the top of the movement.'

'They split up into separately organized areas, that right?'

'Yes. Fergal used to be one of their top men. We don't get much change out of him.'

'I suppose they're always afraid of prisoners turning supergrasses?'

'Not much fear of that with Mourne. He's not in it for what he can get out of it, like a lot of them.'

'What part does the INLA play?'

'Oh, they've got out of hand. Feuding among themselves, now.'

'I'm surprised to hear you mention drugs.'

'That's one issue that splits them. In southern Ireland the IRA are knee-capping drug-pushers, but they're contributing a hell of a lot to funds, all the same. It's a great muddle.'

'You mentioned Fergal Mourne's brother. What sort of petty crime did he go in for?' asked Bob.

'Theft. Silver mostly. He's a bit of an expert at it. Proceeds go to the IRA funds, although I think heroin and coke are proving more profitable to the movement.'

'Interesting. We've had a theft of silver lately, antique stuff. Even more interesting, there seems to be a rumour about Fergal Mourne coming to Full Sutton on Friday. I'd like to change the time of the run.'

'Really? You mean it's become public knowledge?'

'That's what I said.'

'The rumour is strong enough for you to change the time?'

'Yes.'

10

The lot is fallen unto me in a fair ground, yea I
have a goodly heritage.

—Psalms, 16, v. 7

Thursday was the second day after the Dean's death and George
Grindal had a conscience because he had not yet seen Nigel
Parsifal, in any capacity. He should have seen him as a religious
counsellor; as Acting Dean, Nigel's uncle's replacement; as an
old friend; and as a would-be investigator. So as he was drying
the breakfast pots for Lucy he mentioned it.

'I've been in to see the Deanery housekeeper,' she told him.
'In fact I popped in for a few minutes with Mr Barkston to break
the news to her straight after he'd told me, about the Dean's
accident I mean, and I was there yesterday helping her organize
things a bit.'

'Nigel's wife – Maureen – should be doing all that, now,
shouldn't she?' asked George.

'She will be, I'm sure. But Nigel's had a bit of a crisis.'

George regretted more than ever his forgetting of Nigel.

'Oh . . .' Lucy read her father's squashed-looking features as
if he had spoken – 'Not what you're thinking. It's only that his
assistant, Jill – you know the one, she's slim and leggy –
suddenly demanded a few days' holiday, just when Nigel needs
to be away from his shop to deal with the funeral and
everything.'

'You said she wanted to be a cathedral guide,' put in George.

'Yes, and she was very insistent on training straight away.
Julia Bransby, bless her, took her round yesterday and will
again this morning. So with one thing and another, I don't
think what little help I could give the Parsifals came amiss.'

'I'm sure it didn't. I must go along to see Nigel right away.
Where will he be, do you think?'

Lucy glanced at the clock. 'It's my guess that he'll have come in early, dropped Maureen at the shop – she's having to look after it – and he'll have gone to the Deanery for an hour. He'll want to be back at the shop again when it gets busy later.'

George dropped his drying cloth. Guilt added speed to his movements. 'See you later, Lucy, my love,' he said, kissing her forehead lightly.

She beamed with pleasure. George Grindal was always an affectionate father, but, apart from the regular good-night brush of his lips on her cheek when she took him his mug of hot milk, overt caresses were rare. She took the kiss as a mark of approval and wore it with pride.

George found the Deanery looking cheerful in spite of the wet and gloomy autumn morning, but it was a house which could not look anything but cheerful, a long low house, twentieth-century Georgian style, red brick and white paint. He rang, and the door was opened by the housekeeper.

'What an awful thing, isn't it, Canon!' she exclaimed, helping him off with the rainproof cloak he wore over his cassock. After the exchange of a few conventional remarks, George asked her about herself; what was she planning to do, now that her job had obviously come to an end? She was middle-aged and he knew there might be difficulties, but she surprised him by her carefree attitude.

'Mr Nigel will give me a hand if I need it,' she assured him, and he was glad to have this evidence that Nigel was willing to shoulder the responsibilities, as well as the advantages, of being his uncle's heir – as George had no doubt he was.

'Do you want to see him, sir?'

That was George's real errand. He nodded.

'He's in the study.'

Nigel looked up from his informal position – he was squatting on the floor in front of a disorderly pile of books – and his face shocked the Acting Dean. It was white, with an unpleasantly yellow-tinged whiteness; and his eyes were red-rimmed. He had a distracted, drowned look, which was most unpleasant. He scrambled to his feet.

'Mr Grindal!' He came forward with hands outstretched.

117

George took them in both his own and conveyed moral support with his clasp as well as he could.

'How are things?' he asked.

'Not so bad, I suppose, really.' Nigel laughed a little shamefacedly. 'You wouldn't think losing the old bugger would upset me, would you?' He laughed again. 'What with one damn thing and another!' His face crumpled, and he fought to regain control. Tears shook on the ends of his long straight eyelashes.

George remembered that Jill had chosen this time to absent herself, and wondered how much her desertion was adding to Nigel's distress.

'Is there anything I can do?' he asked gently.

'Uncle's in the undertaker's chapel of rest, and the Archbishop suggests holding a funeral service in the cathedral. We're shipping his remains down to Leicestershire afterwards; we've a family plot in the churchyard at Burton Overy and he asked to be buried there.'

'I expect the undertaker's arranging all that.'

'Yes. All taken care of. Music chosen for the service, everything. Flowers ordered.' There was an odd tone in Nigel's voice – between sarcasm and tears.

'You needn't rush to sort his things out, you know,' Canon Grindal said awkwardly, looking at the piles of books. 'The new Dean won't be chosen overnight. You'll have weeks – probably months – to clear the house and sort out his possessions.'

'Yes. I realize that.' Then Nigel went on, a little unexpectedly, 'I saw his solicitor.'

'Oh?' George thought a tone of enquiry would not be unwelcome.

'He showed me the will and gave me a copy. It has to go for probate, of course.'

'Of course.'

'But Mr Hale says everything is in order, so no problem should arise. I'm one of the executors, he's the other. I'm also chief beneficiary.'

'I'm glad,' said George, and meant it. Whether the late Dean had ever actually gone to the length of altering his will George doubted. But Nigel must have been on tenterhooks, wondering whether the death had taken place at a time when the family fortune was willed to others.

'You'll be comfortably off, I hope,' he said.

'It will take a time to sort out after we get probate. Some of the old money – the inheritance from my grandparents – is wrapped up in trusts in which he had a life interest, but where he had the disposal of it fortunately he has willed it to me. Uncle saved a great deal himself, too, and invested it wisely as far as we can see. He's left a lot of small bequests, which have to be attended to first, and I inherit the residue.'

George was satisfied that Nigel openly avowed his pleasure in inheriting; it would have been hypocritical to pretend otherwise. 'I hope he's done something for Mrs Guest.'

'There's a lump sum if still in his service, which she is, of course, and he's contributed to a private pension for her as well as paying her stamp.'

'That's good.'

'I'm wondering if she would come and work for us, living in. Maureen could do with a hand, and we will be able to afford it now. If she would come for a few years, until she's retiring age. By that time the girls will all be older and we shouldn't need so much assistance.'

'Ask her. The Deanery is always beautifully looked after.'

'Yes, I will.'

For a moment they were silent. The room around them spoke clearly of its old master. Apart from the undisciplined piles in front of Nigel, the books were in orderly rows arranged according to subject. Each one looked as if it was consulted too often to gather dust.

The large mahogany writing desk was immaculately tidy. Sheets of thick white paper lay neatly on it, in front of the chair. A few lines were written on the topmost sheet and a gold-nibbed fountain pen lay parallel beside them. George glanced at the even writing. 'Notes on the Fijian language,' he remarked. 'He was an expert in Dutch, too, I understand. Such an impossible-looking tongue. They put Js in the middle of all their words just to confuse. It took the Archbishop to remind me that Dean Parsifal was a great linguist as well as the rather irritating man we knew.'

119

'Irritating? He nearly drove me mad at times,' commented Nigel. 'Yet I feel now as if the sky had fallen.'

George thought of the lump of stone which fell so opportunely. He ought to be questioning Nigel about his whereabouts on Tuesday afternoon.

'He was the last of the older generation,' added Nigel. 'Perhaps that's partly why I feel so bereft. When one is a child the rest of the family form a kind of sheltering tree, an upper layer. One by one they go; now here am I, bare to the world. No branches fretting above me. But I have to take my turn, and become myself the canopy to the younger ones; my own children – well, you would say that's always been the case. But far-flung members, too – cousins, et cetera. I'm now regarded as the head of the family of Parsifal.'

'An honourable estate.'

'Yes, but a lonely one.'

'Were you in the cathedral when it happened?' George had to get to the point sooner or later.

Nigel gave him a surprised look. 'Good Lord, no. I was too busy in the shop to leave even for a pee. Though I would like to have attended that service. The music was going to be particularly fine.'

'Pity we never actually heard it.'

'There will be a chance in the future, I imagine.'

George suddenly began to feel slightly uncomfortable – a hint from his body that he had stayed in one place long enough. He rose to his feet from the carved mahogany chair on which he had perched. 'Let me know if I can be of any help and assistance . . .'

'There is a bequest to you,' said Nigel.

'Really? I didn't expect that.'

'Six books of your choice from his library.'

George was much struck. 'Really? Well, I call that handsome of him. I wonder what I shall choose?'

'Come any time,' invited Nigel. 'I shall be cataloguing every night. I'm going to ask Mrs Guest to stay here for the time being, so that the house isn't left empty, and she will be turning out cupboards and things.'

'I'll do that.'

'And there is something for Lucy.'

'What?'

'Yes. I think the Dean was rather fond of her, you know.'

Coals of fire! thought the Canon. She'll be upset when she hears this. Aloud he said, 'Am I permitted to enquire?'

'Some jewellery,' answered Nigel. 'Not valuable, I would guess. Probably a few old pieces. I expect they were my grandmother's. I don't think he had any of his wife's. He'd actually put them together in a box and labelled them "For Lucy Grindal", although goodness knows, he might have had years of life ahead of him.'

'As well to be prepared. Well, well. One never knows, does one? Poor old Henry. That is certainly a surprise. It never does to judge one's fellow human beings, does it? I'd better get along. I'll be seeing you,' and, unable to think of any further platitudes, George Grindal left the Deanery, picking up his rainproof on the way, and calling to Mrs Guest that he would let himself out.

It was only a short way back home. Barely long enough to decide that he would not tell Lucy yet. No doubt there would be a letter in due course from the solicitor. He would tell her about his books, though. And he would tell her that he was crossing Nigel Parsifal off his list of suspects.

What a strange thing, to leave jewellery to Lucy! George had no illusions about his beloved daughter. Her beauties were those of mind and heart – and they were many. But to all outward appearance she was, let it be said, the slightest bit slatternly. Carelessly dressed would perhaps be putting it more kindly. She was often a kind of walking heap of assorted woollies. Not the type of person to whom one left one's mother's jewellery, he felt. Just fancy the Dean! Well, well . . .

George wondered afterwards what changed his mind when he was at his own gate, what had sent his feet in the direction of the cathedral instead of down his own path. But he certainly went through Chapter Yard, into the cathedral, and was walking near the crypt when Michael Soames seemed to be struggling to open the barrier as if he would burst it apart. He looked hulkingly strong enough to break the wrought-iron bars.

'Is it locked, Michael?' Canon Grindal called out, wondering why Michael wanted to get through. He spoke again. 'Did you want to go in? Renewing acquaintance?' – thinking that Michael must have known the cathedral well in earlier days. By now he was quite close.

Michael went bright red and muttering something inaudible he turned away quickly.

It was only when the young man moved away in this fashion that George began to puzzle over the incident. Michael was not the sort of young man who would have been expected to blush, he admitted to himself, even though George always tried to credit young people with sensitivity. The Dean's death had seemed to bring about a rash of blushes. There was Lucy, when she felt under suspicion; Edmund Jason in his hospital bed; and now Michael Soames. Well! It was nice to know that young people could still blush, these hardened days. He refused to consider the possibility that Soames had gone red with anger, or some kind of guilt.

What could be of interest in the crypt?

It was a fascinating place, of course. There were the vast bases of the old Norman pillars which had once supported a very different cathedral; their great size combined with austere simplicity was one of the most impressive things he knew, and the simple zigzag decoration spoke of the age in which they were made – an airy, open age.

Then there was the Doomstone, a single slab-like stone, carved all over, which anyone who knew of it must want to revisit, to ponder on again and again. The Doomstone always made George think irresistibly of the time of the Black Death. There was the feeling of claustrophobia which must have existed then in the overcrowded medieval towns. The masses of bodies being thrust into the mouth of Hell, the damned being tortured, seemed to bring fetid air, contagion, and all the horrors of death to the senses of anyone regarding it. Was that what Michael Soames had wanted to see? If he had not hurried away so fast the key could have been sought and the crypt unlocked.

On the other hand, he could have wanted to seek out the de Vere tomb, hidden in the dark passages which stretched away under the great building, almost unknown, a secret city. There had been a great deal of talk about the tomb lately. Now George came to think of it, the Dean had muttered something to him over the teacups on Tuesday – something about Verger Soames's insolence in mentioning the matter of the de Vere tomb to him. So Michael's stepfather felt concern for the fate of the tomb, and did not want it disturbed; perhaps that was what had led Michael to wish to see it – though to have been lost from memory for so many years it must be in an out-of-the-way place, not one of the more frequented passages.

Yes. He felt sure he had hit on the truth. It was the de Vere tomb Michael had been after, and because of the fracas about it had not wanted to say so to the Acting Dean.

After a brief visit to the cathedral shop, where already the staff were busy with a group of Japanese tourists, George went out of the cathedral again. He had left home in such a hurry after breakfast that he felt the need to return there and pick up the threads of the day.

At Canon Grindal's, life was proceeding in an orderly manner in its usual direction. Lucy had taken the two dogs for a walk – the visiting bitch, Diamond Lil, had been collected by her owner on the previous day – and then had made the morning coffee, which was keeping hot.

Lucy had not taken the dogs into Dean's Park. She could well have done so, for the key was hanging on a nail by the door; but some delicacy restrained her. Her father was only the Acting Dean, and it had been agreed between them that Dean Parsifal's notices must stay until the next Dean proper ordered their removal – if he did. The notices stayed, so Lucy stayed out. The two dogs had been exercised in the quiet streets.

When George Grindal returned, Lucy was sitting at their breakfast table with a ledger open in front of her.

'Here's Albert Horncastle,' she told him. 'I've found his records for several years now.'

'Where are you?' George looked over her shoulder. 'Nine years ago. Right. Any sign of that Killarney chap he keeps talking about?'

'Not a mention. The old man must have got the name wrong. I've traced quite a few of the people he had asked about, and

I've asked Sister Agape to tell him what happened to them. I've found the name and address of the daughter.'

'Have you found anything about the pension?'

'Yes, she's receiving it as his agent.'

'So that little score should soon be settled! That's good.'

'Yes. Anyway,' Lucy pushed the ledger and her notes away from her, 'I have other things to do apart from chasing memories. I found Michael Soames, incidentally. Did you know he had been an apprentice stonemason?'

'I knew he had been something connected with the building, I wasn't sure what. I had a vague feeling he'd been an electrician. Lucy, I need to see Sam Oglethorpe today. When you went over did he say what he was planning to do with himself?'

'He's coming up to evensong.' She went to fetch the coffee. 'How is your detecting going on, father?' she asked.

'Well, my dear. Not very well, though. I keep eliminating people from my list and will soon have no suspects left. Nigel told me he never left the shop on Tuesday afternoon, so he's in the clear.'

There was a pause, and Lucy looked thoughtful. At last she said, 'But he did, you know, because I saw him when I was out for the meat. He was walking past St William's College carrying a parcel. Going towards the Deanery.'

George looked disconcerted. 'About four o'clock?'

'A little before, I suppose.'

'He told me he was exceptionally busy that afternoon. Perhaps he just forgot. I'll ask him about it, though. Just when I was thinking I'd no suspects left.'

'You don't seem worried?'

'No, because I don't think the murderer meant to kill the Dean.'

Lucy stopped eating her biscuit and looked attentive.

'If that stone was dropped deliberately – and I say, if – it seems possible to mistake Oglethorpe for Parsifal, from above.'

'You mean you think someone wanted to kill Canon Oglethorpe?'

'It seems possible to mistake them.'

'But they were so totally different, father – you would never mistake one for the other!'

'You think not?'

'Wasn't the Dean taller?'

'Maybe a shade. Not much in it. Same-shaped bald patch, same fringe of white hair. I noticed when I stood on the landing and looked down at you both, on Tuesday night, how similar he might look.'

'The slight difference in height wouldn't be noticeable from above . . .'

'What would be noticeable, as we all issued from the vestry into the south choir aisle?'

'There is one thing,' said Lucy doubtfully, after thinking for a minute.

'Well? Come on, what is it?'

'They both limped.'

'Oh, now then, Lucy. The Dean didn't limp. Oglethorpe does of course, with that old war wound. One becomes so used to his way of moving that one forgets about it except on occasions like Tuesday evening when it was mentioned.'

'But the Dean was limping, father. You've forgotten his arthritis and his hip op. I noticed on Tuesday morning when we had our contretemps in Dean's Park. I walked beside him for a little way. He was limping quite badly.'

'Left leg?'

'Yes.'

'That's it! That's it, Lucy. The bell rings, you know, to announce the beginning of service, and that's when we go up out of the door. While we were still in the vestry, Oglethorpe's shoe-lace came undone; he fell out of the row of us going up the steps, to fasten it. Now I think on, as they say, he did seem to be making quite a performance of it – put his foot up on a seat.'

'He has trouble bending,' pointed out Lucy.

'He has trouble climbing those steps, too. Now you bring it to mind I distinctly recall on previous occasions seeing him catch hold of the door jamb to heave himself out of the doorway. I've got so used to the consequences of his wound that I've almost ceased to notice them.'

125

'Did the Dean catch hold of the door jamb, too, when he climbed the steps?'

'Do you know, I believe he did! Now I think of it! So to anyone above, waiting with a lump of rock – they could hide at the side of the walkway until they heard the bell – then move out – they see a man with a limp heaving himself out of the vestry door, making the disability obvious – then limp along the aisle – a man with a bald patch and a fringe of white hair . . .'

'They would be confused if there were two men of that description in sight at once.'

'But there weren't! Because Oglethorpe was still messing about with that shoe-lace while the Dean fidgeted at the back of the procession wondering why the organ hadn't started and then told us to walk forward anyway and . . . down came the stone.'

'Canon Oglethorpe was still in the vestry?'

'Yes. Just mounting the steps to the door when the Dean cried out and fell.'

Lucy looked down at her hands and to her surprise felt her cheeks redden and her eyes water.

'Why, my dear, what's the matter?'

'It's just the relief, father. If it was Canon Oglethorpe they were trying to kill – not Dean Parsifal at all – no one need suspect me of it any more.'

Lucy could not help it; a couple of great tears rolled down her cheeks, and she had to sniff to stop her nose weeping in unison. She felt hastily in her pocket for a handkerchief and pulled out first a dog lead, then a schedule for a Championship Show, then her silver polishing cloth and finally a large and rather mannish handkerchief, in which she buried her face.

George Grindal wondered what to do. With anyone but his own daughter there would have been no problem: his long training and experience would have told him. He wished his wife – many years dead but still missed – were there to help him.

At last, as Lucy showed no signs of recovering, he adopted her own method – a recourse to the hot drink department. He

126

patted her arm and picked up the coffee-pot. With a fair copy of her own intonation, he said, 'Come now, I'll water the pot.'

'You make it sound like tea,' sniffed Lucy. 'There's some milk left in the pan, if you want to make some more.'

George felt free to leave her. Through two open doors he still felt in touch as he made more coffee. Then in a couple of minutes he returned, to find Lucy red-eyed but emerging from her cotton covering.

'Why should anyone try to kill our Samivel?' said George, remembering his Pickwick. He sighed. 'It's been bad enough trying to find a murderer for Henry, where suspects abounded. Now I have to start all over again.'

'But how awful,' said Lucy. 'How awful to be killed in mistake for someone else.'

'I don't know that it's any more awful than to be killed for yourself,' replied George. 'It really does make his death accidental. An act of God.'

'We don't know, do we? We don't know when our work on earth has ended, when our purpose is fulfilled. Perhaps Canon Oglethorpe still has work to do, more important than the Dean's.'

'I don't think we ought to be led into these conjectures. It's still murder, whether accidental or not, whether one man has done his work on earth and the other hasn't, it's still murder.' George sounded a little repressive.

He considered the two men. The Dean had been constantly pugnacious and irritable; Canon Oglethorpe was the spirit of goodness and generally beloved – and he had lived a life of unblemished virtue and constant care for others. All through his work in the prison service . . .

George stopped there. Of course. In some way he was a danger to an ex-con, that must be it. But how could he possibly endanger anyone?

At that point George Grindal could take his line of reasoning no further. He – George – had searched in vain for a motive powerful enough, a personality faulty enough, among those recently upset by the Dean; in his long experience of men and women he could not see that any of them had that disregard for society, that otherness, which was, he thought, necessary

127

before a premeditated crime could be committed. Such a rash, impulsive, yet premeditated crime! One so very likely to miscarry! As it had, indeed, if his supposition was correct.

Just then there was a pounding on the door, a most indignant and furious assault on it. The Canon and his daughter looked at one another, rose together, and rushed out into the hall. Whatever had happened now?

As they opened the door a young man almost fell in upon them.

'Where is he?' he shouted. 'What have you done with him?'

'Who?' said the Canon.

The young man had a mass of curly black hair, a reddish face and a frantic expression.

'Where's Edmund?' he shouted.

'Edmund Jason? He's in hospital. Wait a minute – you must be Simon!'

'I thought he would be all right here of all places. As if he hadn't suffered enough! What have you been doing to him?'

'Well really, it's more what he's been doing to himself . . .'

'I can read the papers!' shouted Simon.

'It's not our fault!' said George.

'We're very fond of him,' put in Lucy.

'Why didn't you take more care of him, then?'

'I thought you were in Cambridge,' George heard himself saying.

'I was.'

'Look, calm down. Everything is going to be all right. Edmund will fully recover, we hope. No one will do anything but be supportive to him. We think we have a treasure in his musicianship. There is no need to behave like this.'

'You can't leave him on his own a minute without something happening,' said the young man more calmly.

'Have a coffee,' said Lucy.

'Tell me how to get to him. I must see him at once.'

As soon as he was sure how to reach Edmund Jason, Simon turned on his heel and without another word slammed out of the door again. He seemed to leave a vacuum torn out of the air of the hall, as if he had sucked life and oxygen away with him.

George and Lucy looked at one another.

'Goodness, what a very fiery young man!'

'What a contrast!'

They were silent, recovering. Then George announced, 'I'm going to go back to the Deanery right away. Nigel wants me to choose these books. If he's still there I'll ask him outright about your seeing him on Tuesday afternoon.'

'There must be lots more urgent things, father . . .'

'No, my dear. Nothing more urgent than clearing up this problem. Cathedral business is up to date. If anyone wants me you know where I'll be.'

Lucy wished her father would forget about the whole matter and leave it to the police. Soon she would have to think about lunch and before that there was some housework to do, and first of all she had better take those ledgers back to the Chapter Office and call in at the cathedral to see if she could spot Julia and Jill, although it was often very difficult to find anyone in such an enormous building, crammed as it usually was with visitors.

Mealtimes and cathedral services formed the divisions of Lucy's day. Later, at half-past twelve, she began preparing a simple meal, hot soup and cold salad. George came in as she was setting the table.

'Still horrible out,' he said. 'Not a thick mist, but one of those hazes like the ones in cinemas in the days when more people smoked. As things come towards you they gradually change from pastels, becoming brighter until they're in full technicolor.'

He set a great pile of books down on the table perilously near the salt and pepper.

'Oh, what have you chosen?' cried Lucy.

'Nigel was very generous, you know. The bequest said six books – but what is one to do when a book is in several volumes?'

'Father! You're incorrigible!'

'They would only have gone to the saleroom and fetched nothing at all,' replied George Grindal cheerfully.

'Books! You soon won't be able to move in this house!'

Lucy did not look as fierce as she was trying to sound. The soup was quite safe on a low heat in the kitchen, she remembered. She came round eagerly and began to look.

'Richard Hooker's *Ecclesiastical Policy*. You've wanted that for a long time. Several volumes, though, father!'

'And look here, Lucy! William Temple's *Readings in St John's Gospel*, published by Macmillan in 1939 – and not only that, it's *autographed!*'

'Two volumes,' said Lucy, shaking her head. 'First and Second Series. Well, I suppose one wouldn't be much good without the other.'

'Yes! Autographed in both of them!' exulted the shameless George. 'And Thomas Traherne's *Centuries of Meditations*, you remember that, Lucy, he was 1636 to 1674, but the manuscript wasn't discovered and published until after his death.'

'It says here first printed in 1908,' remarked Lucy.

'And Walter Hilton's *The Ladder of Perfection*, and look here, John Henry Newman's *Apologia pro Vita Sua*.'

'Don't say you've chosen a modern book as well,' Lucy teased, taking up J. A. T. Robinson's *The Priority of John*. 'This was only published in 1982.'

'Wasn't that another posthumous publication? Did I ever deny that the present day can produce items of value?' asked her father.

'You have a distinct preference for older books.'

'Well, they were books, weren't they? So pleasant to handle, good paper, proper typesetting, decent margins, nicely bound.'

Lucy looked at her father's face. It bore a wistful expression. She operated her skills as a mind-reader.

'There were others, weren't there? Other books you would have liked to bring?'

'I thought I might go to the sale,' admitted George. 'There were two works by William Law which I would have liked very much indeed. And a copy of Edward Schillebeeckx's *Jesus – an Experiment in Christology*.'

'Wasn't that the book Schillebeeckx got into trouble with the Vatican over? You've got a copy, father.'

'Henry's was in much better condition. I bought mine second-hand and it is rather battered.'

Lucy decided to fetch the soup, or they would be there all day talking about the books. She served it steaming into the dishes as George moved his new darlings to a side table.

'Did you see Nigel? Yes, you must have. Did you challenge him?'

'I'm afraid I didn't.'

'Oh, father! You should have!'

'The way he's reacted to the Dean's death convinces me that he certainly didn't wish it. And as for Oglethorpe – I can't see any suggestion of a motive there either.'

'So he's crossed off your list again?' Lucy sat down.

'Yes. He definitely is.'

11

Their mouth is full of cursing and bitterness,
their feet are swift to shed blood.
—*Psalms*, 14, v. 6

Earlier the same morning Jill's radio shrilled into life. She slowly
sat up among the warm and crumpled sheets as the set awoke
her. With a sigh and a glance at Terry's still-sleeping face, she
responded to the call.

'Plans changed,' came the terse message. 'Superstar moving
from Wakefield tomorrow morning pretty damn quick. Expect
leave six forty-five a.m.'

'Right, we'll be ready for the earlier time, then, no problem,'
responded Jill.

The set went dead. She looked at her watch. Thank goodness
the whole thing was tomorrow and not today, she didn't have
to get up and do anything – not yet, anyway. Life with Terry
was so delightfully free and easy. No set mealtimes, lovemaking
whenever they liked – instead of when Maureen wouldn't find
out, as it always was with Nigel. Jill was the most fastidious of
women, yet she didn't care that the one room Terry rented
could only be described as sleazy. She didn't care that when he
had finished using the hand-basin it was left filthy and the
towel showed his individual hand marks in grime. She didn't
care that the floor was scattered with spent matches and that
fag ends had been stubbed out all over the place as well as in
the overflowing ashtrays, and one was unfolding itself into a
tobacco flower in the remains of a glass of whisky. She didn't
care that the clothes he had flung out of the night before were
scattered on floor and chairs.

She sighed again. Today she would have to go back home,
making out that she'd been in London staying with a friend for
the last couple of nights. Well, needs must; and tomorrow the

great adventure was to take place, and she and Terry and Mike and Fergal would set off together and she'd never have to live at home again.

She remembered the day they had first met. He had come into the shop when Nigel was at lunch and asked the price of a silver tankard, Chester, Britannia standard silver of 1715. They'd talked about various items in the shop for a few minutes and then he'd asked her to meet him for a drink in her lunch hour. She'd agreed at once, and that had been the start of it . . .

Lying back in a daze of imagined glamour and adventure she touched Terry's curls softly, twining them about her fingers, remembering how the muscles of his back felt under her hands when he possessed her, how completely they were at one, losing their identities. She willed him to wake.

They wouldn't have to be too long about it, though. They had to have some breakfast and then she was to meet Julia Bransby at the cathedral at ten o'clock. There was something in Jill that didn't want to be late for the appointment, that wanted to continue training and one day to walk round explaining things to a group of tourists. She'd better put her country clothes on when she got up and go straight home after the cathedral.

Julia hardly recognized Jill when they met. The girl was in a long tweed skirt and long boots so that not an inch of leg was to be seen. She wore a white ribbed sweater under the soft leather jacket and a tweed hat on her head, and carried a small overnight suitcase.

'I must ask you,' Julia said when she remembered, 'about the pop star you were talking about and the concert. My son Adam would like to go, I'm sure. How much are the tickets?'

'Oh, they're sold out,' Jill replied instantly. 'He's very popular and he hasn't been to York before.'

'Is he on tour?'

'He's just been at Wakefield. It was a sell-out there too.'

'I don't think I've heard of him.'

'You wouldn't have.'

Julia didn't like this reply. It sounded as if she was too old for the latest trends and she didn't think she was. At least she tried hard to keep up with Adam and his evolving tastes, and he was a darn sight younger than Jill.

Jill twirled alongside Julia as if she was disco-ing all by herself. Her lids were down, shielding her eyes and thoughts, but there was that excitement emanating from her which Julia had noticed the previous day. There was something else as well, in her walk, in the sometimes languid gestures, in the tremulousness of her lower lip, in a sort of satisfaction to which the widowed Julia had become a stranger.

'She's made love about half a dozen times since I saw her last,' thought Julia, and felt envy and also – surprisingly – fear for Jill. She knew that state of honeyed bliss was often followed by disillusion and the pit of despair.

'Let's get on with it,' she said aloud. 'What did I tell you yesterday about this chapel? What's it called and what did I tell you about the dossal curtain?'

It was early afternoon when Lucy heard a knock at the door. She had been washing the dogs' feet, and, fearing wet paw marks all over the caller, she pushed them into the breakfast room and shut them in.

Lucy opened the door on to a vision of loveliness, Maureen Parsifal, Nigel's wife.

'Do come in, Maureen.' Lucy was immediately conscious of her untidy hair and the fact that Clementina Crosspatch had affectionately scratched a hole in her tights.

Maureen hung up her expensive soft woollen coat, which was a deep shade of amethyst.

'A cup of tea?'

'Well, I will, Lucy, as you offer it. But I really only came round to thank you for being such a help, and if you're busy . . .'

'Nothing that won't wait.'

'What a pretty jumper you're wearing. I had one just like it once.'

Lucy fell into the trap. 'Haven't you still got it? This seems to be wearing very well.'

'Goodness no. I gave it to a jumble sale long ago.'

134

Lucy thanked her lucky stars that the long elegant Georgian sitting-room had been tidied, and that a fire lay ready on the hearth. She hastily assembled a kettle full of water, cups and tea things, on to a tray. The situation was desperate. There were no biscuits left, no scones or cake, either homemade or bought. She'd been going to spend the next hour baking. As a last resort she cut a few squares of the fudge she had made earlier for her father and put them on a little plate, then led the way upstairs where she could plug the kettle in and set a match to the fire.

'So cosy.' Maureen sounded approving. 'I didn't think we were allowed to burn solid fuel any more. How nice that you still can.'

Lucy looked alarmed. 'I thought logs didn't count,' she said.

'You'd better check, my dear,' said Maureen. She was as tall as Nigel, and now folded herself gracefully into a low chair by the hearth. She wore a light grey dress with matching tights and shoes, and an amethyst-coloured cardigan in cashmere to match the colour of the long nails on her pale hands.

'If only I had fair skin like that,' thought Lucy, 'and that soft fine baby hair.' She felt awkward, as she always did with Maureen – though they got on very well, as everyone supposed. 'It must be something to do with being married or unmarried,' her thoughts ran on, very conscious that she had only achieved heartbreak and not conquest in the game of love.

'What a business, isn't it,' went on Maureen. 'Nigel's quite upset about losing that horrid old man. I can't say that I am, though.'

Lucy pushed the idea to the back of her mind that Maureen ought to show gratitude for the money the Dean had left them if for nothing else; then she said, 'He could be disagreeable at times.'

'Never anything else. A death makes a lot of work, though. Mrs Guest has been busy.'

'She's done very well.'

'With your help and guidance, Lucy, and we're very grateful.'

'It was the least I could do.'

The kettle started to sing.

'Nigel's asked her to come to us. He told me at lunch-time

135

that she's agreed. It will be useful to have her, though I wouldn't be surprised if she drinks like a fish.'

'Mrs Guest!'

'You're so trusting, Lucy. You know what I mean – the old Bristol Cream over the chocolates when she's off duty for the evening.'

'One could hardly blame her.'

Maureen drew out a cigarette, perfunctorily offering one to Lucy, who refused. 'You don't mind if I do?'

'Please. I don't object in the least.'

The cigarette had a tiny band of flowers above the cork tip.

'So annoying for you that Jill had time off just now.'

'Jill? Oh, you mean Nigel's bit of fluff.'

'Do you think she is?' said Lucy weakly.

'About the fifth, by my reckoning. Don't worry. Nigel knows on which side his bread's buttered. He has these little foibles from time to time.'

'Don't you mind?'

'It gives me a useful hold over him – not that I ever need to employ it. While I'm bringing up the girls I've enough to do without considering his every whim. When I've more time to devote to him these . . . others . . . won't be necessary. But meanwhile they flatter his ego immensely. They keep him happy and are probably cheaper than golf.'

Lucy was glad to be able to make tea. This was not her idea of the relationship between man and wife. She imagined wanting to be with someone, and they with her, devoted to one another's interests – not a bit like the picture Maureen was conjuring up, a sort of power game.

On the hearth the flames were licking round the thin apple logs. The room was not really cold, because of the background central heating, but as Lucy poured out the tea the cups steamed slightly. Maureen took hers with a thin sliver of lemon, and delicately helped herself to a square of fudge.

'Lapsang! Heavenly.' She breathed out two long straight bars of smoke, which gradually broke up and dispersed. 'Lucy, I wanted to ask. These things the Dean has left you. They won't be any use to you, will they? I wonder if you wouldn't like us to have them valued and give you the money instead?'

136

Lucy sat up of a sudden, very straight. She took some fudge and bit it and her eyes became bright.

'What things?' asked Lucy.

Maureen leaned forward to put down her cup. She had taken only a neat small nibble from the fudge, which lay in the saucer. Even in the thin winter light her amethyst necklace in its fine golden setting sparkled prettily.

'You don't know about them? How typical of men. Nigel told your father about the bequests. He must have forgotten to tell you.'

'Bequests?'

'Dean Parsifal left your father his pick of six books from his library. Rather him than me. I don't suppose there are six books worth reading in the whole lot.'

'Something to me, did you say?'

'A box of oddments, I believe,' Maureen said offhandedly. 'As I suggested, Lucy, we'll have them valued and give you the money.'

'If the Dean has been kind enough to remember me I think I would like to have his bequest.'

'You don't mind if I look them over first, do you, Lucy? Just to check that he hasn't put any pieces in that should go down in the family – we do have daughters, you know. They love things that have belonged to great-grandmothers and so on.' Maureen waved the hand with the cigarette in it, vaguely, and a sideways trail of smoke joined the growing haze. 'It isn't that I am at all bothered for myself, though the expected thing, the right thing, one might say, would have been for them to come to me.'

Lucy's spine seemed to be made of a ramrod and her eyes were brilliant, either with anger or unshed tears.

'If the Dean left anything to me I'm sure it was his own to leave,' she said.

'Oh, of course. But men don't understand these things.'

'I'd like the bequest exactly as he meant it, please,' went on Lucy.

'I didn't mean to offend you, my dear. But it isn't as if you bothered about your appearance, now is it? Old jewellery won't mean anything to you.'

(Jewellery? thought Lucy.) 'The Dean's bequest means a great deal to me,' she said aloud. 'I'll go and get it now, if I may.'

'I'll come with you. We'll look through the box together, dear.'

'That won't be necessary, thank you, Maureen. I can manage perfectly well on my own. I take it Nigel is along at the Deanery at present?'

'Yes. But you'll find this bequest totally unsuitable, Lucy. Don't forget, I'll take it off your hands.'

'Sweet of you, Maureen. I will remember. Would you like another cup?'

'No, dear. If you're really sure that you wouldn't like me to come with you and look through those oddments . . . .'

'I'm quite sure.'

'Then I must be getting back to the shop. I've left our eldest in charge. That was delicious, quite delicious.'

Maureen did not look very pleased, but defeat was unavoidable. Even she could not push the point any farther. Rather slowly she left the house, pausing at the door to add, 'Next time you want to make fudge, Lucy dear, do tell me and I'll lend you my sugar thermometer.' Then she walked in the direction of Petergate.

Lucy rushed her arms into a coat, ignoring the whines of Prince Rupert and Clementina Crosspatch from the breakfast room. She walked smartly along to the Deanery, thinking kind thoughts about Jill.

Nigel had just returned and had not yet begun his afternoon's work. He was standing looking out of the window, his hands in his pockets, when Mrs Guest showed Lucy into the room. When he turned, the troubled look on his distraught face more than the few words of formal greeting put Lucy in the picture as far as his state of mind went.

He gave her a warm smile in spite of everything. They were much of an age. If it had been Lucy in whom he had shown an active interest, Maureen would have been far from complacent. The idea, though, had not occurred to either Nigel or Lucy.

'Maureen and I have just had afternoon tea,' she remarked, 'and I hear the Dean left me a bequest. May I have it?'

'It's irregular,' said Nigel. 'Humphrey Hale is going to write

138

to you about it. But under the circumstances we don't see why there should be any delay. I'll fetch it. Will you mind giving me a receipt, Lucy?'

'Of course.'

Nigel had had a most unpleasant lunch with Maureen, who could not be brought to see that wills and their provisions were not to be lightly disregarded. If it had been up to Maureen the bequest would quietly have been set on one side and forgotten. It said a lot for Nigel, and for his liking for Lucy, that no taint of that unpleasant and melodramatic scene clung about her in his eyes. He could look at her face without seeing Maureen's angry one interposed between them.

The box was of brown cardboard, fairly shallow, and about a foot long. It was firmly sealed with tape and written on a white stuck-on label were the words 'For Lucy Grindal.'

'Maureen seemed to know what was in it.' Lucy examined the sealed box.

'In the will it says, "A box of jewellery, labelled, to Lucy Cordelia Grindal". And if you shake it there's a bit of a rattle.'

Lucy took one of the sheets of paper on the desk and the Dean's pen – quite as if she used it every day – and wrote a receipt.

'I'm busy cataloguing the books.' Nigel seemed to want to make conversation, though Lucy was not inclined for any. 'Most of them will go into specialist sales, I'm afraid. Your father has chosen his six, and I'm keeping those my friend Robert Lacy bound for the sake of their binding. But books aren't really my thing. And he had such a lot.'

Lucy gazed round the book-lined study without comment.

'Mrs Guest has been sorting out the household linen. There's some nice old family stuff put away – crochet edges, embroidery, that kind of thing. Maureen seems quite keen on it. Even the girls want what they call "lace" in their bedrooms. I prefer to keep the expression for bobbin lace, or beautiful old needlepoint. I'd hardly want to keep the kind of antique shop which is muffled in household linen.'

Lucy spoke at last. 'No, of course not. But it has gained amazingly in popularity. In jumble sales ten years ago you could hardly give it away. Now they fight over it.'

Nigel tried a laugh. 'We're at opposite ends of the same trade, Lucy. You with your jumble sales for charity and me with my shop.'

'It's amazing how often things from my end appear at your end the following day.'

Lucy's sternness was mellowing a little. She could not be unkind to Nigel. She felt like petting and soothing him, whatever the hurt he was suffering. As that was impossible, she only said, 'Now, I'll leave you to it.' But a thought had crossed her mind which would not be stifled. 'Didn't I see you on Tuesday afternoon, Nigel? Walking past the cathedral, carrying a parcel? It looked like a book.'

Nigel thought for a minute. 'I didn't go out of the shop on Tuesday afternoon,' he said. Then, 'Oh yes I did! You're right, Lucy. Uncle left a book behind that morning. When Maureen came in I took the opportunity to pop round with it for him. I'd forgotten all about that.'

'I thought I'd seen you. Well, I'll be off,' and with that she went, firmly, as if he might try to detain her, clutching her box.

Once at home, she could not open it. The whole thing was too emotional. She carried it up to her bedroom, which was along both a corridor and the balustraded landing which ran from the sitting-room across one end of the hall at first-floor level.

There was a window facing west and oddly positioned close to one corner, so that on an autumn day like this the room was dark. The tall panelled walls and the Georgian fireplace and the big old-fashioned furniture were shadowy, almost unreal. Lucy put the box on her dressing-table and stood looking out of the window for a few minutes.

She could see the whole massive bulk of the cathedral and the spiky foreground bauble of the Chapter House, like the topknot of a crown; also the flat green of the grass of part of Dean's Park. Just out of sight was the bit of grass where on Tuesday morning she had been mating Diamond Lil of Drinkwater with Jacobite Prince Rupert, and the Dean had come out so indignantly.

Most women at the present moment would have been regarding themselves in the mirror, or eagerly breaking open the box. Lucy was thinking of God and death and destiny.

After standing there motionless for a few minutes she looked at her watch. Four-thirty already on this Thursday afternoon. In the building just opposite, evensong would soon be drawing to a close. For the worship of God did not cease, through all the small troublings of mankind.

A quarter of an hour earlier in the middle of evensong a bullet had hummed across the choir and buried itself in the panelling beside Canon Oglethorpe's head.

George Grindal was standing next to him. There had been no sharp report, but he heard a sound like something travelling swiftly through the air and he heard a faint thwack and rending of fibres as the bullet buried itself in the wood. George's head spun round but he could not interpret the sound he had heard – or had he heard it? It had been so faint against all the other sounds of the service.

Canon Oglethorpe came upright again and did not seem to have noticed anything at all. George Grindal could hardly believe it himself. He looked round the choir area. Evensong was said, not sung, that day; there was only the murmur of voices to hide what had sounded uncommonly like a silenced shot. It seemed so incredible that his mind failed to admit the evidence of his ears and eyes. He concluded that he had been mistaken.

Oglethorpe had a small boy to thank for his escape. His stall was near to a little girl in a coat of scarlet rimmed with white swansdown, behaving herself beautifully; and a little boy beside her who was planning mischief. He had secretly gathered up a handful of the smooth golden hair from the little girl's shoulders and what he was going to do next Canon Oglethorpe could guess only too well. Hastily he had bent over the wooden division between, and touched the back of the boy's hand.

'Don't do that,' he had whispered, stern but not unkind.

The boy could not have looked more surprised if a hand had come down from heaven. He dropped the hank of hair. Canon Oglethorpe straightened up.

The assassin was cramped in a narrow space above the housemaids' cupboard full of brooms and dusters. The

141

cupboard was near the cathedral policeman's office and the only secret vantage point he could find. He had waited patiently for an hour without moving for the right moment to shoot and now when he had aimed exactly right and the bullet had gone home it had not finished off its target.

The Canon's intervention in the affairs of the congregation caused a small stir. People looked round at the two children and the old man to see what was going on.

A superstitious fear swept over the hidden assassin. His skin crawled and his hair prickled on his neck. This was the second time that Oglethorpe had failed to die. He must be under some sort of protection. Centuries of superstition rose up. Perhaps silver bullets would have done the trick. He could perfectly well have fired again, and again, and again, and in the end there would have been no chance of escape for Oglethorpe. Yet he would certainly be tracked down if he tried anything else and that would threaten the larger enterprise. In a sudden panic he began to scramble down.

George Grindal felt extremely uneasy. Ever since he had concluded that Oglethorpe, not Dean Parsifal, had been the object of attack he had wanted to protect him in some effective way and had not been able to do it. Now he decided that the minute evensong ended he was off to talk to the police. But first he ought to tell his friend of the danger he believed him to be in. He ought. But he wasn't going to. What good would warning him do?

As soon as they were in the vestry he said, 'Sam, when you were in the prison service, did you know someone called Killarney?' George was praying that for once his friend would be able to remember names and relate them to people. The mild, gentle face looked back at him.

Leaving the box on the dressing-table for later, Lucy went down to the kitchen to begin cooking the evening's casserole. There was just too much to think about altogether. Clementine Crosspatch complained bitterly about having been left alone for so long shut up in the breakfast room and lovingly pawed another hole in her mistress's tights. Today, Lucy had not had to bother with afternoon tea for her father; he had said that he was going from evensong straight to the hospital, to see Edmund Jason.

'You might look in at Mrs Hassock's,' he had said. 'I am supposed to be going there with Sister Agape, but I'd be pleased if you would take my place. Just to see how the old man is doing.'

'You mean Mr Horncastle?'

'Yes.'

Lucy had by now briefly met the old tramp who had once been a verger, and rather liked him, so she did not mind.

'He's really settled very well,' said Sister Agape as she skimmed along beside Lucy at her usual rapid pace. They were walking down the small terraced street.

'I should have thought Mrs Hassock's incessant chatter would have upset him,' Lucy said. 'We won't be seeing as much of her in the cathedral as usual now, I suppose. When did he leave the shelter?'

'Yesterday tea-time. We'd approached her, and got agreement in principle, and cleaned him up and sorted him out – luckily there were some very good men's clothes I knew of that were going to go to Oxfam which just fitted him. We got a barber to go and trim him up as well. So he really looked quite different by the time we brought him along.'

'That was lucky.'

'Yes. Then, I came last thing and saw him, and again this morning. You were worrying about the way she talks all the time? Oh, he doesn't mind that, dear. It's company, and he switches off, you know. I could see that already by bedtime last night. Sister Lauren says it's a technique lots of mental patients learn. Very useful for most of us, I should think. I wish I could practise it sometimes. Here we are.'

Sister Agape reached up to the gleaming knocker and pounded energetically with it.

Dora Hassock opened the green door with a flourish.

'How lovely! You've come to see Mr Horncastle, I'm sure. Do come in. He'll be so pleased.'

'How is he?' asked Lucy.

'Very well, really, considering what he's been through. I knew him years ago, you know. I knew his daughter too – if you can call her a daughter.'

Mrs Hassock ushered them into her front room, with the window on the street, the window through which Lucy, when walking that way, had glimpsed her after dusk on a winter evening. The picture of Mrs Hassock sitting in peace by the fire with her knitting was Lucy's favourite image of her. Now the old man was sitting at the other side of the fireplace, where he could see anyone who happened to pass outside.

'Here's Miss Grindal and Sister Agape come to see you, Mr Horncastle, aren't you the lucky one?' Mrs Hassock let out the words in a shrill shriek.

Albert Horncastle sat by the fire, clean, tidy and respectable. His hair and beard had been trimmed. Lucy had preferred them as they were before, but she knew that in this she would be in a minority of one – or two, since her father probably felt the same. However, Horncastle appeared surprisingly happy, although he looked up at them without much enthusiasm.

'Good afternoon, Sister, good afternoon, miss. I know, you're the Canon's daughter.'

'She's the one with the dachshunds,' shouted Dora.

'I'm not deaf, you know,' he said.

'I'll get some tea.' Dora Hassock bustled off.

'She's a good-hearted girl,' Albert Horncastle remarked in a patronizing voice. 'Sit down, do rest your feet.'

'Are you feeling better?' Lucy asked. 'Will you be happy here?'

He looked at her with full attention for a minute. 'Yes, thank you. Glad to be back in York, and so near the cathedral again. I hope to get to the services soon, but Mrs Hassock tells me you've had a lot of changes.'

'We've lost our Dean.'

'Very sad. Parsifal you said his name was.'

'Henry Parsifal,' said Sister Agape.

'I knew a Henry Parsifal once, but it wouldn't be the same.'

'When was that?' asked Lucy.

'When I was in the RAF. We were stationed at Full Sutton, and I was courting my wife, she lived at Gate Helmsley, and

144

this pilot officer, Parsifal, was courting the young girl who was staying at the manor. She was their niece from London. He got married before we could. She was going back home, you see. Only up in Yorkshire for a holiday. Terrible, it was.'

'Terrible?' prompted Lucy, but Horncastle's thought had wandered off on another tack.

'There'll be a lot of changes now. New stonemasons, new vergers, new policemen. We used to have a good time. Cricket. Not in the Dean's Park, of course.'

'I never knew the Dean had been married,' said Lucy.

'Oh, I don't suppose it was him,' said Sister Agape.

'Parsifal's a very unusual name.'

Horncastle's voice was running on, still obsessed by cricket. 'That young man, the best bowler we ever had. You couldn't trust him, but he could send a ball like nobody's business . . .'

'Just now you were telling us about a pilot officer you knew, called Henry Parsifal. What was terrible about him getting married?' asked Lucy again.

Horncastle's eyes cleared and he answered her directly. 'She was lovely, like you, my dear, no offence.'

'I'm not lovely,' replied Lucy.

'I'm not thinking of looks, but I mean in her nice ways, and her voice, the way she'd come straight out with things, and she loved dogs, always had them round her. She had a little Yorkshire terrier, I remember. Used to tuck it under her arm. The old dog at the manor followed her everywhere, as well.'

Lucy's eyes filled with tears.

'That was a back-handed compliment if you like,' said Sister Agape, 'lovely but he isn't thinking of looks.' She got up briskly as she spoke to confront Mrs Hassock and the tea tray and shield Lucy from those penetrating eyes. She didn't know what was the matter; Lucy hadn't even liked the Dean; but something was wrong, that was obvious.

Over the late cup of tea the conversation was monopolized by Dora Hassock, who was most anxious to know more about the young cricketer who was so often in Albert Horncastle's thoughts. 'What happened to him?' she asked.

Albert could not remember anything more and could only

145

repeat, 'Clever with his hands, but no good, too pleased with himself. All the young men are like that now.'

As they left Dora Hassock murmured to her guests, 'I went in to see Mr Jason today, he's much better. I hope to have him home next week. That friend of his, Simon, is using his room while it's free. He's a live wire, he is.'

'I'm so glad,' Sister and Lucy said together.

'I don't mention him in front of the old man, only upsets him, I find. But they'll be good friends, I'm sure of that. Mr Horncastle loves music.'

'It's just as well,' remarked Sister Agape as they walked away. 'He'll have to put up with music whether he likes it or not.'

The autumn mist was thickening again. Yellow street lamps looked lurid in the greyness. Something marshy in the fogs of the wide vale of York seemed tonight to poison the gathering vapour. Lucy shivered in her thick coat and scarf. The rumble of the traffic was deadened until it reminded her of distant aircraft.

12

Though an host of men were laid against me, yet shall not my heart be afraid, and though there rose up war against me, yet will I put my trust in him.

—Psalms, 27, v. 3

Canon Oglethorpe's puzzled expression had cleared as he repeated several times, 'Killarney? Killarney? Yes, of course I remember, George. It's only a slight problem I have with names. They come back, you know, if I wait a minute. He was in Parkhurst for manslaughter. Got six years as far as I remember. It was a death on a building site, there'd been some sort of barney and a man struck his head on concrete and died. The suggestion was that Killarney had hit him, in fact he admitted as much, but no one had seen the incident.'

'Would you recognize him if you saw him again?' pressed George.

'Of course. It isn't long ago, only a year or so. I strove hard with him. Do you know, now you mention it, I think I did see him sometime recently.'

George breathed a deep sigh. 'I'm going to go down to the police station,' he said. 'If you'll hang on here a few minutes while I rush to the Soames's and back – I want to ask Mrs Soames something but I'll be very quick – I'll walk along home with you, I can go past your house.'

Oglethorpe looked surprised but he agreed and soon afterwards the two set off together on the same route they had travelled on the Tuesday evening, when two young men had reared up so quickly in the mist and then gone running off.

When George arrived at the police station in Clifford Street he asked for DCI Southwell.

'I'm afraid he's not on duty at present, sir,' said the constable

147

at the desk. 'Would you be willing to speak to someone else? Detective Inspector Smart is here.'

'Very well.'

'If you'll wait in the interview room?'

Dave Smart came in and held out his hand.

'How can we help you, Canon? Everything is under control as far as the Dean's inquest goes, I think.'

'I did have a word on the telephone with Mr Southwell late on Wednesday night – last night. Did he mention it to you?'

'No, sir, what about?'

'Mr Smart, I am convinced the Dean's death was not accident but murder. It was only accidental in that the stone was intended for someone else.'

Dave Smart decided he had better humour the old man. 'And this is what you told DCI Southwell?' he said.

'That is what I told him and I'm telling you now. The stonemasons are sure that the stone did not flake off naturally.'

'In humid weather limestone can be much affected, we were told.'

'Yes, yes, we know that. Look, Mr Smart, I've been conducting an investigation of my own. I want to tell you – since Mr Southwell isn't here – what my conclusions are, and I want your help. My colleague Canon Oglethorpe is in great danger.'

'It is better to leave investigation to us, sir.'

'Are you taking notice of what I have to tell you or are you not?' asked George Grindal tartly.

Dave wrote busily on a pad of report forms.

'Dean Parsifal irritated nearly everybody and Canon Oglethorpe is generally popular, so of course at first I thought someone had lost control and murdered Parsifal. But the more I looked into it the more I eliminated people from my suspect list. Then I realized how similar the two men looked from above, and at the time they both had a limp in the left leg. The wrong man was killed by the assassin.'

'We had concluded that it was an accident, sir.'

'Canon Oglethorpe was until recently a prison chaplain at Parkhurst. There he knew a young man in for manslaughter, who I believe to be Michael Soames, the stepson of one of our vergers, who has recently reappeared in the city after allegedly

148

touring Australia. I believe that he was imprisoned under his own father's name of Killarney, and that for some reason he is so afraid that his spell in Parkhurst will become known that he is trying to kill the Canon before he can reveal the truth. He attempted to kill him and got the wrong man.'

'Who is this Soames, did you say, sir?'

'He's the stepson of one of our vergers. Before I came here I went to see his mother and verified that his original name was Killarney before her second husband adopted him, and it was under that name that Oglethorpe knew him in prison.'

'That's all very well, Canon Grindal, but why should this Soames – or Killarney – want to kill him? He's done his time and is out, you say? So what's the big deal, if you don't mind me putting it that way?'

Canon Grindal was past the stage of studying motive. 'Canon Oglethorpe needs protection,' he said impressively. 'I've just escorted him home and I want to know that he'll be safe. Can you station a constable outside his house?'

'Well . . .' Dave was taken aback. 'I don't know about authorizing a guard for the Canon. We'd have to be very convinced of danger to take that step,' he temporized.

'You mean that his danger is all in my imagination?'

'I wasn't at all implying . . .'

'Yes, you were, Detective Inspector.'

'The Canon is a danger to this young man . . . That's plausible, I suppose . . . but surely only if he is still engaged in some unlawful activity? Have you any evidence what that might be?'

'I see what you are thinking. That the disgrace to his parents and having his criminal history made public is not a strong enough motive?'

'Exactly. And as for the falling stone, Canon Grindal, we investigated and decided that it was an accident. There was no way anyone could have done it. The evidence will all be produced at the inquest.'

'Have you written all this down?' asked Canon Grindal sharply. 'Are you refusing a guard on Canon Oglethorpe?'

'We do have guide-lines, sir. I don't see how we could justify

149

the expense of it. But I've written everything down, yes, I surely have.'

'If another attempt is made and succeeds, the responsibility for Oglethorpe's death will be on your head, Inspector Smart. If you refuse to take action I must make an official complaint.'

'I'm sorry you feel like this, Canon Grindal. As you know our Detective Chief Inspector personally, you can contact him even though he is off duty.'

'You know that I would only break into his free time as a last resort. I have done it already once on this case when I phoned him and I felt guilty about that. Everyone is entitled to some private life. But I do consider this is a matter of life and death. If you do nothing I *will* put in a complaint.'

'I'm sorry,' said Dave Smart. 'In the morning I'll talk it over with the boss and see what can be done.'

'You don't believe me,' the Canon said angrily. 'Leave it until morning by all means, Detective Inspector Smart. On your head be it.' With that, he left the police station.

'Bloody hell,' said Dave Smart, drumming his fingers on the table.

At the home of Verger Soames, Mrs Soames was worried about Michael.

'I don't like him out so late.'

'He'll be all right, mother! It's natural for young men to want to drink with their friends. Don't treat him like a child. He's more at home in a pub than here, I expect.'

'He's been back only four nights. You'd think he'd want to spend a bit of time with us. I don't like it, John.'

'It's going to be all right, I tell you. He'll settle down. He's sown all his wild oats. I'm pleased that he's taking an interest in the cathedral again. When he broke his apprenticeship I was afraid he'd go right off the place. It always used to fascinate him.'

'I think it still does, darling.'

'Yes. You know, on Monday when I took him to see the de Vere tomb he was very impressed. He even asked me for the key so that he could go back later on and have another look at

150

his leisure. I noticed it on his dressing-table and took it back yesterday afternoon, and then he asked me for it again this morning. He is really intrigued by the carving. If a young man is sensitive to history there must be hope for him. We'll see him turn into a good citizen yet.'

'I'd like to think so – though he'll never go back to the mason work, I'm positive.'

'It's a pity, we could have done with him in the stone-yard.'

'But there's that bad violent streak in him, John. He gets it from his father. You think it's subdued and gone, but then it flares out again.'

'He certainly didn't get it from you, my dear,' said Verger Soames, giving her grey hair a kiss in passing. 'I'm making a cup of tea. Do you want one?'

'Please.'

Mrs Soames sat with the sock she was darning drooping idly on to her lap. 'John thinks he understands my Michael,' she pondered, 'but he doesn't. I've never told him about his father's rages – he seemed almost insane at times. I've hinted at it, but never liked to tell him that I used to get knocked about. It isn't something you want to confess to another man. John would be indignant and angry on my behalf but it would change things if he knew. Telling someone you've been a battered wife is a bit like telling them you've been raped. They can never quite forget. You are changed in their eyes, as if the victim inaugurated the crime. If you hadn't been a doormat you wouldn't have been trodden on – that's what doormats are for. But it's his father's unpredictability that I see in Michael – that's what's got him into trouble in the past – and I don't believe we're out of the wood with him yet.'

John Soames came back into the firelit sitting-room with the teapot and two cups and saucers on a tray. 'Still brooding?' he said. 'Shall I pour?'

'Yes, you do it, love.' She accepted the fine china cup with its delicate design of harebells. The fragrant tea soothed her. 'You make a good cup of tea.'

'Long hours of patient study.' Soames's husbandly enjoyment of the moment was shattered by the peal of the door bell.

151

'Something's happened to Michael,' said Mrs Soames instantly.

Soames returned from answering the door accompanied by the young architect, Holdernesse.

The cosy lamplit room looked good to the young bachelor. The taste might not be his – Mrs Soames liked crinolined ladies holding their skirts daintily, patterned wallpaper on the walls, and lots of little mats – but the homelike atmosphere and the kindliness of the two middle-aged people always charmed him.

'I was passing and saw your light, Mrs Soames. I wasn't going to come in but your good husband insisted.'

'Very pleased to see you. Please sit down.'

Verger Soames had fetched another cup. 'I was telling Mr Holdernesse in the hall, my love, that I *had* mentioned the de Vere tomb to the Dean. But it's all irrelevant now.'

Holdernesse took the fragile cup and saucer. This was something else he liked. The ritual quality of their lives. The attention to detail. He was sure they did the same things on the appointed day each week, and that Mr Soames probably made tea at the same time every night. He liked, too, the attentive way they always listened to him. He sipped his tea and prepared to ride his hobby-horse.

'I can't help hoping that we get a co-operative dean for a change. Someone who will care that so many things are misrepresented. One of the archbishops is not buried where the cathedral guides keep telling people he is, for instance. Most of the notices in the building are half-truths at best. The structure is perfectly clear if they will only tell people to look at the arcading at the bottom of the walls. And another thing, the de Vere tomb should not be moved from its historical position.'

'It'll all come out right,' soothed John Soames.

'Well, yes. I think it might. The Surveyor of the Fabric has looked at the tell-tales and thinks we will have to do some work on the pinnacle, which isn't too big a job at all.'

Mrs Soames said nothing. She was sorry to feel so inhospitable tonight. It was nice of Holdernesse to call occasionally. But now she was looking at the hands of the clock as they crept round later and later and wondering where Michael was and had a feeling in the pit of her stomach which would not go away.

Michael and Terry were sitting in a crowded bar. It was noisy, hot, smoky and the smell was of sweat and spilt beer overlaid with perfume and aftershave. Terry's thin vivid face under its lock of hair had the tense look of anticipated fear. Mike's had a more uplifted expression.

'No unnecessary violence,' said Terry. 'All we need to do is get him out when they stop. There'll be all hell on. It shouldn't be too difficult. All we need do is threaten them.'

'Aw, boys' stuff,' said Mike. 'You've never been involved in much, Terry. Oh, you're a nice lad all right. You've taught me a lot. I wouldn't be in this party now if you and I hadn't shared in Parkhurst. But you've always avoided anything heavy – even in jug. You should have done more boxing, like me.'

'I'm more agile than you, mate, I'll tell you,' replied Terry.

'Give you that, mate, give you that.'

'So none of your old flare-ups, see? This has got to go straight.'

'When we're in Ireland . . .'

'That'll be different. With Fergal back at the head of his division there'll be a place for both of us.'

Mike ran the scenario through in his head. He liked it. He could savour Belfast now; the upper room with a naked light bulb swinging, the old table among a medley of chairs, the elbows forming a ring round a Guinness or ten maybe, the cloud of smoke above: and the talk about what really mattered – explosives, times and methods; calculations of the best places to do psychological damage; jockeying between different factions for prestige – that's the stuff – the war of liberation from the old British occupation force and vengeance – that's on – that's what life is all about. And if anyone got in the way – too bad. Too bad for the old Dean. (But he'd really get Oglethorpe in the end, no doubt about that.) Too bad for anyone who was not important.

'I don't know that Oglethorpe can do us much harm,' said Terry, as if he caught Mike's thought.

153

'He bloody can. If they knew I'd been inside there would have been hell on and no way we'd have carried out our preparations quietly and set it up like we have. He can identify me.'

'I don't know that it would have mattered as much as you think.'

Mike was shaking. 'I tell you he's not bloody human, that old creep. I tell you it's more important than you know.'

Terry's attention had gone back to his own preoccupations.

'Even if the trigger-happy English bastards got the hell out tomorrow we wouldn't be free,' he remarked.

'Of course we would.'

'No. Not until we've kicked every last capitalist swine into the sea as well. We'll still be slaves to English firms and to the international companies who own the factories. The land for the people not the outsiders, whoever they are. We want our own factories, our own shops, our own churches, our own schools. To hell with everybody else's. Until we've cleared them out we can't be free.'

'Whitehall's bloody khaki bandits first!' objected Mike.

'Right on. The Army of Occupation first.'

'And with plenty of hard cash backing from sympathizers abroad, we'll blow their lousy arses to hell and back!'

'Maybe you're right. But things have changed. I've raised money for the cause and there's plenty from places near to home. We needn't go begging from outsiders – we can cope fine on our own.'

'Since when have they been outsiders?' Mike gave a deep and noisy yawn and stretched his arms like a tired wrestler, hitting a fancy glass-shaded wall light with one upflung arm and a framed Art Nouveau print with the other. He thought money from sympathizers had formed the reliable backbone, though he wasn't going to argue with Terry. Yes, true enough, cash was coming through in other ways now, they'd proof of that. Plenty of funds for the war – that sounded good. In the right cause. And if the tommies were gone, a start on the factories . . .

'We've got to get this next bit over first,' broke in Terry, licking his lips nervously.

'No sweat.'

'Get 'em in, Mike.'

Mike got up to go over to the bar. On one of the tall stools was a lad in a collarless shirt, workman's overalls and a punk hair-do, gazing absent-mindedly at Mike.

'Who do you think you're staring at, mate?' Mike asked him.

'Not staring at nobody,' said the youth nervously.

Mike grabbed hold of the shirt with one hand and twisted the other into the dyed black hair. 'Look here, matey, you keep your bleeding nose clean, geddit?'

Terry rushed up. 'Mike! It's all right! Cool it!'

'This shit was staring at us.' Mike gave the youth a shake.

'Take your friend out of my pub!' the landlord yelled at Terry.

'Come on, Mike! This is the last thing we want! We've things to do tonight, and there's tomorrow, remember?'

Once outside the pub they stood on the pavement arguing.

'Leave off Oglethorpe,' Terry said.

'Look, he can get me twenty years, mate.'

'You nearly got twenty years in there just now.'

'Don't be daft, you don't know what you're on about.'

A bobby on the beat strolled towards them. 'Move along now, gentlemen,' he said politely.

'Yeah, all right, officer.' Terry took hold of Mike's sleeve. 'Come on, Mikey. Home to mother. Everything's got to look normal just now, right?'

155

13

Hear my voice O God in my prayer, preserve
my life from fear of the enemy.

—*Psalms*, 64, v. 1

Canon Grindal had been fuming when he left the police station.
He knew he was right. In Michael Soames he had found
someone who was in conflict with himself and with his world.
Someone who had both motive and opportunity, for although
George had not worked out the 'how', he could see that Michael
had the background knowledge to have found a way to do what
he did. Someone who had difficulty in adjusting to the different
expectations and demands made on him, and who was so split
apart inside and unable to express himself that the only
response was violence.

George did not want to go home in an agitated condition. For
the time being, locked in his own house, Oglethorpe should be
safe. Remembering the young assistant organist, George walked
to the hospital. In spite of his conviction about Michael, there
were other points that needed clearing up, if Edmund Jason
could now speak.

Simon was sitting in the corridor outside the door to Jason's
room, heartily asleep in an uncomfortable upright chair. The
nurse walked past him and showed George Grindal in.

'You can only have a few minutes,' she said.

'Hello,' said George, and then paused, looking round the
room, before inspecting the pale face on the pillow.

The pause gave Edmund Jason time to adjust to his presence.
This time there was to be no nonsense. The facts must out.

So far Jason had not spoken, although he had smiled.

'It's been a beastly, damp, cold kind of day,' commented
George. 'But you're all right in here.'

George knew how after a traumatic experience people

reverted to thinking of tiny things as if they could no longer think about big ones. But he could spare no time, not knowing how long he might be allowed to talk to Jason. If Simon woke up that was trouble. He came right to the point.

'Something puzzles me about Tuesday,' he said. 'Can you tell me what delayed you in striking up the introit? We were to process to music, I believe? After the procession had formed, we were waiting for the organ; in a few seconds the Dean said, "What's keeping Jason?" more or less – then set off without the music – and at that point the stone came hurtling down and struck him. As far as I remember, it was quite a time after – while we were fetching the cathedral policeman – that you began to play.'

George decided he had gone too far and too fast. Edmund Jason looked as if he was about to faint.

'We'd had an awful scene,' he whispered at last. 'I was so upset, I – I – I don't know how I managed to play at all.'

'When we came to tell you that the service was postponed you were in a very agitated state – but then it was difficult to persuade you to leave off playing.'

'Music is such a help . . .'

'What was the scene about?'

The nurse came back in, and took Jason's pulse. She looked sternly at George Grindal.

'If this patient is excited it will be very bad for him,' she said to George, 'and you will have to leave.'

'I'm sorry, nurse.' George was not repentant at all. 'But until he unburdens himself there will be no peace for this young man.'

'I want to talk,' said Edmund Jason in a hoarse whisper.

'Not much, or you will do more damage,' the nurse said. 'I'll be back in a few minutes.'

'At Pottaugh, the school where I was music master, I made friends with Simon.'

George had always regarded Edmund Jason compassionately, because of his shy, awkward, withdrawn qualities. He was glad that this difficult soul had made at least one friend, and one as stalwart as Simon.

'We became very close.'

157

'Lovers?' probed George's gentle melodious voice.

'Not really,' muttered Jason.

'Was it only Simon that you were so close with?'

'Oh yes. How could there be anyone else? There is no one like Simon.'

With this sentiment George agreed. 'I've met him. Is he much younger than you?'

'Four years. He was eighteen and I was twenty-two.'

'This was a deeply emotional friendship, then?'

'I love him.'

'Well. Unfortunate when he was a pupil still.'

'He's at university now. But then he was in his last term; they found out that we loved one another and I was dismissed.'

'What's called a "case" if I remember correctly. Usually at my school it would be the boy who got the chop – although such affections were usually among us and did not involve the masters, anyway.'

'It was so near the time of his leaving, and he was sitting scholarships.'

'So they let him stay and sacked you?'

'Yes.'

'On your application form for the post here you didn't declare the fact that you were under notice, then?'

'No. That was why the Dean was so furious with me. He found out and came into the organ loft directly.'

'Very distressing for you.'

'It was, the way he did it. I know I was wrong in not revealing it before. But it was my private life and I was afraid that I would be ruling my application out of court if I said I was under notice at the time. But the Dean was suggesting that I was attracted to little boys – as if I would!'

George Grindal was pleased that he could turn to the bedside cabinet and take up the feeding glass containing orange juice. 'Drink a little of this,' he said, holding it to Jason's mouth.

Then, when Jason had sipped and George had had the chance to think a little, he went on, 'As you say, it was your private life, and as such should not influence the Dean and Chapter in considering your application for the post. But at the same time

I can see that when the matter came to the Dean's attention he would rightly feel concern.'

'I love Simon. No one else in the world matters to me in that way. And anyway the papers say there are lots of gays among the clergy. Not that we think we're gay. I'm not sure about it. I suppose we might find out that we are.'

'Quite so.'

'In my opinion the Dean was inclined that way himself, otherwise he wouldn't have been so nasty and had such filthy ideas,' muttered Jason.

Dear Henry! One did wonder! So rigidly suppressing all natural instincts! 'We must not pass judgement,' said the Acting Dean. 'Dean Parsifal has gone to a higher jurisdiction. But you know, dear Edmund, that relationships of the kind you and Simon have – or might well have – are notoriously short-lived.'

'Not with me.'

'So what did keep you . . . What did delay you in commencing your music?'

'I was sitting in front of the keyboard with my head in my hands, thinking it was the end of the world.'

'Hmmm.'

'Are you going to dismiss me, Canon Grindal?'

'Certainly not. Neither was the Dean, I'm sure. He intended to give you a fright, I've no doubt.'

'I thought you would have no alternative – that he would have given instructions.'

'You were quite mistaken.'

'Oh . . . and that's why I decided . . .'

'I thought so. Did it seem as if you were thrown out from heaven?'

'Yes.'

'You have no need to fear at all. Tell me more about Simon. Before he wakes up. He's asleep outside at the moment.'

'He is coming to spend his Christmas vacation with me,' whispered the assistant organist. 'He's only here now because he heard about – about . . .'

'I know,' said Grindal.

'When I'm back home and he comes to stay, if you would

come round one evening, to hear a little music – my extravagance, I have changed to compact discs – you will understand about us.'

George Grindal looked at him kindly. 'I would be happy to spend an evening with you and Simon.'

Does he realize his own pathos, he wondered. Is their bond in reality an intellectual one, or only protective on Simon's part? Remembering the way Edmund played the organ, George was inclined to think that Edmund lived for his music and any human relationship – even with Simon – was on the periphery.

As he left Edmund Jason's room George was pleased to see that Simon was still slumped in an abandonment of sleep. He did not want another antagonistic confrontation with that young man.

After his visit to the hospital Canon George Grindal had returned home to the evening meal. Over it, Lucy told him of the events of her day, and of the box upstairs on her dressing-table.

'And you've not looked in it yet?'

'No, I haven't.'

'Let's look together. It will be like Christmas.'

They ignored the dishes until later and sat one on either side of the sitting-room fire. George took out his pocket-knife and with it Lucy slit the sealing tape.

'I'm trembling,' she said.

'Quite natural,' said her father.

He sat back and waited. She eased the lid upward and off and sat looking into the box with a comical expression on her face. George Grindal remembered Pandora.

'Tell me,' he said.

'They're mostly old pieces.' Lucy began to take out brooches and rings. 'Bulky. Some good old-fashioned paste brooches. A gold bracelet.' She passed it over for his inspection. 'Lots of semi-precious stones, coral, turquoise, garnet – here's a garnet necklace. Cameos, seed pearls.'

She lifted solid Victorian pieces for him to see and began to lay them out on her knee with shaking fingers. He realized that these things would suit her. They would give her a kind of grandeur, a timelessness. Inwardly George blamed himself for not thinking of it before. At Christmas he would hand over to her her mother's small store of jewellery.

Lucy found something wrapped in tissue paper in a corner.

'Look, father!' She was holding up a smaller brooch which twinkled in the light. She passed it over to him. It was a Royal Air Force brooch, brilliants and enamel, the kind RAF wives once proudly wore.

'Who do you think it was made for?' she asked.

George turned it over in his fingers. Henry Parsifal had been in the Air Force during the war, he knew. 'People had these made for mothers, wives, and sweethearts,' he said. Lucy was silent, still waiting for his pronounced wisdom.

'I would guess this was made for his wife, and never given to her.'

'This afternoon Albert Horncastle said something which made me realize the Dean had been married. I had had no idea. Why do you think the brooch was never given to her?'

'It's a sad story. Your mother knew her vaguely, that's how I heard it. I'd forgotten, actually, but it's coming back to me. Henry met and married this girl all in the course of one short fortnight. Then she went to her parents' home again and he went back to his squadron. He was in Bomber Command, you know, operational. He hadn't taken orders then. On his first night's flying after the quick honeymoon they were on a big bombing run. The same night, back home, his wife was killed by a V2 rocket on London.'

'Oh no!'

'I'm afraid so. Ironic, wasn't it? But many things were, during the war. That's why he was never able to talk about it. He tried to pretend that the whole episode hadn't happened. In fact if you had not unearthed this little thing, I don't believe I would ever have remembered.'

'There was something Nigel said, when he gave me the box. He said they were probably his grandmother's things.'

'They wouldn't be the wife's. Her home and everything in it were completely destroyed.'

'So she never got this little brooch!'

161

'You will be the first one to wear it, Lucy.'

'I don't know if I will be able to now I know its story.'

'He gave it to you, didn't he?'

'Yes,' she whispered.

Although she had not finished looking through the box or realized half that it contained, she decided to take it back upstairs again and George did not stop her.

'No dogs'. . . and yet, 'Jewellery to Lucy Grindal'. . .

Lucy put her head on her hands and let the tears, which she had had to choke back earlier in Mrs Hassock's house, come in a flood. The tensions of the last days found release. How topsy-turvy life was. If only she had known that the Dean cared something for her. And now it was all too late. Too late to be kind to him and not aggravating. Too late to turn into a swan. It was a long time before Lucy dried her eyes.

Later, after father and daughter had washed the dinner things together, she picked up her knitting and forgot herself by becoming absorbed in a difficult pattern, the Canon found a book, and the rest of the evening passed.

When the time came for bed George didn't feel at all ready for it.

'I can't stop thinking about things,' he said fretfully, and went on to tell her his suspicions and conclusions and how they had been received at the police station.

She listened with astonishment. 'No wonder you can't stop thinking about it.'

'I'll take the dogs for a walk,' he said.

'Very well, father.'

On this Thursday night, the fourth of November, Canon Samuel Oglethorpe was also unable to settle to his usual routine of preparing for bed. He couldn't make out what was the matter, but at last decided that a stroll around the city could do him no harm and that when he came back his bed and his book might be more appealing. There was something troubling him and he wasn't even sure what it was.

That was the problem with being over seventy. As he fastened his front door behind him he looked back over his life –

'such as it has been,' he added humbly, out of long habit. He had been born in a vicarage and expected to die in one, like his father and grandfather before him. He had carried on their tradition of dedicating his life to spiritual things. 'A life is not long enough,' he mused, looking up at a distant glimpse of the cathedral towers.

It must be later than he thought. The floodlighting had been turned off. The towers presided over the city lit only by the fleeting light of a shifting moon.

He trod heavily on his good leg, more lightly on his bad leg. How long ago the war seemed – the minesweeper wending its slow way over the dusky sea. For once a good war, fighting evil. He was glad to have borne his part in it, glad even to the point of giving thanks when the old wound troubled him. The shut-in sky of the town irked him for a moment and he made his way towards the cathedral for a wider view of heaven.

Whatever it was that he could not bring to mind must lie in the past. His early posts after ordination ran through his head like the pages of a well-thumbed Bible. From Missions to Seamen to the busy inner-city parish in Leeds, then the Prison Service and Parkhurst, then his old friend the previous Dean had persuaded him to take this tiny church and his honorary canonry, but died before he had actually come to York, so it had been Dean Parsifal instead . . . But then, he had his other friend George and his god-daughter Lucy . . . Well, he was content. A parish congregation of five old women and a dog (and sometimes only the dog) hardly taxed him.

As he rounded the corner and came into the purlieu of the cathedral his heart was full of gratitude and a love which spilled over and embraced the city. The building in front of him was so gracious, so unbelievably big, so grand, so beautiful whether by night or day. It uplifted him, as it always did. He stopped worrying over the troubling knowledge which he could not quite remember.

Going out into the night George Grindal also hoped to find peace. He liked the pattering of eight little feet beside him; it was companionable. Taking with him the key to Dean's Park, he walked the dogs right round the cathedral. They went along the east end, between the largest gothic window in the world, the Alpha and Omega window soaring above them on their right, and the more homely Renaissance sundial on its grass plat on their left.

They walked along Deangate past what fire had left of the Early English south transept built by Archbishop Walter de Gray, with its mass of scaffolding around the doorway which had been restored in Victorian times. George Grindal remembered that some twelve feet below him lay the remains of a Roman city where once Constantine was proclaimed Emperor. He liked having the quiet of the night to think of such things.

He reached the west end with its twin soaring towers flanking the Heart of Yorkshire window, and glanced up as he always did at their strong sculptural shapes, mistily seen. He loved the west front's mass of intricate detail, its doorway with the niches. This walk should have the effect of settling his mind and of enabling him to sleep.

Without a thought of Dean Parsifal's notices, George Grindal let himself into Dean's Park and locked the gate behind him. He was enveloped by the cold damp calm of the winter's night among grass and trees. On his left was the Purey Cust nursing home behind its railings.

Treading more briskly now, he passed the flying buttresses of the north side and the great simplicity of the north transept with the five lofty lancet windows named the Five Sisters. The north choir aisle. The Chapter House.

It was after he had paused to unlock his exit gate and lock it again after him that he glanced over once again to the north side of the cathedral, deep in shadow. At that moment his peaceful contemplative mood vanished.

There was a parked car in Chapter Yard, close up to the side of the great building, barely visible in the darkness. A flicker of light came from near the ground.

George knew the door in that position; it should be locked. He had not seen the source of light – a thick buttress of stone jutting out from the wall was in the way. But it was certain that he ought to investigate; and not, he thought, with the help of Clementina Crosspatch and Prince Rupert.

Hastily jog-trotting to his house he pushed the two dachs-hunds into the hall and shut the door again. As he rushed back down his path to the gate he saw a burly figure approaching from the Queen's Walk; he did not need the evidence of the limp to recognize his old friend.

'Sam!' he called out. 'Well met by moonlight. Come with me. Something's up.'

'Up?'

He'll be better with me, George thought, than wandering about the city on his own at night; I knew he should have had a policeman on guard outside the door.

As the two men went the way George had just come, he explained why he thought something was up. They found the widest gate standing open. George had not noticed this before. He wondered how on earth he could have missed seeing it. They went over to the parked car. It was a Ford Escort of an unobtrusive colour. They walked round the buttress to the door; it was indeed open, yawning on to a deeper blackness.

'Did you see that? Another flicker of light!'

'No. I didn't see it.' Sam Oglethorpe was whispering. 'But it might be the cathedral policeman doing his rounds with a torch.'

'Yes, it might. Come on in. I want to know why this door's open.'

As they went through the door two things happened. There was a distant clamour, a braying and banging and shouting, very muffled and indistinct, and there was a great luminous white shape bobbing at them, an inhuman shape yet with bold black eyes and nose and a spreading black grin . . .

They both confessed afterwards that they thought it was a ghost.

George stepped back smartly on top of Samuel, who was still going forward. It took them seconds to pull themselves together and reorganize themselves. The white shape hung there in the blackness of the short corridor inside the entrance to the cathedral, grinning at them. George stepped forward cautiously. The clamour, whatever it had been, had died down. George advanced further through the doorway. The shape ahead remained motionless, then swayed eerily.

165

He put out his hand. It was still there, and seemed to be waiting for him. He touched it – the tips of his fingers made contact with the pale face. It moved away skittishly. He drew in a long breath and spoke low.

'You know what it is?'

'I've no idea. I don't think I want to know.'

'It's one of those gas-filled balloons the children bring in sometimes. If you let them go they float up right into the vaulting because of the warmth rising from the crowds. At night the building cools down and so they drop again.'

'We could have done without it,' said Oglethorpe.

They walked further into the darkness of the building. George Grindal returned to the doorway and fumbled around on the wall, wondering if there was a light switch. He found something, and switched, but no light came. Probably it's something else, not a light switch at all, he thought. Where are they? Blessed if I can remember. On a panel somewhere? But there must be one near a door as well?

'I think I've got my flashlight in my pocket,' whispered Oglethorpe. He felt around and pulled out a small but efficient torch, but did not put it on fast enough to stop George going flying over an unexpected obstacle with an involuntary cry and then a groan of pain.

As he scrambled to his feet and turned to see what he had fallen over, the muffled clamour broke out again, further into the building.

There was a suitcase on the floor of the short passage.

'What's this?' George pulled it towards the lesser blackness near the door. 'Shine your torch.'

It was not locked. When it was opened the thin probing beam of light picked out the brightness of silver. A number of silver objects, only partly hidden by clumsy wrappings of newspaper, filled the suitcase.

'Whatever these are, they shouldn't be here like this,' whispered Sam. 'Look, I'll put them outside.' He took the suitcase and hid it, away from the door and the parked car.

'Come on.'

'I'm coming.'

George, creeping on in the darkness, was by now near the

166

wrought-iron gate into the crypt. Sam Oglethorpe's narrow beam of light showed it to be swinging open. Deep within the bowels of the building was another flicker of light, no sooner seen than gone, but reflecting from its hidden source on to pale limestone.

They ought at that point to have gone in search of the cathedral policeman, but the two elderly gentlemen were feeling like adventurous boys, their pulses racing, and the thought never entered their heads.

'Down here.'

The two crept as silently as they could down the steps into the crypt. It was like a pleasant room under the raised floor of the choir area. There was the elaborate cover to the font where the founder of the building had been christened many, many centuries ago. There was an altar, and hanging panels of beautiful old embroideries. They turned right. Dark even in daytime, the next part had been done up fairly recently and was also attractive in a modern way. Then there was the beginning of the emptiness, the yawning gaps through which could be seen the bases of the ancient Norman pillars which had once held up a very different cathedral. On the right there were no pillars, but gaps still, blocked up by wrought-iron grilles. A few yards further, and they could see that one of these wrought-iron barriers was also open. The grilles had been put up to stop any member of the public getting into the maze of unlighted stone passages which wound their way under the building.

In this eerie journey from the barely glimpsed but familiar towards the unfamiliar, George Grindal had had time to think about what lay under the cathedral. Apart from the Undercroft, which was a great tourist attraction, there were all these other passages and empty gaps, into which people rarely bothered to penetrate. They had been mapped, he believed, by someone or other, but where the map was he was not sure. All that he did know was that they stretched way, way ahead. They wound and wandered under the great fabric of the building above, cold, unvisited. For a moment a shiver ran down his back as if a great goose at the very least had walked over his grave.

Ahead of them was a scraping sound as of something being

167

dragged along the ground. In the crypt itself, near the open wrought-iron barrier, was another suitcase.

Trying by cupping his hand over the clasps to avoid the penetrating clicks of opening, George lifted the lid. Under the thin beam of Sam Oglethorpe's torch they saw that the second suitcase was full of guns.

14

Draw me out of the net that they have laid
privily for me, for thou art my strength.
—*Psalms*, 31, v. 5

Lucy had heard her father open the door and had called out,
but was only answered by the decisive sound of the door
shutting behind him. She ran downstairs and leaned from the
doorway in time to see him and Canon Oglethorpe walking
briskly past and turning into Chapter Yard. The sound of low
voices came to her ears, but she was not able to make out much
of what was said.

She went thoughtfully back into the house and stood looking
down at the two dachsies who had been left with their leads
still attached to their collars and trailing over the floor.

Picking up the leads, she wondered whom she could talk to
about this. She didn't feel at all able just to shrug her shoulders
philosophically and go upstairs again into the sitting-room.
There was something wrong, that much she felt sure of, and
those two silly old men were going off on their own to
investigate it.

Although her father was extremely active and ten years
younger than his friend, Lucy sternly classed them together at
that moment as a couple of elderly babies on their way to stick
their fingers into goodness knows what forbidden sort of pie.
Then she remembered how close she was to her friends, the
Anglican Sisters. Surely they wouldn't all three have gone to
bed?

If they were surprised to see Lucy and two small dogs on the
step at going towards midnight, they were polite enough not to
show it. On the face of it there seemed little enough cause for
concern; the Acting Dean and an Honorary Canon had gone for

169

a walk together, into Chapter Yard, or Dean's Park, or somewhere; well, no doubt they had matters to discuss. Theological or procedural matters too deep for such as Lucy and themselves. On the other hand, Lucy must be acknowledged to know her father better than anyone, her godfather likewise – and dear Lucy was exceedingly perturbed. And if dear Lucy was so agitated, it behoved them to do something about it. Definitely, said Sister Agape.

Sister Lauren had already gone to bed. They would not wish to disturb her. Sister Susan hesitated about sallying forth at such a time of night, but Sister Agape had no such hesitations.

'Five minutes, my dear, and I will be following you,' she said. 'Never fear, reinforcements are here. Mafeking will be relieved.'

Lucy wondered whether to offer to wait for her reinforcements to be ready – the preparations involved, she guessed, exchanging the ease of un-nunlike pink furry slippers for something more practical – but decided to set off alone.

Not quite alone. She still held the two dachshunds on leash, and took them with her – forgetting the 'No Dogs' notice on the gate of Dean's Park and her resolve to abide by it.

The two Canons, having discovered the suitcase full of guns, turned off the thin beam of their torch and held a whispered consultation.

'Worse than we thought,' breathed Samuel Oglethorpe softly.

'Dangerous people,' replied George Grindal.

Their eyes almost glowed in the dark, they were so excited.

'Hide this,' added Sam, and with cautious use of the light they slid the suitcase into a less conspicuous place. Distantly above them went the sound of banging, urgent, persistent, but through the thicknesses of stone they could no longer hear it, even in the silence of the night.

Now was the time when they should have gone for reinforcements, to notify the police, to find the cathedral security policeman, to investigate the noise which they had heard earlier, or do anything, rather than what they did. If they had been giving advice to others in their place, they would have suggested these things. They would have urged that George should run to his house to use the telephone, leaving Samuel in a safe corner with a watching brief. Instead of that . . .

'After them?' enquired George, in the spirit of Greyfriars School.

'Certainly.'

In the last few minutes they had both grown fifty years younger.

They set off warily, their light only a glow of pink through Canon Oglethorpe's fingers, down the winding passages. They were doing their best to be quiet, in that entombed silent place where the scrape of an insect's leg would have seemed loud, and to manage with hardly any light, where Styx itself would have seemed sparkling. The passages did not go straight, but turned at right angles and ran into one another in an apparently random fashion.

They shuffled along slowly, almost holding their breath, knocking their feet on projecting stones or deposits of discarded weatherworn carvings, for these passages were used as store places. In less than two minutes they were lost. The fact was that they were desperately enjoying themselves. They were not thinking of the holy edifice about them. Their thoughts were concentrated on the mystery ahead. Every step was pure magic.

They had been stumbling along for some time, trying to be as quiet as possible. The air in these underground passages was cold, chill as the water in a deep well. George was in front, Sam, holding on to his shoulder, behind. Sam's free hand, clenched over the torch, was out at his side, giving them both the faintest glow of light.

As their eyes grew more accustomed to the place and their ears attuned to the quality of its acoustics, they became afraid. The excitement gradually left them and the boyish sense of adventure seeped slowly away. It would have been hard for either of them to say when one heightened emotion changed into another. Perhaps when Samuel Oglethorpe shivered with cold and the shiver passed down his arm into George Grindal's shoulder. Or when George's toe struck a stone, giving him intense pain which he could hardly contain soundlessly. He bit

171

his lip until he could taste the salt of blood and Samuel flinched with him.

Ahead of them they could hear something; a thin scraping, a bump, a footstep; made, they knew, by human beings – human beings who were trying to act quietly but who felt pretty secure.

The two old men felt anything but secure. As they crept along they could not help wondering what they would find.

They found the de Vere monument.

When the pink whisper of light first touched it they could hardly believe what they were seeing, as it loomed up eerily from the farther darkness. Crisp but sensitive carving; delicate panels of lace-like gothic tracery surrounding an oblong tomb; a reclining figure in fluted robes; exquisitely fine and precisely carved long bands, decorating the robes, showing coats of arms alternating with religious symbols. Round the base of the tomb a horizontal strip of carving in deeper relief, with little scenes of people – the would-be saint's miracles, guessed George. Then the *memento mori* – the skull, the bones. Familiar things and themes enough to life-long churchmen, but they were used to seeing them scarred by centuries of exposure to the hazards of life among destructive man. Above the reclining figure of John de Vere was lifted a canopy on slender pillars, a canopy of wrought stone so fine that it looked as though a breath would stir it, yet so steel-strong that it might last for ever.

Their whole purpose in visiting the crypt was forgotten. They stood entranced, now both silently agreeing with the late Dean that this lovely perfect thing should be moved to a place where everyone could see and enjoy it.

As they stood off guard, two young men both carrying suitcases sprang out from the passageway behind the tomb. One of them was using a much more powerful torch than Canon Oglethorpe's, without any attempt to conceal its light. Its beam shone full, breaking into their eyes now accustomed to darkness.

While they were momentarily dazzled and amazed the two strong youngsters, with a great shout like a war-cry, burst between them. Wielding the heavy suitcases like battering rams they caught the old men on the shoulders, brutally bruising, enough to break bones, bearing them downwards.

172

Their ears full of the shouting, shrieking and cursing, the Canons did not cry out. As they were assaulted and broken away from one another their hands reached for some support, wrinkled fingers finding only the infinite hardness of sheer stone walls. As the two old men fell, heavy feet, trampling and kicking feet, caught their shins and their heads banged into contact with stone. Completely winded, they lay stunned and confused, unable either to defend themselves or fight back.

The two young men took the length of the crypt at a run and were up the steps and into the north choir aisle in no time. Their soft-soled trainers made little noise and the heavy suitcases were no burden to them.

They were making finely for the inconspicuous side door they had left open when two small brown dogs flew at them, barking madly and snapping at their legs. The sharp din of a cacophony of barks cut the cathedral air like the staccato utterance of a machine-gun.

'What the hell!'

One man went head over heels, letting go of his suitcase, his head hitting the stone paving. A dog started snapping at his face which he instinctively guarded with his hands.

'They've got bloody dogs!' The other tripped and fell on his knees but quickly regained his feet, kicking at the dog attacking his ankles. 'Get off me!' He tried to get hold of a thin glossy body which would not be got hold of, and caught bites on his fingers. The shouting and barking echoed in the large space of the cathedral and somewhere a muffled voice could be heard shouting, 'Let me out!'

Lucy Grindal had been poking her nose in at the open door and wondering whether to wait for Sister Agape when the two dogs had broken from her, jerking their leads from her slack fingers and racing ahead.

Instinctively she ran after them into a whirling tangle of limbs and fur, shouting 'Come here Clem! Rupy!' with no time to consider her actions. If she did think, it was to realize that these shouting struggling men were up to no good. Her dogs were familiar with everyone who might legitimately be in the cathedral at that time of night.

At first she tried to catch the dogs' leads, then she tried to get hold of the men instead. Her fingers slipped from sweaters and jeans. She tripped over a case and landed full on top of the larger of the two men. Though winded, the impact seemed to startle him into a state of panic. With extraordinary strength he struggled to his feet, knocked Lucy's hands away, kicked her legs, heaved her to one side and bolted for the open air.

Without an instant's pause to see what had happened to his mate the fleeing man ran to the parked car, wrenched open the door and fell in. The engine started at once, he reversed and tore with a screaming of tyres on gravel through the gate on to the road and, narrowly evading a police car which was approaching, he roared off into the night.

Lucy had fallen desperately this way and that, bruising her knees, scrambling up, catching a dog instead of a man, falling over a suitcase again, getting up, and receiving a blow in the face from the torch which the other man was using as a club. The near darkness was lit only by the faint moonlight filtering through centuries-old stained glass and by the whirling light, now here, now there, from the heavy torch, which now came down viciously with a heavy crash across the back of Clementina Crosspatch who slid from under it with a shriek of pain.

Sister Agape, rushing forward in her strong black shoes, her habit streaming behind her, encountered the second fleeing man and felled him with a flying rugby tackle, his own impetus jerking him forward on to his face.

No sooner had he hit the ground than she was on him, sitting across the hollow of his back, firmly twisting his right arm up behind to the level of the nape of his neck.

'Got you,' she said with quiet satisfaction. He felt the whole of her compact solidity, as heavy as she could make herself, and her capable hands immobilizing his arms. He remained still and tried to gather his wits.

Some minutes earlier, PCs Brown and Todd had been on routine patrol when requested by radio to proceed quickish to the back of the cathedral and see what was going on, in response to a 999 call by Sister Susan, who had rung as soon as Sister Agape had left the house. It was now, having narrowly avoided one of

174

the fleeing men as they entered the cathedral precinct, that they arrived at the scene of the struggle.

'This man is some sort of criminal, officer, but I don't know what he's done,' panted Sister Agape from her seat on the small of the man's back. Though breathless, her serenity was quite intact.

PC Brown put a pair of good sturdy handcuffs on the captive and then fastened him to a convenient iron railing.

'Just stay there,' he said unnecessarily, 'till we find out what's going on.'

'I'll keep an eye on him,' volunteered Sister Agape. Terry Mourne flinched. He would have preferred the policeman.

Out of the door came a bruised and winded Lucy and the two dogs. She was bending half double and holding their leads, but it looked as though they were taking her for a walk, not she them. While she was hobbling, they, after the few seconds' rest, were perky and frisky once more, shrugging off the blows they had received. In their opinion this was something that ought to happen every night.

PC Brown ran his strong torchlight over Lucy. She looked disreputable. It was fortunate that he knew her or she might have finished up handcuffed to the other end of the railing with Sister Agape keeping an eye on her too.

'Miss Grindal?' PC Brown said doubtfully.

'Mr Brown! What a relief to see you!'

'You aren't supposed to take dogs into the cathedral, ma'am, or in the park, there's a notice, "No Dogs".'

What a stupid thing to say at this moment, thought Lucy. But people did say the most stupid inconsequent things when surprised.

'I know all about that, Mr Brown,' she replied as tartly as she could. 'Now do go and see if you can find Canon Grindal and Canon Oglethorpe in there, there's a good chap. All sorts of awful things have been happening.'

'You don't look well, miss,' said PC Todd.

'I don't feel it.'

'Would you like to sit in the police car for a minute?'

It was parked where the Ford Escort had been parked moments earlier. Lucy nodded.

'Are you coming to sit with me, Sister?' she asked Sister Agape.

'No fear, this is all much too exciting. But you go and sit down, dear. Even in this light I can see you look quite done in.'

Lucy never knew a police car could feel so luxurious. Clementina Crosspatch and Prince Rupert climbed on to her lap and licked her face. She was too exhausted to stop them. She clasped the two small warm bodies to her and wept a little on to their coats. Her eyebrow had received the blow from the torch and had begun to throb; she could feel a trickle of blood.

Within the cathedral the two policemen swung their lamp's strong beam around the vast spaces. Inside the door leading into the building there were signs of the scuffle; two suitcases flung anyhow – wet footprints and blown autumn leaves – tiny scraps of fabric torn away from clothing by sharp teeth, a trace of blood, a roll of dog hair.

But their attention was attracted to the sounds which arose in the background – a sort of confused hammering and shouting. They made their way over to find out what was going on.

The cubby-hole of a police office between choir and south choir aisle was locked, the key was in the door on the outside. Flung on the floor near by was an official-looking walkie-talkie. From inside the office came the banging, muffled by the stoutness of the woodwork and masonry.

When they let Tockwith out he was almost purple in the face.

'Took your time, didn't you?' he gasped.

'Nobody knew you were locked in there, chum.'

'What's been happening? What have they stole?'

'We don't know yet. Miss Grindal said to look for Canon Grindal and someone else.'

'Come on, then,' said Tockwith. 'What are we waiting for?'

Then they saw him properly. Two of his front teeth had been knocked out and blood was running from the corner of his mouth. His nose was a purple pulp. He was shaking all over but did not seem to notice his own condition. His eyes were full of war lust and he was ready to rush off and attack his assailants, to give them more than he had got. He was twice their age but nothing would have stopped him had not the door and the lock been so strong. His hands were bloody with battering at it.

It did not take long for the three to put the electricity back on, and at once everything seemed more normal. They began a tour of inspection and almost immediately discovered the wrought-iron crypt gate swinging open.

When at last they found the Canons among the underground passages, the two old men had begun to recover themselves a little. They had been able to speak to one another and it was the sound of their murmuring voices which had first helped to locate them. The three entering the passage called out, 'Canon Grindal! Canon Oglethorpe!' and soon heard answering weak shouts.

'Look here, officer,' said Oglethorpe as they followed the strong beams of lamplight out of the maze of passages towards the normal electric lights of the crypt itself, 'here by this wall I put one of these fellows' suitcases. Just wait till you see what's in it.'

PC Brown was hesitant.

'I don't know that we can do that here and now, sir. We ought to get you back home and report all this at the station.'

'Shine your light here.' The elderly Canon's voice still held something of the quarter-deck.

The policemen gave in.

Oglethorpe snapped open the case.

'Guns, you see!' he said triumphantly.

'Kalashnikovs!'

Suddenly the whole thing took on a different aspect altogether.

15

The heathen are sunk down in the pit that they
made; in the same net that they hid privily is
their foot taken.

—*Psalms*, 9, v. 15

Jill had gone back home on Thursday afternoon and she got up
early on Friday morning knowing nothing of the chase in the
crypt the night before. Terry had said that he wouldn't phone
her, so she did not expect any contact except that which came,
brief and crackling over her headphones.

'All set?' was the query.

'All set,' was her reply.

She had made a mug of coffee and a slice of toast at the farm
table among the general clamour of her father, brothers, and
their dogs. Jill's mother had died five years before and if she
had not struck out for her own life, Jill could easily have slipped
into being a general housekeeper and maid of all work on the
farm. As it was, a middle-aged woman cycled in every day from
the nearest village, and the household tumbled on its rough
and ready way.

When Jill was at home there were jobs she was expected to
do; and at half past six in the morning she had finished eating
and went out into the rapidly emptying farmyard. The air was
chill and mist-hung. Jill stood for a few seconds and sniffed it,
and thought of the effect this recurring mist would have on
their plan. It was for the good, she decided.

Her brothers had left her one of the tractors. They were off to
take advantage of the comparative dryness of the ground before
winter set in properly.

She grimaced as she looked at the tractor, sure that they
would have left her the worst of the bunch. Not that she needed
one for what she was about to do, but on the farm they had all

got used to jumping on the nearest tractor instead of using their legs.

At least it started first time.

She headed out for the pasture at the end of the farm lands where the sheep were grazing, taking with her extra feed on the trailer at the back. Her dog Tip kept up easily. Arrived at the pasture, Jill glanced at her watch. She was early. Timing must be precise.

The sheep clustered round the tractor, looking up with hope. Grass was nice but the field was well eaten down, and what Jill had in the trailer smelt very good.

She climbed down and walked round the flock, looking them over carefully. Mist clung to their fleeces, droplets of condensed water crowding into the fibres. They regarded her without fear. None of them was limping. They all looked fit and healthy. No signs of trouble. She spent twenty minutes on this examination. None of those who knew her in her independent life in York would have recognized her at that moment. She wore old jeans and wellingtons, a thick plain jumper and a Barbour jacket too big for her, no make-up, and her hair was pushed into an antediluvian tweed hat which came well down towards her eyebrows.

Then, before feeding the sheep, she and Tip rounded them up into a compact flock near a gate which led out on to the dual carriageway ring road. She started the tractor engine again and positioned it with care. The sheep looked up expectantly. Surely the food could not be much longer in coming?

Jill stood waiting, judging that the time was right.

The call came.

Superstar was on course – that meant they were passing Askham Bryan College.

Jill swung open the gate. She had checked it over and oiled it during the previous week. She put the tractor into gear. At this time in the morning traffic was still fairly sparse – sparse, that is, for such a busy bypass. Minute by minute it was building up. The faint mist was not making much difference to speeds. Traffic loomed up suddenly in the disconcerting way it has in mist, but visibility was fairly good.

Jill drove out the tractor and trailer rather slowly. There was a break built into the dual carriageway at this point on purpose for her father to drive across his farm stock when necessary. He had agitated for an underpass to reach his fields on the other side, but without result.

The sheep, with Tip at their back, came slowly after her. At the cross-over point she stopped the tractor and trailer and got out. By now one or two vehicles had already had to stop. The sheep were frightened. They had never before been herded on to the road and then brought to a halt.

Jill, subtly, began to do all the wrong things.

As the sheep poured out they began to stray, terror-struck, in all directions and break from their tight pack formation. Puzzled by Jill's contradictory orders, Tip was helpless.

At the back of the waiting cars arrived a police car closely followed by a Land Rover with a red stripe down its side. They came to a halt. One of the policemen got out of the police car and came towards Jill.

'What do you think you're doing, miss?'

'We have a perfect right to take our stock across this road, officer.'

'You don't seem to be doing it very efficiently.'

As the PC made a grab at one of the sheep, intending to help her move them out of the way of oncoming traffic, the animal eluded him and, tossing its head, it ran towards Leeds.

An unobtrusive dark saloon had stopped at the rear of the traffic jam which was rapidly forming.

Jill wondered desperately where Terry and Mike were. This was it; this was the opportunity they'd organized so carefully. The pair of them ought by now to have jumped out of the ditch at the side of the road. She had noticed the Ford parked a few hundred yards away in the shadow of one of the flyovers.

Mike scrambled up from the roadside ditch and into her line of vision. He looked incredible. His clothes were torn and seemed as though he had slept in them for at least a week. His face was bloodstained, swollen, covered in bites and scratches. There was no Terry.

Mike dashed across the road towards the Land Rover, approaching it from the front among the bobbing sheep.

180

The police constable who was trying to help with the sheep said, 'Hey, where are you going?' but Mike did not reply.

'Hey!' the PC said again. Mike was level with the bonnet of the Land Rover. The driver and the man in the passenger seat were watching the sheep and did not notice him.

'What do you think you're doing?' The PC left the awkward sheep who had now been joined by another twenty or so. Mike was among the creatures, level with the side of the Land Rover and nearing its back.

The constable grabbed him by the shoulder, his fingers slipping on the smooth pad of muscle and, turning, Mike gave him a straight punch to the jaw which knocked him down nearly senseless.

'Right fracas we've got here,' one of the men in the front of the Land Rover remarked to the other. 'Sheep all over the bloody place. Girl doesn't know how to control them. We'll be here all day. Bugger up our schedule. One of the escort has tripped over among them now.' For he had only seen a blur of navy blue as the PC fell backwards.

In the back of the Land Rover were Fergal Mourne and Prison Officer Clark. Fergal did not look much like a hero. His keen fine-drawn face was tired and subdued. He seemed the least interested of anyone at the scene. Withdrawn into himself he waited for the journey to get under way again.

Prison Officer Clark had been brought up on a moorland farm. He knew sheep. He opened the rear door of the Land Rover and began to climb out.

The dark saloon car at the back of the hold-up had disgorged its driver and the man from the front passenger seat. While most of the drivers in the rapidly increasing jam were just sitting there tooting their horns or twiddling their thumbs, worrying about their schedules and the growing mist, the two men walked purposefully forward.

Now, as PO Clark was climbing out of the Land Rover, they came up to him. Mike had left the fallen police constable and was making his way, as best he could for sheep, the few feet to the same point.

'You Mike Killarney?' One of the men came towards Mike as the other reached PO Clark.

181

'Yeah . . .' Puzzled, Mike realized that these men must be the back-up team.

The man spoke very quietly. Only Mike could have heard him among the growing noise and confusion of the hold-up.

'Change of plan. We're going to deal with this. You keep out of it. Where's Terry Mourne?'

'Got caught,' said Mike.

'Bloody idiot.'

'What's all this hold-up about?' said the other man, at the back of the Land Rover, to PO Clark.

He spoke in a casual way as if he was just one of the chance passing car-drivers and the prison officer looked at him ready to give a civil reply, but before he could answer the man had extended his left arm past Clark's shoulder and shot Fergal Mourne through the heart. There was hardly a sound. Fergal had looked up at the sound of the voice; an expression of surprise came over his face as he clutched at his chest, a momentary action – then all was over.

'Look here!' PO Clark grabbed at the man in an automatic reflex. He hardly realized what had happened, only that the prisoner in his care had been attacked.

After retracting his arm slightly the moment he saw Fergal Mourne slump forward, blood coming from his Fair Isle jumper and gushing out between his fingers, the man from the saloon car now shot again, this time aiming precisely at Mourne's bending head.

Clark had hold of his right arm, but still using his left the man thrust the muzzle of his gun to Clark's temple and pulled the trigger for the third time. The prison officer's grip relaxed and dropped from the man's sleeve as his body fell to the road.

Mike was only a yard away but was prevented from seeing what was happening by the corner of the Land Rover and by the other back-up man, who stood squarely in front of him.

Then at the faint sounds of the silenced shots Mike furiously tried to get past the man from the saloon car. The policeman behind him had dragged himself up to a sitting position on the road and was getting ready to take action again.

'What the hell?' yelled Mike. He was looking dangerous.

'You keep out of things that don't concern you, son,' said the man.

Mike had seized the man, trying to thrust him to one side and get past him, but although the man did not look much, he was deceptive. For all Mike's strength he could not move him an inch. He had met his match.

He shrieked, 'Terry's brother's in there, we're springing him!'

'Tell Terry we've sprung him.'

The policeman behind Mike was on his feet. Fury lent him strength. Hands like iron bars caught Mike from behind. In front the man from the dark saloon had knocked Mike's grip and now waved the gun close to his eyes.

'He's been sprung, right?' he hissed, and then abruptly turned. The two men ran off on either side of two sheep who decided they would run the same way.

The whole thing had taken a minute at the outside.

By the time the prison officers in the front of the Land Rover had begun to realize what had happened and got out into the mêlée of baaing sheep, the two men had reached the dark car and reversed as far as they could. Then they drove straight out over the grassy intersection between the two carriageways and, accelerating in a way no car that make had ever been known to accelerate before, they vanished into the hazy darkness before anyone even got their number.

Jill had been too busy creating havoc to keep up with events. Shouting and noise and sheep held her in a whirl of action without getting anywhere.

'It's all up, Jill,' shouted Mike as he was bundled into the back of the police car.

'Are you involved in this, miss?' asked the officer, struggling towards her as soon as he had disposed of Mike.

'I don't know what you mean.'

'If you're taking them sheep over there, how come you haven't opened the opposite gate yet?'

'Oh . . . I didn't think . . . how silly of me, officer!' Even though she had not put on any make-up that morning, there was enough left-over mascara round Jill's eyes to make her upward glance very effective.

183

'Criminal conspiracy perhaps, silly, no. You know this man.'

It was not much use denying it when he had shouted to her. Where was Terry? What did it all mean? What was she to do now? The policeman told her.

'Can you get these sheep off the road, miss, before any more of them are killed?'

Jill cared deeply for her sheep. She straightened up and took a general view. Then she went white as she saw blood on the road and the two sheep which had run along in such a friendly way between the two terrorists lying in unnatural positions in the fast lane.

There really did seem nothing else to do.

Shouting to Tip, she began to round the flock up and get them back into the field they had come from.

Traffic was piled up on either side of the road and she worked to a chorus of sarcastic remarks from the drivers. She had to run hither and thither among the stationary vehicles, fetching the straying sheep. But once she was working with her usual efficiency the job seemed to the watching policemen to be soon done, in spite of the panic which had gripped the animals.

At last – it had seemed like years to Jill – the sheep were all in and she clanged shut the gate. As the traffic started gingerly to edge forward she ran to her two dead sheep, seeing now that another had been hit and was lying injured and dying on the other side of the road. Tears streaming down her face, Jill picked one after the other up in her arms as well as she could and half dragged them to the verge.

Then with the policeman holding up the traffic she backed the tractor and trailer until they were safely parked in the field entrance.

Once the sheep had been moved, cars had begun thrusting forward, eager to be on their way. When the road was finally clear they began to speed through, nipping round the police car and the Land Rover.

The policeman was standing beside Jill. Seeing that all was safe, he said, 'If you'll come with us, miss.'

'I don't understand what this is about,' was all she could think of to say.

She could see Mike in the back of the police car; after that

184

first shout he had taken no more notice of her. She could also see something was wrong in the Land Rover, because in response to a radio call from the police car an ambulance had come screaming up and several men in uniform seemed to be busy at the back. A stretcher had been brought from the ambulance.

The policeman who had been telling her what to do had lost his hat and his face was bruised. Her sheep were dead. Terry had not come. She had no idea what had happened to his brother, and no understanding of how their lovely plan had gone so obviously wrong. She'd done her bit all right, even at the cost of losing some of her flock.

Somehow she hadn't reckoned on that. Not on the sheep getting killed. Terry wouldn't have let that happen, if he'd been there, she was sure he wouldn't. Where was he? For Terry was what it was all about, for Jill. She couldn't care less about Fergal Mourne and she didn't like Mike, but for Terry she would have gone through hell.

She looked with puzzled eyes at the scene before her, the ambulance men carrying a stretcher, and then another stretcher, and did not comprehend it. Some sort of accident. If she thought anything it was that a car must have run into the back of the Land Rover in the hold-up.

'Come on, miss,' said the police officer quite gently.

'Where?'

'Down to the station. You've got a lot of questions to answer.'

'My dog,' she said. Going to the field fence she leaned over and shouted to Tip, who was standing looking lost. 'Home,' she said to him, 'home, home, Tip.'

When he started to go towards the farm, twisting his head every few paces to look back at her, she turned away and walked obediently to the police car.

16

Their sword shall go through their own heart;
and their bow shall be broken.

—*Psalms*, 37, v. 15

Colin Holdernesse came through the backyard of Canon Grindal's house and knocked on the kitchen door, bobbing his head across the window so that he saw that Lucy was in the kitchen. There was no escape.

'Good afternoon, Colin.' She opened the door to him.

'The Canon about?'

'No, he's down at the hospital seeing Edmund Jason. Can I help?'

'What a week!' remarked Colin, making himself at home in the large cosy room. He sat in a Windsor chair on top of a knitted cushion. 'I expect you know all about what happened this morning?'

'Yes. Though what happened last night was just about enough for me.'

'Can you imagine the IRA intruding on our peaceful life here?'

Lucy turned and looked fully at him. For the first time he noticed that her face was bruised to several different colours, there was a plaster over her eye, and she moved stiffly. For all that, she was dressed more neatly than usual, in a grey blouse under a loose salmon pink jumper, and a dark skirt. At her throat was a pleasing old-fashioned brooch in coral and seed pearls.

'After this week I don't think life will ever be the same again,' she said.

'It's a nuisance for you, not being able to take the dogs into Dean's Park,' Colin Holdernesse went on. 'I'm surprised Canon Grindal hasn't taken the notices down.'

'He's only Acting Dean,' replied Lucy.

'Anyway, I've come round because I think I've got the solution to your problem, if you'd like it, that is.'

'Tell me,' said Lucy, who was in no mood for prolonged chat. She wished Colin would go away. She had a lot to think about, and there were things she ought to do. As far as the Parsifals went, she thought they could now manage without her; but there was poor Mrs Soames – she was going to need a shoulder to cry on – and Lucy felt a certain concern about Jill. Then, too, she had noticed this morning that Prince Rupert was paying undue attention to Clementina Crosspatch and if she was coming into season – Lucy must look in the calendar and see how long it had been since her last one – they would have to be kept apart for a while and she'd have to decide whether or not to have Clem mated this time . . .

Colin Holdernesse was in no hurry to tell her. Having a gift-wrapped parcel of a piece of news he was not going to divulge it too quickly.

'I've been looking through the records of this property,' he said. 'My house and yours. Fascinating.'

'I'm sure they are.'

'The various people who've lived here. The customs which have changed over the years. Did you know, for instance, that until ten years ago nearly all the garden of my house was used by the inhabitants of yours?'

'No I didn't,' said Lucy. She couldn't see that that was particularly useful or helpful information.

'And at the time the Canon living here allowed the Surveyor of the Fabric of the time the use of the garden for the term of his tenancy.'

'Did he?' Lucy still felt a complete lack of interest.

'Yes. Canon Watson was not interested in gardening. He was glad that my boss's predecessor was willing to take it on.'

'Very sensible,' said Lucy.

'But he only ceded the garden for the term of his *own* tenancy of this house, aware that the next Canon Residentiary might wish to have it again.'

'Nothing was said to us about it.' Lucy's voice was still dull and uninterested.

187

'I'm afraid our last Surveyor of the Fabric was at fault there. He liked having a large garden and hung on to it – strictly against the agreement. Nor did he mention it to me when he retired to Devon and I took over the house six months ago. You remember that our present Surveyor of the Fabric owned a house in York already.'

Colin was beginning to be a little irritated by her lack of excitement. She looked at him as though she were thinking of something else.

'So now I'm proposing giving your garden back to you,' he said, reaching the point at last in some desperation, wondering if his words were going home at all.

'You're going to give us your garden?'

'It's *your* garden, Lucy. I've been trying to explain that to you. Come and have a look at it.'

He led her unresisting into the cold misty air, through the small yard outside her kitchen and out of the door at the other side. This opened into a small paved area shared jointly for access by several houses, and one of the wooden doors led into his garden.

It lay partly behind the house Canon Grindal and Lucy were occupying and partly behind the house used at present by the assistant cathedral architect, and it was easy to see how it could conveniently belong to either.

'I don't think I've ever been in this garden,' said Lucy, 'although some of our bedrooms look out on to it. It's quite large, isn't it?'

It was a roomy, comfortable garden, with a few mature trees, and several square formal rose beds in the spreading grass. Although it had obviously been well maintained in the past and much loved, it was already beginning to show the signs of Colin Holdernesse's lack of interest.

The grass had been mown perfunctorily and there were young weeds establishing themselves in the beds. Lucy bent down and absent-mindedly pulled up a plant of groundsel and then shook the soil from its roots. It seemed, as she stood looking round with the weed dangling from her hand, that what Colin had said was beginning to sink in.

188

'Do you mean – have I heard you right – do you really mean father and I can use this garden, Colin?'

'I've been telling you. It goes with your house. My predecessor only had the temporary grace-and-favour occupation of it. I don't want it. That little strip under my window will be quite enough for me to look after. I'm no gardener.'

'I can't believe it . . . The dogs will love it,' said Lucy, 'and so shall I. And Father. Look at that garden seat! How pleasant it will be to have afternoon tea there!'

'I knew you'd be pleased.' Holdernesse was beginning to feel some of the warm glow he'd looked forward to experiencing.

'Pleased!' She turned to look at him with eyes to which the life had returned. 'Pleased isn't the word. Oh, it isn't the word at all. Are you sure we're entitled to it, Colin? How can you bear to part with it?'

'If I'm not entitled to something I can part with it very easily. And I'm sure you'll let me come in to sit awhile if I want to.'

'But of course! You must feel that it's just as much yours as ever!'

'I shall be delighted to be your guest.'

Lucy put her hands over her face.

'It's too much,' she said. 'Too much to take in, all at once. I won't need Dean's Park at all. Our own garden, Colin! And look at the roses!'

Even in this cold weather, with remnants of mist still drawing chilly veils to obscure the middle distance, and so short a time to go to Christmas, there were a few brave blooms flaunting frost-browned red and pink and amber,

Colin Holdernesse felt all the warm glow he had hoped for. But he could not help wondering why, when women were happy, their eyes became so suspiciously bright.

'And to think it's only Friday,' said Lucy.

Detective Inspector Smart came back into the office.

'You were right, sir,' he said.

'I'm always right, aren't I, Dave?'

'Of course, Bob. You surely are.'

189

'Anyway, what was I right about?' Bob Southwell had become immersed in other things.

'You asked me to check on the lad that was arrested last night – as to whether or not he was Fergal Mourne's brother.'

'And is he?'

'He is.'

Bob drew a long breath and leaned back in his chair. He took off his glasses and bent his head. 'Tuesday afternoon Fergal's brother walks in here to report, because he's out on parole. What's he out on parole from? Stealing silver. What have we just had? A burglary of valuable antique silver.'

'That's right.'

'None of us made the connection between Terry being in this area and Fergal being moved to Full Sutton because Terry reported routinely to uniform branch and they don't know about every little job we do. We realized something might be up to do with Fergal but thought we'd forestalled it.'

'Right.'

'So it took two old clergymen to show us that we were wrong, that the silver and the IRA were connected, and that we'd had a murder on our patch and put it down as accident.'

'Right.'

'We very nearly had two murders in the cathedral.'

'Right. Michael Soames told us he'd shot at Canon Oglethorpe and sure enough there was a bullet in the woodwork.'

'We had two murders out on the ring road.'

'Right.'

'I wish you'd stop saying "right", Dave. I think we ought to ask Canons Grindal and Oglethorpe to join the force and resign ourselves.'

Dave Smart daren't say a word.

'OK, you got me,' said Terry Mourne. He glared at the policemen like a cornered animal. 'But you'll never defeat us, never.'

'Never is a long time. We hardly need to defeat you, Mourne. You are busy defeating yourselves.'

'What do you mean?' The young man saw something else in

Bob Southwell's face, not the straightforward oppression he expected.

'Well – you're out on parole, right?'

'Yes.'

'Signing on here in York – yet what do you do? Carry out a burglary of antique silver from a country house – exactly the kind of crime you were committed for in the first place. Your trademark all over it. The first person we're going to suspect is you. You'll be straight back inside again. We've found the silver, with your fingerprints, so you haven't benefited IRA funds. All quite useless. And anyway they are making so much money from importing drugs into Ireland now that your feeble efforts are a drop in the ocean. They don't need you and your silver money, Mourne, any more than they needed your brother.'

'What do you mean, drugs? Ireland's a fine pure country. We don't have drug addicts like you decadent lot in England or America. The IRA fight for freedom, they don't import filthy drugs to corrupt our young ones. Drug dealers get kneecapped in southern Ireland.'

'A lot of things have been happening while you were in Parkhurst, Mourne.'

Terry Mourne leaned back in his chair. He felt sick. This copper wasn't exactly like the usual sort. He hadn't got the attitude at all. Seemed as if he knew something Mourne himself didn't; as if not everything he had to say was said yet. Of course it wasn't true! The Cause wasn't poisoning the Emerald Isle with drugs. He wasn't swallowing that. The uneasy feeling persisted.

'What were you aiming to do with your stuff, Mourne? The Kalashnikovs and the grenades? Join the girl on the bypass, was that it? Join in the confusion? And do what, spring your brother?'

'If you're so bloody clever you tell me,' replied Mourne.

'I don't need to tell you. We know what you were planning. Jill lets the sheep out, when the Land Rover halts you leap out of the ditch, armed, and attack it, rescue your brother, then he speeds off in the getaway car that comes up behind at that moment and you lot scarper. Everyone meets up in Ireland,

191

your brother takes his place again at the head of his bit of the IRA and everything in the garden's lovely, right?'

There seemed little point in denying it.

'If you say so, smart arse,' said Mourne.

'Well, thanks to Canon Grindal and the cathedral staff you were intercepted, and couldn't carry out your part in this precious plan. So what do you think happened, when the road was blocked?'

'Nothing.'

'You imagine that your brother is now in Full Sutton prison, safely in their High Security section, incarcerated there for the next twenty years?'

'Not if I can get him out he's not.'

'He isn't there, Mourne.' Bob Southwell spoke seriously, gravely, but gently.

'What happened?' Mourne's voice was suddenly husky.

'You don't know?'

'How can I? I wasn't there, was I?'

'He was shot, I'm afraid.'

'You bastards! Where is he? Is he going to be all right?'

'It wasn't us bastards that did it, Mourne. Look, let's have a cup of tea.'

Southwell motioned to the constable who was sitting quietly in the corner, making the word 'sweet' silently with his mouth, and the constable went out, leaving the door ajar.

'Tea? I don't want your bloody tea. I want to know what happened to my brother.'

'The getaway car came to the blockage and stopped. Two men got out. They went up to the Land Rover to ask what was happening. One of the prison officers was getting out of the back and one of the men from the getaway car took the opportunity to lean past him and shoot your brother.'

'What?'

'The prison officer grappled with them and they shot him too. Then they ran back to their car – which was far enough behind not to be entangled in sheep – made a U-turn on to the other carriageway, and drove away. By the time we realized and were in radio contact, they'd given us the slip. It all happened in seconds.'

192

'Our side didn't do it. You're making this up. We wanted to release him so that he could go back to Ireland and lead the movement again. This isn't true.'

The constable reappeared with the cups.

'Look, Mourne, whether you believe me or not, drink this tea.'

Mourne's cup was heavily sweetened.

For a moment Mourne thought of dashing the cup from the constable's hand. Then he saw his own hand trembling. He needed that tea. He took it and sipped. The man opposite began to drink his too. He seemed to be looking down at the table, and his thin-jawed face was serious. The light glancing on the large lenses of his spectacles prevented Mourne reading the expression in his eyes.

'Did you bring yourself a cup?' Bob asked the constable.

'No, sir.'

'Get one.'

The constable went out and got one, and a strange peace fell on the room. Mourne was trying to pull himself together. The strain of the last days told. He shivered all over. Grateful for the warmth of the cup he cradled it in his hands, a hemisphere of comfort.

'Another cup?' asked Bob presently. Mourne nodded. 'You'd better bring the pot,' Bob said to the constable.

For several more minutes there was absolute quiet. Bob contemplated the top of Mourne's bowed head. The tumbled dark curls were all he could see.

'You've got to realize how things have changed,' he said quietly. 'Your brother was an idealist, right? In the old mould. Plenty of people sympathize with the long sorrows of the Irish and wish them free and happy, plenty of people in England too. Though the violence, the hatred, the mob action – many of the ways in which the struggle manifests itself are seen as wrong. You make your own chains. Yet people burning with idealism gain a certain respect, even from those opposed to them, right? Though you may not realize that. Idealists, that is. Not terrorists.'

'My brother is dead?'

'Yes, he is dead. We didn't shoot him, Mourne. You can't

193

blame us for it. He was executed by your own side. That's a fact, whether you like it or not. And, don't forget, the prison officer lies alongside him in the mortuary. A man with a wife and two small children.'

'Executed? Why?'

'Because the IRA has changed, Mourne. And the INLA have got out of hand and are feuding among themselves. They told you to spring him, yes. But they didn't want him going back to Ireland and taking his place at the top again. In any case they would have wanted him to spend two years in the community, a sort of quarantine, in case he'd become a supergrass.'

'Don't you say that of my brother!'

'It's the standard safeguard they take, Mourne, you ought to know that. And if they'd let him back in at the top, what then? He would have seen at once that his old associates had become rotten and corrupt and he wouldn't have stood for it. They've become like the Mafia, Mourne. They control organized crime, some of them import drugs, they terrorize shopkeepers and demand protection money. The last thing they wanted was an idealist coming back amongst them, with all the popular sup- port he would have commanded. He would have reacted as Christ did to the money-lenders in the Temple. No way were they letting him go back to Ireland. You would have released him only to his execution.'

'Why did they want him out, then? Tell me that. Why not leave him in jug?'

'Why? Because while he was alive he was a focus for the old ideals. Dead he's a martyr. They can deal with martyrs.'

'You mean they would have killed him anyway?'

'I'm sure of it. Probably during the journey back or in a country lane over there. A car exploding, maybe. But when things went wrong – when you didn't show up as expected, and on his own Mike Soames couldn't cope – then they seized the moment. Chance played into their hands. The prison officer opening the back of the Land Rover when he did sealed Mourne's fate and his own.'

The young man with the dark curly hair had no reply to make. He put the drained cup down on the table.

'Back you go to the cells, then, Mourne,' said Bob Southwell,

194

not unkindly. Internally he decided that, if he had any influence on events, this young man would at least be able to attend his brother's funeral, to say farewell properly, to help him come to terms with both past and present and perhaps to prevent his further term in prison from twisting him inevitably to the bad. It might even, in the end – if he was lucky – produce a better man.

All three rose. Mourne was escorted back to his cell.

'Keep an eye on him,' Southwell told the constable in charge. 'He's in a state of shock and might do anything.'

Then he wondered. He went back to his desk and checked the reports. The men must have got out of the getaway car before Mike Soames had time to do anything – they reached the Land Rover before him. So if Terry Mourne had been there it would have made no difference. They would presumably have still got out of the car at the same time. Had they never intended to rely on Mourne and Soames at all? Had the intention all along been to execute Fergal themselves? If so, if Terry had been there, would they have left him alive?

Bob Southwell shivered. He felt convinced they would not. Mike Soames presumably did not matter.

A knock came on the door and DI Dave Smart entered.

'I'll tell you what, Bob,' he said. 'There must be someone in this with inside knowledge from Wakefield nick. Probably somebody working there talks to a pal or a lover, not realizing the gossip's going straight to where it shouldn't go. The girl had a radio set. We changed the time of the journey yesterday. She must have known to set the blockage up for this morning.'

'That's right. They would have co-ordinated her movements with the journey to York.'

'So the contact – whoever he, she, or it is – has got to be found.'

'Get on to it, Dave. Liaise with the prison governor and also the Wakefield force. How's the pursuit of the two gunmen going?'

'Hopeless, I think. If someone had noticed the number of the car we might have had a lead. At least we'll get the ballistic report on the bullets.'

Dave left the room and Bob turned to Mike Soames's statement, which was short as he had refused to answer most questions. Oddly enough he had confessed to taking a pot-shot at Canon Oglethorpe, as if it was something he had to get off his chest, when the police didn't know of it and would most likely never have found out. About the events on the motorway he had mainly been dumb. 'What did the man out of the car say to you?' He had at least answered that one. 'He said, "Where's Terry Mourne?"'

'Odd that Mike should have admitted to that,' thought Bob. 'I suppose he thought it didn't matter, as it doesn't. It didn't implicate Terry any more than he was already. But it tells me something. It is now my opinion that if Terry had been there they would have shot him too. Perhaps they meant to get the two brothers later and changed their plans at the last minute, to killing them on the spot. The only thing that surprises me is that they let Mike Soames off.'

Dave Smart put his head round the door. 'Canon Grindal is here,' he said, looking worried.

George Grindal looked very serious.

'I owe you an apology, Canon,' said Bob. 'Other events made me forget to act on your telephone call of Wednesday night, and DI Smart was not very helpful yesterday when you asked for police protection for Canon Oglethorpe. We now know that he did indeed need such protection.'

'Well, all that's in the past now,' replied Grindal.

'How is everything?'

'Everything?'

'You have been having rather an upset at the cathedral.' Bob could see various scrapes and scratches on the Canon himself.

'Edmund Jason our assistant organist is recovering nicely. His friend Simon arrived and has been standing in for him music-wise.'

'He plays too?'

'He's an Organ Scholar.'

'What's he like compared to Jason?'

'It's like exchanging Johann Sebastian for Beethoven. Simon is a very forceful young man.'

'So that's sorted out,' said Bob comfortably.

'Albert Horncastle – oh, you don't know about him – '

'Tell me.'

'An old man who turned up in a bad way. Now lodging with Mrs Hassock. We've dealt with his daughter and recovered his cathedral and old age pensions and he's improving from day to day. Only this morning he volunteered to help Canon Oglethorpe at St Helen's on the Walls by being a verger there. The cathedral is a bit too high-powered for him now but he thinks he can manage St Helen's and it will keep him occupied and busy as well as helping Oglethorpe. It's a matter of having a body there, really, to answer questions from visitors and give the pews a bit of furniture polish.'

'That's all very good. And what can I do for you this morning?'

'I'd like to speak to the prisoners.'

'All of them?'

'Terry Mourne, Michael Soames and Jill.'

'Yes, of course you can.'

'And later Canon Oglethorpe will be coming down, he wants to speak to them too.'

'They might not appreciate the visits.'

'I can't help that,' said George Grindal. He sounded weary. Bob was not to know that what was really oppressing him was that during his interview with Smart the day before, he had lost his temper. He who was always telling other people to read Luke.

17

Our soul is escaped even as a bird out of the
snare of the fowler, the snare is broken, and we
are delivered.

—*Psalms*, 124, v. 6

'Soames,' said Bob Southwell, 'how can you explain this?' He
threw a bunch of keys down on to the table.

Mike shrugged. 'What is there to explain? They're just keys.'

'Keys to parts of the cathedral. This one, for instance, fits the
door of the stair through which one can reach the walk along at
triforium level and over the south choir aisle. This fits the
wrought-iron doors to the crypt.'

'So? They're just old keys. How am I expected to know what
they fit?'

'They may be old but they've been used recently. They are
clean and oiled. They were in your pocket. Come on. How did
you get them, in the first place?'

'My old Dad's a verger, isn't he?'

'That's not how you got the stairs key, and you know it.'

'Had it a long time,' said Mike.

'That explains it, then. Did you get this key when you were
an apprentice stonemason at the cathedral?'

'They get lost sometimes.'

'And over the course of years it is forgotten that a key went
missing . . . So the cathedral policeman knew that no keys had
been signed out for the stairs. But he didn't know about the
existence of this one.'

'More fool him.'

'When you saw Canon Oglethorpe it must have been a shock
to you. You last saw him in Parkhurst. You realized that he
could identify you as an ex-convict to your parents who thought
you'd been abroad, and to the police, and that he could tell us
that Michael Soames was the convict Michael Killarney, and

you imagined your IRA activities might be endangered by him
. . . It was easy enough for you to go up to the walkway over
the south choir aisle, and prepare a stone which would look as
if it had fallen naturally . . . And hide at the end of the walkway
until the bell signalled the start of the service, when the clergy
come out of the vestry – then whip out quick, and hurl the
stone on to the man you thought was Oglethorpe. It was easy
enough, too, for you to get through that housemaid's cupboard
and take the pot-shot at the Canon.'

'Sez you.'

'That's what you did, wasn't it, Soames?'

'My name isn't Soames.'

'Your name is whatever I choose to call you. That's what you
did, isn't it?'

Mike shrugged and made a rude gesture.

'Murder will be the charge, Soames. Manslaughter last time,
wasn't it? This is worse. You were bound to get it, sooner or
later, the way you were going. Your temper's getting you quite
a reputation.'

'I want to see my lawyer. You can't pin anything on me.'

'I'm going to have a damn good try. It will hardly be necessary
to bring in the IRA job. We might let the charge of assaulting a
police officer lie on the files as well in case we need it later.'

'Pig,' spat Mike. Frustration and rage were fighting for the
mastery over him.

'Here's your book back,' said the pig. 'You might want
something to read in jug.' He tossed a battered copy of the *Life
of James Connolly* on to the table between them.

'You aren't fit to touch that,' said Mike, snatching it up.

'Have you been boning up on all the old heroes? Not such
heroes, after all, were they?'

'They fought for their ideals.'

'I've been reading it, you see. Amusing when Connolly
addressed that meeting in 1911 at Cobh. The Irish people were
against him – the Catholics and the women charged him and
smashed his soap box. He had to be rescued by the police and
escorted back to the hotel where he was staying, then under
police protection to the railway station. The police force being

199

useful in time of need – abused other times, eh? Rescuing the hero from the Irish themselves?'

'Don't put dirt on him. He was shot by the English. They carried him in a stretcher to be shot.'

Bob Southwell sighed.

'True enough. There's evil done on all sides. No one comes out clean. All the same, Soames, wouldn't he rather have died like that? He became one of the martyrs that way, don't forget. It was short and quick. He had the last rites. He would have died slowly otherwise of his gangrene; there was no possible escape from that. Wouldn't he prefer the sharper end?'

'What about the shoot to kill policy?' shouted Mike. 'What about the interrogations – the hoods over the heads – the leaning against the wall – what about all the other things you filthy lot have done? What about the hunger strikers who died in Longkesh?'

'Two wrongs don't make a right, Mike. Never have and never will. The oppression of one side doesn't excuse the terrorism of the other. The end never justifies the means.'

Southwell got up from his perch at the end of the table. There was something he couldn't understand about Michael Soames. He'd now reacted in anger, yes, and he'd confessed to shooting at Oglethorpe, but he also seemed smug, self-satisfied, as if all the charges that had been thrown at him were not what he was afraid of, as if there was something else that hadn't been found out. Why had he really thrown his lot in with his friend Terry and the IRA? Southwell knew that Terry had been for a while Soames's cell-mate in prison, but that didn't seem enough. Neither did the possibility of Oglethorpe's identifying him as Killarney seem enough for two murder attempts on the old man.

'I don't know why I'm talking to you like this, Soames. You're beyond reason. You killed a man in case he identified you – and you weren't even able to identify him correctly. You're going to do a minimum of twenty years for the wrong man. Your mother's outside, waiting to see you. For heaven's sake try to be halfway decent to her. You've caused her enough suffering.'

Mrs Soames entered fearfully into the room where her son sat. She glanced round, not knowing what to expect. White

200

ceiling, cream walls, grey paint, grey lino tiles on the floor, a bare table, a couple of plain blue moulded plastic chairs with tubular iron legs. Apart from the policeman sitting silently in the corner it could have been anywhere. It was just a little lockable room in a police station. The actual cells with beds were a few yards down the corridor. From them came no sound.

In that first glance she took it all in without knowing that she had. The second glance – and all the subsequent looking her eyes did – was at her son.

'Micky,' she said softly. He looked up. 'Micky, why have you got involved in all this?'

There was too much to separate them. All the years he had been away, all the years since he was her little boy.

He lifted his head with pride.

'It was the Cause, mother. The Cause of a free Ireland. I had to follow, you know. He was my father, Michael Killarney. A hero. I had to follow him.'

'I don't know what you are talking about, Michael. It's hurt your stepfather a lot, you stopping using his name. He loves you. He's been a good father to you. He's really hurt and rejected. I couldn't get him to come with me today.'

'He's an old fart.'

'I can't understand what you're going on about, about your real father.'

'He was Michael Killarney, wasn't he? That's something to live up to, you know.'

Mrs Soames hesitated. 'His name was Michael Killarney. But he was never mixed up with the IRA. You mustn't think that, Micky. A decent man, he was.'

'What do you mean, mother? He was one of the great republican heroes – died in 1967, shot by the occupation forces in Ireland . . .'

'Yes, he died in 1967.'

'In Belfast.'

'Yes. He was working on a building site over there at the time.'

'Shot down, a martyr's death . . .'

'Well, no dear. You've got mixed up, somehow. I have heard

201

of the Michael Killarney you're on about. Your Dad told me he was a second cousin. I never met him.'

Michael looked at her, stupefied.

'It's true, Micky, my love. That wasn't your Dad. Your Dad died accidentally.'

'But . . . but you've always refused to talk about him – and he died in Belfast in January 1967 . . .'

'To be sure he did, love. So no doubt did a lot of other people. No, I didn't talk about him. Because just before he set off we'd had a fearful row and he'd told me he was in love with another woman. He'd got his job in Ireland and it was because of what he said about this other woman that you and me didn't go over with him. He was a first-class brickie, you know that. One night he'd stayed having a drink with the lads so it was dark as he was walking back to his lodging and a van skidded on some black ice and mounted the pavement and crushed him against a wall. Well, it was a judgement, I thought – and I was too upset to want to talk about it – I've never been able to talk about it.'

Even now, tears welled up in Mrs Soames's eyes and she had to rush her hand to her pocket for a handkerchief.

'And the martyr Michael Killarney wasn't my father?'

'I'm sorry, love. They were cousins. Not that I ever met the other Michael.'

Michael saw the cell in Parkhurst so clearly. He saw himself and Terry Mourne sitting side by side on the bed. Saw himself confessing shyly to being half Irish, and giving his father's name. 'Not *the* Michael Killarney?' Terry had asked excitedly. 'Not the hero Michael Killarney?' That had given Michael something he'd never had before, a sense of pride and identity. Terry had told him about his brother Fergal and they'd felt as if they were brothers themselves. Terry had told him all about what the bloody Brits had done in the Maze and all that and about the potato famine and centuries of oppression and they'd planned how to get back at them. It had been great, had that. Then Terry had gone out on parole and he'd shared instead with the Beezer and they'd planned that diamond merchant job and he himself had panicked somehow and shot that bloke and enjoyed shooting him and then he'd had to go into hiding and take cover under his step-father's name and join in with Terry and Terry had promised that in return for his help the Movement would give him sanctuary and he'd started to get really interested in the Martyrs and all that and what they'd be doing when they were all safe in Ireland together, and it had been like when he and Terry were sharing, like brothers, all marvellous but there was a description of him broadcast on the radio and there was that creep Oglethorpe who knew that he was Killarney and not Soames and who knew that he'd shared with the Beezer on account of the Beezer being religious and that creep always coming to talk to him, and the Beezer had been captured by the fuzz and had shopped him, he knew that, and if Oglethorpe said anything it meant twenty years only because of some little sod at the jeweller's and an end to everything with Terry.

His mother had started to cry.

There was no point after all in anything.

'A Rite of Reconciliation,' said the Archbishop. George Grindal had gone out to Bishopthorpe and the two men were sitting together. 'Now Michael Soames has confessed to the murder of the Dean we must have a Rite of Reconciliation as soon as possible. It still surprises me that he was able to aim accurately at a moving target.'

'I understand he's quite athletic and good at bowling and shooting.'

'A pity he couldn't use his skills for a better purpose. Now. It's still quite early. Do you think we can arrange it for tonight?'

'Tonight!' George looked astonished.

'The sooner the better. Tomorrow there's the funeral service for the Dean to fit in, and it's Saturday anyway. I see no need to make a great fuss about this, you know. We don't want the public to know about it if we can help it. I thought just the Chapter, as many of them as can be assembled, and late this evening after the building is closed to the public.'

'Well, I suppose we could.' George thought of all the telephoning he would have to do, round at least the Residentiary

Canons, if not everyone. Yes, it had better be everyone. Twice in one week was really a bit much.

'We could arrange it quite quickly. I've been thinking about it. Here's the form of service I suggest.' The Archbishop passed over a piece of scrap paper.

'Psalm 51, yes, the Penitential Psalm. Psalms 103 and 84.'

'Or 42,' put in the Archbishop. 'The Litany with the suffrage added – I've written it down there – "That it may please thee to cleanse and bless this church and sanctuary to the glory and worship of thy Holy Name, We beseech thee to hear us Good Lord."'

'And a confession?'

'Yes. I thought either the one from the Eucharist, or the one from the Book of Common Prayer, the commination service.'

'I know.'

'And the Prayer for the Departed.'

'Yes, that ought to be in.'

'No music, of course.'

'Followed, I think, by the Eucharist?'

'Definitely.'

'I'll have to work out the Collects and Readings,' said George Grindal thoughtfully. 'If you could take the service, Archbishop?'

'Certainly. It would, I think, be proper. What time do you consider . . .?'

'Late, I feel, don't you?'

'Should we say ten o'clock?'

'Very well. Then perhaps I could offer everyone a hot drink before they went home. It will be cold in the cathedral at that hour. With so many of us not as young as we once were, it is wise to take precautions.'

'So that was it,' Canon Oglethorpe remarked to Canon Grindal. 'I knew that I'd seen him before. Of course it was at Parkhurst. I remember well, now. But it threw me seeing him in such a different place, and with the Soames – such a nice couple. We knew him as Killarney, you see.'

'Old Horncastle as good as told us. "I knew his father," he

said. That's why he never called him by his stepfather's name. Did you know him well, Samuel?'

'Oh, yes. I used to visit his cell mate. He was a bad lot unfortunately, under a mask of piety. The minute he got out he took some irresponsible young hooligan on a hold-up at a diamond merchant's or something like that, and a young assistant was shot, murdered. But about Michael Killarney. It was not easy to make an impression. But I thought I had made one. Yet he can commit murder – the poor Dean! Let alone storing arms in the cathedral and siding with the IRA.'

George Grindal stared hard and silently at his old friend.

'Oh well.' Oglethorpe gathered up his things. He always had a great deal about him. His Bible would be in an inside pocket, but the library book he was carrying to read at odd moments, his pipe and matches, a bag of humbugs he had just offered to George, his glasses, and his gloves, made a pile on the table. It took quite a time to stow them all safely or put them on. At last he got up and went limping towards the door.

George rose too and held the door open as Samuel Oglethorpe went through it.

'I'm going along to see him now,' added Oglethorpe. 'One of my failures, I'm afraid!' He shook his head. 'Still there might be something I can do. One of my failures!'

The members of the Chapter who had been able to assemble walked quietly in the night across to the cathedral from the Deanery. The Deanery had a larger room than the house Canon Grindal occupied, and it seemed the most appropriate building to use, both to meet in, and for the hot drink afterwards. Lucy Grindal and Mrs Guest were preparing that.

The feet of the clergymen made little sound, and the few street lamps blurring in the faint mist, combined with the floodlighting on the great building, gave them enough light to see their way. They did not speak. Their cassocks swished hardly at all. Those who were to wear the vestments had gone ahead to don the purple and the silver and the black. The night was still and fine, only the mist once more lowered the horizon and instead of being like a sharp black and gold print the

205

cathedral looked softened, out of focus, all in subtle shades of grey and peach.

Once inside the little side door into the dark building Verger Soames handed each person a candle, and lit it for them. He shook as he did it, but his will was steadfast. He had specially asked to help with this service.

The candle flames flickered onward to assemble within the shell of the carved choir of the great building.

The voices joined in chant, without the benefit of any instrument; the organ was silent.

The Archbishop's sonorous voice sounded out the spoken words, 'O Lord God Almighty whom the Heaven of Heavens cannot contain much less temples made with hands, who are yet pleased to have thy habitation here upon earth; Visit we beseech thee this church with thy wonderful mercy, cleanse it by thy grace from all pollutions, and ever keep it pure; and as thou didst have respect unto the prayer of thy servants David and Solomon, so accept our prayers and offerings and with thine abiding favour and mercy, bless this ancient house, hallow it, sanctify it, cleanse it, through Jesus Christ Our Lord, who liveth and reigneth with thee and the Holy Ghost, one God for ever and ever. Amen.'

As the eerie beauty of the service progressed, George Grindal looked over at his old friend Oglethorpe.

'It hasn't occurred to him,' he thought. 'I wonder if it ever will. It hasn't occurred to him that he was the target. He knew Killarney's history and sympathies – he could give him away – he was a threat. The Dean meant nothing to Michael Killarney, nothing at all.'

Canon Samuel Oglethorpe was singing now, with his heart and soul praising his Lord. His face was transfigured. No one to look at him would have realized that he knew perfectly well that one had tried to return evil for good, that the stone which struck down the Dean had been meant for his own head. Oglethorpe had faced that fact earlier that day and overcome it. It would make him strive all the harder for Michael Killarney's soul.

'It isn't my responsibility to tell him,' thought George. 'I hope he never realizes, for his own peace of mind. But if he does, I believe he's strong enough to cope with it. His faith is as a strong staff. Oh well! The snare of the fowler . . .'

Oglethorpe too had a quotation running through his mind. It was, 'Ye that by night stand in the House of the Lord, even in the courts of the House of our God, lift up your hands in the Sanctuary, and praise the Lord.'

The floodlighting on the outside of the mist-clung building prevented passers by from noticing the flickering light of the candles; the swish of the traffic stopped them hearing the sound which within was ascending so clearly to God.

Also by Barbara Whitehead

Crime fiction (The York Cycle of Mysteries)
Playing God (Quartet, 1988)
The girl with red suspenders (Constable, 1990)

Historical fiction
The caretaker wife (Heinemann, 1977)
Quicksilver lady (Heinemann, 1979)
House of green dragons (Methuen, 1982)
Ramillies (Methuen, 1983)

Timeswitch fiction
Shadows end (Kimber, 1984)

Non-fiction
Dig up your family tree (Sphere, 1986)

The Dean it was that died

In the hours before the Dean died more than a few people swore they would like to kill him. A self-important, irascible man, feared and disliked by his colleagues, Dean Henry Parsifal was felled by a knob of carved stone in his own cathedral on All Souls' Day.

Although the police regard the falling masonry as an accident, one of the Canons Residentiary, George Grindal, is not so sure. Pursuing his own investigation with the help of his friend, Canon Oglethorpe, ex-Chaplain of Parkhurst Prison, Grindal uncovers a veritable nest of vipers. A young employee of the cathedral attempts suicide by hanging; a bullet is fired at Canon Oglethorpe during a service; and a cache of IRA arms is discovered in a consecrated place.

Barbara Whitehead's third novel in her York Cycle of Mysteries (the previous two are *Playing God* and *The girl with red suspenders*) combines a riveting story of prejudice, culpability and pursuit among the ancient and beautiful buildings of a cathedral city with a formidable knowledge of church lore and the social life of the modern clergy.